W9-BOA-908

WESTON PUBLIC LIBRARY
3 4053 10362 2667

SHAKEDOWN

SHAKEDOWN

Charlie Stella

PEGASUS BOOKS
NEW YORK

Ste

SHAKEDOWN

Pegasus Books LLC
45 Wall Street, Suite 1021
New York, NY 10005

First Pegasus Books edition 2006

Library of Congress Cataloging-in-Publication Data is available.

ISBN: 1-933648-05-8

Printed in the United States of America
Distributed by Consortium

Business bad? Fuck you, pay me.
You had a fire? Fuck you, pay me.
The place got hit by lightning? Fuck you, pay me.

—*Goodfellas*

For Craig McDonald

For answering a letter from my wife five years ago . . .
For introducing me to Ken Bruen . . .
For all your support. . . .
For the e-mail that was the start of this book . . .
For being a dear friend . . . now you're famiglia.

SHAKEDOWN

CHAPTER 1

FOUR DAYS BEFORE the start of the Feast of San Gennaro a group of local volunteers were still stringing lights above Mulberry Street in Little Italy. On the corner of Mulberry and Grand, tourists were herded together by guides alongside tour buses.

An oppressive heat wave had recently invaded New York City. The air was stagnant. People fanned themselves with newspapers or whatever they could find. Some stood under awnings for shade.

Two men stood on Grand Street between Mulberry and Baxter. One was an older man, somewhere in his fifties, with slicked-back gray hair and piercing blue eyes. The other was at least half his age but was huge by comparison. Both men wore sports jackets and were feeling the heat. The constant flow of people traffic forced them to stand near the curb.

"These fuckin' people," Tommy Agro said. "They're like roaches."

He spoke at the big man, John Forzino. It was near noon. The sidewalk traffic on Grand Street was heavy with mostly Chinese, many carrying fresh produce in orange plastic bags. A tiny woman crashed into Agro's back before stepping aside to pass him without excusing herself.

"Jesus Christ!" Agro yelled after the woman.

Forzino and Agro had first met a few minutes earlier in a parking lot on Broome Street. The new acting skipper of Agro's crew was Forzino's uncle. The kid had been sent to Agro to be trained and tested on the street. A career-ending knee injury during his junior year at Ohio State had cut short Forzino's NFL dreams and college education.

Now Agro sized the kid up. He stretched both arms out wide to grab Forzino's broad shoulders.

"You're big enough," he said. "And I know your bloodlines are solid."

Forzino turned sideways to avoid an elderly Chinese man walking with his head down.

"They must love the bumper cars in Coney Island," Agro said.

Forzino smiled. His uncle had told him Tommy Agro could be funny, especially when he was pissed off or when he went on a rant, but there was a darker side to the wiseguy Forzino's uncle had warned him about as well. Tommy Agro was a stone killer.

"We're waiting on a guy, an Irishman friend of mine, before we go see this other guy," Agro said, "although I'd rather wait in a fuckin' zoo than stand out here with these roaches crawling all over the place. My old man must be doing cartwheels in his grave."

Forzino thumbed toward Mulberry Street. "At least it's still Italian over there," he said.

"Yeah, one block in an entire neighborhood," Agro said. "It's no consolation, you ask me. Even the feast next week, San Gennaro, Italians'll be outnumbered twenty to one."

A Chinese woman wearing thick glasses coughed as she passed Agro. He covered his face with both hands.

"I'm telling you," he said over the tops of his hands. "It's up to me I quarantine all of them before another STARS thing they brought here."

"You mean SARS."

"The fuck I just say?"

Forzino was sure Agro had said STARS, but he let it go and stepped in front of the fifty-two-year-old wiseguy to shield him from more passersby.

"Thank you," Agro said. "Although you should earn combat pay fending off these noodles."

"The guy we're going to see here or on Hester?" asked Forzino, hoping it was closer to Hester so they could get out of there.

Agro started walking. He put on his sunglasses. "Yeah, this way," he said, "between Grand and Hester. My Irish friend has the address, he don't see us on Grand."

Forzino followed Agro to the corner and then south onto Baxter Street, where the people traffic was minimal. The address Agro was looking for was in the middle of the block. When they got in front of the building, Agro pulled a cigarette from a pack of Marlboro, lit up, and rested against a parked car.

"We goin' up?" Forzino asked. He was blocking the sidewalk with his huge frame. Two Asian teenagers had to step off the curb to get around him.

"In a minute," said Agro, bending down to examine his Bruno Magli loafers.

He hooked his Ray-Ban sunglasses into his shirt pocket, squinted up at the sky, and turned his focus to a group of Chinese women crossing the street. Two of the women were eating something from a plastic bag with Chinese writing.

"The shit these people eat," he said. "Used to be Italian, Little Italy. Now you gotta step over these Chinks to even find one of our own. I don't know how the holdouts do it, tell you the truth. Must be some axe to bear."

"Cross," said Forzino.

The wiseguy squinted. "Why the fuck I wanna cross, the guy lives over here?"

"Cross to bear," Forzino said.

"The fuck you talkin' about?"

Forzino realized he shouldn't have corrected the wiseguy. He made a mental note never to do it again.

"We'll hang here a couple more minutes," Agro said. "Maybe he looks out the window, it gives him the runs he sees us here."

The humidity was getting to Forzino. He removed the gray sports jacket he was wearing.

"Could use that for a circus tent, kid, you know that?" Agro joked. "How much you bench? Your uncle said you could lift cars from their bumpers."

Forzino blushed from the compliment. "Yeah, sometimes," he said. "Small cars. We used to do that on campus sometimes, move cars around like that."

"Serious, how much you lift?"

"Five hundred."

"Jesus H. Christ. The fuck your mother feed you?"

"I also weigh close to three hundred, so it's not that big a deal."

"Bull-fucking-shit it's not. Five hundred pounds is five hundred pounds, my friend. We had a guy a few years back, legend on the street this kid was. Jimmy Mangino. Everybody called him Jimmy Bench-Press. Could lift like four hundred, I think. Something like that. And he was tough as a Mandingo's dick is long from what I heard. He got sent up by a rat, maybe forever. Just got made the day they bust him, talk about shit luck."

"The same day he was straightened out?"

"Same day, morning after," Agro said, "something like that. Rats. What you gonna do nowadays? They're like these people, like roaches, they're all over."

He pointed up at the building they were standing in front of.

"This guy we're seeing today?" Forzino asked.

"What your uncle is thinking. Yeah, maybe. He was running book for the other guy before he did a flip, the rat cocksucker."

"You mean Nicky D'Angelo."

Agro nodded. "He was skipper of this crew before your uncle got upped, yeah. The guy upstairs ran book for Nicky. Seems kind of funny how this guy retires three months before Nicky does his back flip into the witness protection program, no? Makes people think. At least your uncle is smart enough to think."

"You guys safe after Nicky flipped?"

Agro chuckled. "We fuckin' hope so, I'll tell you that much. But who knows? The reason we got moved to this crew was to keep it tight after the fallout. Your uncle got upped and I'm his man to take care of things. It's the only way to keep this thing of ours in one piece anymore. We can't take chances no more."

Forzino grew nervous wondering if they were about to kill someone. He wiped his forehead with a paper napkin he had stashed in his pocket.

Agro slapped him on the back. "God bless," he said. "I envy your age. You don't smoke, right?"

"No, never."

"Good for you. It's a bad habit. So's the drugs, which I'll assume you're not involved with. Drinking, too, is bad enough, but a guy's gotta have something to take the edge off once in a while."

Forzino nodded obediently. "I hear you," he said.

Agro tossed his cigarette butt into the curb, lit a fresh one, and glanced at his watch.

"Looks like my friend ain't gonna make it," he said. "Him, too, you can learn from. Tough son of a bitch, he is. Not afraid to swing a bat he has to. And it's what you can do with a baseball bat that counts. Don't ever forget it. I seen guys bigger'n you go down from scrappy little pricks my size wielding a pipe, a bat, a two-by-four, whatever the fuck. The thing is to never blink, you gotta go to work on somebody. You just do what you gotta do and get out of there."

Forzino swallowed hard.

Agro said, "You're gonna be tested sooner or later, and then you gotta have it on the spot, soon's it's called for."

"We doing anything right now, over here?" Forzino asked.

Agro squinted at him. "Here? You been playing too much football, my friend, maybe without your helmet. Not here, ever, no way. No beefs allowed around these parts. Last crap that went down here was Crazy Joe when they whacked him eating dinner around the corner in Umberto's. Before they moved the place couple blocks north to Broome Street. It caused all kinds of problems, that cowboy hit. Don't you know that?"

Forzino shook his head. "No, I didn't. Joe who?"

"It was part of the Colombo wars," said Agro, clearly upset that Forzino was ignorant of mob history. "This place, Little Italy, is ours, in spite of the Chinks infested it. How could you not know about Joe Gallo getting whacked at Umberto's? They give the fuckin' tours around the corner, in front of Ferrara's, to the mopes step off the buses there. It's one of the highlights, they talk about that hit. Maybe you should take one."

Forzino shrugged again. "I thought we're the Vignieri family."

Agro stared hard at the big man until Forzino shrugged from embarrassment.

"Forgetaboutit," the wiseguy said, running the words together. "Let's go see this guy."

CHAPTER 2

Bobby Gennaro frowned at the bouquet of yellow roses in the vase on the dining room table. He had set it there a few minutes ago alongside the engagement ring he'd bought while his girlfriend was away on business. He had originally planned to let her find the ring by itself on the table when she walked in the door. Then he thought he might set it alongside a piece of her favorite chocolate raspberry cake, but a friend had suggested roses were the way to go.

Now he was confused.

He looked back and forth from the cake to the flowers when the apartment buzzer sounded and interrupted his dilemma. Bobby walked to the window and looked down to the street. Whoever had buzzed was already inside the building.

He grabbed the engagement ring and slipped it inside his front pants pocket, then moved the vase of flowers from the table to the kitchen counter and stood it alongside the piece of cake. He circled the table once more to look down at the street but stopped short when he saw his reflection in the glass. The scar along the left side of his face was clearly visible from across the room; a permanent reminder of where he'd once spent eighteen months of his life, in Sing Sing penitentiary. He forced himself to turn away and headed to the door to look through the peephole.

Bobby frowned at the sight of a big, young bruiser followed by an older, shorter man he immediately recognized as they stepped off the elevator into the hallway.

"Shit," he said.

Tommy Agro was a wiseguy with a mob crew rival to the one Bobby had been affiliated with before he retired from the bookmaking business three months ago. Seeing Agro traveling with muscle wasn't a good sign. Bobby had been expecting a visit from someone with the Vignieri crime family since the day he read about his former boss cutting a deal with the federal government.

Agro stepped in front of the big man out in the hallway and was approaching the apartment door first. Bobby opened it before the wiseguy knocked.

"You brought my gold watch?" Bobby asked without emotion.

"Yeah, sure," said Agro before thumbing over his shoulder. "This is Johnny-boy Forzino, Joe Quack's godson. I'm showing him the ropes."

Bobby ignored Forzino. He stepped back inside the apartment to open the door wider. Forzino nodded as he passed. Bobby did not return the gesture.

"What's it about?" he asked Agro.

The wiseguy was already walking through the dining area into the living room. Forzino had stepped inside the kitchen off to the left. The apartment was a top-floor, loft-like duplex with a twenty-six-foot cathedral ceiling. It featured an open space from the kitchen to the bedroom and bathroom in the rear. The stairs were off to the right behind the closet facing the apartment door.

Agro glanced up the stairs leading to the second floor and then looked straight up at the ceiling.

"Nice," he said. "Looks like a fuckin' church, that roof."

"We like it," Bobby said. "What's up?"

"Nicky D'Angelo, the rat cocksucker."

"What about him?"

Agro forced a chuckle. "Can I at least sit, have a cup of coffee?"

Bobby glanced back at Forzino. He stood like a statue blocking the kitchen.

"Sure," Bobby said. "I'll put up a pot."

He thumbed toward the dining room table as he sidestepped the big man. "Have a seat," he said.

"I'd rather stand," Forzino said.

Bobby had wondered who would take over Nicky D'Angelo's businesses. When his former boss was pinched middling drugs to the Russian mob, D'Angelo had flipped to avoid a thirty-to-life sentence. Bobby had already retired a few months earlier. Another three months, he had thought, and he would've been home free.

Agro and Forzino had come to remind him that he wasn't off the hook yet, not really.

"So, how's life?" the wiseguy asked. "Looks like you're doing okay."

Bobby spoke over his shoulder while filling the coffeepot with water. "Looks can be deceiving," he said. "My girlfriend makes a lot of money. This is her place."

"Yeah, what's she do?"

"Videography."

"Video what?"

"For lawyers," Bobby said. "She films depositions for lawyers. She's working one of the big corporate scandals out in Texas now."

"She's a Chink, no?" Agro asked.

"Jerk-off," said Bobby under his breath.

"What's that?" Agro asked.

Bobby turned the water off and turned to face the wiseguy. "She's Chinese," he said.

"No disrespect intended," Agro said. "She's got money, she's a beautiful thing."

Bobby had never dealt with Agro in the past, but he'd been told by a few people the Brooklyn wiseguy was a first-class asshole. Now he was learning it firsthand.

Agro pointed to the flowers on the kitchen counter before leaning forward to try to smell them. "Nice," he said. "Tokyo Rose, right?"

"Excuse me?" Bobby said.

Agro looked to Forzino for support. "You know, like in the war there. Tokyo Rose."

"She was Japanese," Bobby said. "Lin Yao is Chinese."

Agro was instantly confused. "Huh?" he said.

Bobby shook his head.

"Anyway," Agro continued, "Joe Quack's got your old crew. They moved me over with him and brought the kid on to learn the ropes."

"It wasn't my crew. I ran an office. It was Nicky's crew."

"Nicky's a rat cocksucker. How we prefer to refer to him now he's flipped."

Bobby came out of the kitchen and sat at the table across from Agro. Forzino continued to stand and stare from just outside the kitchen.

"So," Bobby said. "What's it all got to do with me?"

Agro removed his sunglasses from his pocket and set them on the table. He said, "There's concern you knew something before the rat fuck flipped, tell you the truth. There's concern from what's left of his crew, and there's concern from the new guys running the show there, your old office."

Bobby maintained eye contact with Agro. "It's wasted energy, all that concern. I didn't flip on anybody. I didn't know Nick was going to flip. I decided to get out was all that happened, end of story."

Agro smiled. "Just like that, three months before D'Angelo turns?"

"Just like that," Bobby said. "I won't even bullshit you and tell you I saw the writing on the wall. I didn't have enough to do with Nicky or anybody else in his crew to give a shit. I didn't know he ran drugs. I ran the office and took care of my own accounts. When people were slow, I went after them. I didn't use muscle, and I didn't miss a beat for ten years. Never skimmed a dime or was accused of skimming. That's the reality of it."

Agro sat back on his chair. "Except the only word you got on that is you're own and that rat cocksucker, Nicky D'Angelo. Question is, did you rehearse it?"

Bobby could see where it was going. He shook his head. "You guys," he said, "you just don't know when to leave a good enough thing alone."

Agro sat forward again, this time looking pissed off. "Excuse me?" he said. "You guys?"

"I left the office in good shape," Bobby said. "If it's not doing as well now as it was before I left, then it's probably a management issue. Or maybe the new guy is skimming. I wouldn't know, because I haven't cared since the day I left. As for the bullshit about flipping, what the hell do I have to flip about? In case you don't know, I did a bid. Almost two years, stand-up." He pointed to the scar along the left side of his face. "Where I got this," he said. "As far as D'Angelo, I'm out of the loop. And don't forget I can still be indicted myself. I ran his office, it can come back to me the same as you whatever he's giving the feds."

Agro smirked. "You remember another guy named Gennaro they found dead on the Garden State last winter?" he asked. "Frank Gennaro his name was."

"Yeah, I do," Bobby said. "And he's no relation, nor did I ever meet him. He gave up Jimmy Valentine, I'm not mistaken, but I read that in the papers same as everybody else, probably in one of Jerry Capeci's Gangland articles, same as everybody else."

Agro glared at Bobby a long moment. "Yeah, well, Quack thinks there should be a tax," he said. "It's his thing now, your old office. He's the new skipper, so it's his law."

"Except I was out three months ago," Bobby said. "New laws don't apply to me."

Agro smiled at Forzino this time. "Oh, really?" he said. "What are you, the Prince of fuckin' Bel-Air, new laws don't apply?"

Bobby was doing his best not to insult the imbecile sitting across from him, but it was impossible, exactly the way these conversations were meant to go. "I'm just saying," he said, "I was out, Tommy. How can Quack tax me now? At least call it what it is, a shakedown."

Agro pointed a finger. "You'll want to watch your mouth about now."

Bobby took a deep breath. He let the air out of his lungs in one long exhale of frustration.

"And keep the huffing-puffing routine to yourself," Agro added. "We're here to tell you what the deal is. You retired three months ago you no doubt socked some scratch away. Quack wants his end of a new tax. A percent or two of whatever you grossed for a month out of the office there. Consider it a luxury tax, you need to feel it's justified."

Bobby smirked. "Yeah, right," he said.

"Well, that's what it is, so there's no use arguing. I don't know how much you did in a month, gross I mean, but I'm sure we can come to an agreement on it."

"I did a million a week minimum," Bobby said. "Figure five million a month. A percent of that is a fantasy, I can tell you that right now. I'm not paying it. Even if I had it, I wouldn't pay it. I thought you guys left extortion to the Chinese."

"Again with the commentary," Agro said.

Bobby had ten thousand dollars in cash sitting behind the stereo receiver on the wall shelf in the living room. If he thought it would get rid of Agro now and forever, he would hand it over with a smile, but he knew it would only encourage the wiseguy to press for more.

"I'm not wealthy, just retired," he said. "There's a difference."

Agro pointed at Bobby's arms. "You were always a tough kid, I can see you're still working out, hitting the weights, whatever. Maybe you think you're strong enough. It happens sometimes. Guys get out of a thing, forget who they were involved with. I can see it, how that happens. Your arms look bigger'n last time I saw you."

Bobby rolled his eyes.

Agro pointed at Forzino. "The kid here used to play ball in the Big Ten," he said. "Monster, ain't he? Benches five hundred pounds."

Bobby said, "With a pause or without?"

"What?" Forzino asked.

Bobby turned to him. "With a pause or without? Did you stop the weight on your chest or bounce it for momentum?"

"Five hundred pounds is five hundred pounds," Agro said. "The fuck's the difference?"

"He bounced it it's more like four fifty, maybe less."

"Oh, yeah, how much you bench?" Agro asked.

"I don't know," Bobby said. "I haven't tested myself since I was away. I'm retired, remember?"

"You're also a smart-ass, I can see that," said Agro, again pointing a finger.

"You wanna test against me?" Forzino asked.

Agro smiled. So did Bobby.

"What's so funny to you?" Agro asked.

Bobby said, "You must be hurting, this is the best you can do, try and shake a guy down with another guy is gonna challenge him to a weight-lifting contest."

Agro's eyes narrowed. His face turned red.

Forzino said, "I didn't mean a contest, asshole. I meant a fight."

Bobby turned to him again. "Oh, then excuse me, I had it all wrong."

Agro was standing. He pointed down at Bobby. "A point on five million," he said. "Your words, and that's what I'm taking back to Quack from here. Whatever he decides is the number, you'll pay it. You might get a visit anyway, for being such a rude cocksucker of a host."

"I think the coffee's ready now," Bobby said. "You want?"

Agro was headed for the apartment door. He ignored the offer. Forzino glared at Bobby as he followed his boss.

"I'll get the door," Bobby said.

He waited until they were in the hallway before letting it close. He watched through the peephole as Agro and Forzino walked the length of the hallway to the elevator. He could see Agro was still pissed off and animated as he motioned back toward the apartment. Bobby waited until they disappeared inside the elevator before turning away from the door.

When he did, he noticed Agro's sunglasses on the dining room table. "Fuck," he said, and wondered if it was just a coincidence the wiseguy had left his glasses or, more likely, if it was an excuse to send Forzino back to get them later.

CHAPTER 3

LIN YAO JI dropped the sunglasses on the dining room table as soon as she learned who they belonged to. She looked at Bobby and set both her hands on her hips.

"One of those goons was up here today?"

"Two, actually," Bobby said. "And I'm expecting one of them to return, maybe more, for the glasses later tonight."

Lin Yao took a moment. She glanced from the flowers that had been waiting for her to the sunglasses and sighed. She had just flown home from Dallas after eight days of filming corporate depositions. She was tired and anxious to relax. She was also hoping Bobby had some good news about finding a legitimate job while she was away.

"Maybe we should just throw them out?" she said about the glasses.

Bobby shook his head. "Won't stop them from coming back. I'm pretty sure Agro left them here on purpose."

"Well, I don't want them up here where we live. I thought that was against the rules anyway, bothering people here, in this neighborhood."

"It is, but Agro is an old-world wiseguy and he needs to remind himself. He was schooling some wannabe, a big kid played college football. Agro was probably feeling his oats lecturing the kid. He has to save face now, because I told him I wouldn't pay, so the kid'll come back, maybe with somebody else, and he'll try and intimidate me."

"And?"

"And I'll teach the wannabe a lesson," Bobby said. "Hopefully, I won't have to mark him up and escalate the thing. Either way, though, Agro won't like what happened. They'll offer me a sit-down they know I can't agree to. Then it'll either step up or they'll go away."

Lin Yao wiped sweat from her forehead with a paper napkin. "Yeah, right, sure they'll go away. Those Mafia assholes, I doubt it."

Bobby smiled at his girlfriend. She was one of the toughest people he'd ever known. She was also beautiful. At thirty-three years of age, Lin Yao looked as if she was still twenty-five. She was five foot four, 119 pounds, most of it muscle. Her black hair was straight. Her ponytail reached the small of her back.

Although she no longer practiced, she had once qualified as a black belt in karate during her senior year of college. To sometimes complicate matters, her older cousin was the head of a local Chinatown street gang, the Mott Street Shadows. Lin Yao's relationship with Bobby had been a problem when they first met, because of her cousin. It was only her strong personality that had kept the problem from becoming a war. In a face-to-face confrontation with her cousin, Lin Yao had stared the street thug down until he saved face by calling her crazy and leaving the apartment.

Now Bobby winked at her. He was thinking about showing her the ring as she stood there tough as nails in a navy blue pinstripe skirt suit. It was one of Bobby's favorite outfits.

"Try on the glasses," he told her. "We can play teacher-student."

"Don't be an asshole," Lin Yao said. "I'd like to take a shower and have a back massage while I'm watching *Jeopardy,* if you can manage to find the time. Four hours on a plane and another four in airports, and then the goddamn humidity outside. I was feeling good about coming home. I was actually looking forward to it."

"Your wish is my command," Bobby said. He reached into his pocket for the ring.

"What are you going to do about those assholes?" she asked. "You want to get married and start a family, but now here they are back in our life again."

He let go of the ring inside his pocket. "I'll handle it," he said.

"How?"

"That's my business."

"Not if they're coming here it isn't. It's my business, too."

"They won't do it again. I promise."

Lin Yao bit her lower lip. She had heard the promise before.

Bobby pulled his hand from his pocket. "How was the deposition?" he asked, to change the subject.

The job had been long and tedious and she wasn't in the mood to discuss it now. Instead, she stared daggers at her boyfriend for avoiding a problem they both knew wasn't going away.

"What?" Bobby asked.

Lin Yao headed for the bedroom. "I'm going to take a shower and soak in a bath," she said. "When I come out, I want to discuss what we're going to do about those assholes you used to do business with."

"Yes, ma'am," Bobby said.

Lin Yao flipped him the bird.

He waited until he heard the shower before heading out of the apartment with Tommy Agro's sunglasses. One way of avoiding a return visit from Agro and his goon was to visit them instead. It was also a way of keeping Lin Yao from being way too angry for him to ask her to marry him later.

Outside on the street Bobby dialed a number he had promised Lin Yao he'd never dial again, his old bookmaking office. He spoke to a clerk he didn't recognize before he was passed on to the new guy supervising the operation, somebody named Joe. Bobby asked Joe to contact Tommy Agro and to have the wiseguy call back.

He decided to smoke a cigarette while he waited for the return call. The last thing he needed was for Agro or his muscle, or anyone else they sent, to show up while Lin Yao was home alone. She just might call her cousin on Mott Street and start a war with the mob before she finished watching *Jeopardy.*

The return call came at the same time Bobby finished his first smoke.

"Speak," a deep voice said.

It sounded like the big kid, Forzino. Bobby wanted confirmation. "Who's this?" he asked.

"Who are you?"

"Who's this?" Bobby asked again.

"What's the difference?" the voice said.

Bobby was sure it was Forzino.

"I'm on my way uptown," Bobby said. "Where are you?"

"I'm in transit."

"Aren't we all?"

"Hey, don't be an asshole."

Bobby couldn't resist. "Speaking of assholes, which one am I speaking to?"

"Tough guy, huh?" the voice said. "I was at your place earlier."

Bobby smiled. "Yeah, well, I'm heading up to Murray Hill," he said. "You tell me where to go and I'll leave the glasses there for you."

"No good. You hand them off to me."

"Excuse me?"

"Put them in my hands. My friend likes those glasses, he don't want anything to happen to them."

Bobby chuckled. "That's rich, pal. I'll meet you out in front of Christina's on Second Avenue off Thirty-fourth in fifteen minutes. You're not there in twenty, I'll leave them with the girl tends bar there."

"You better be around when I get there," the voice warned.

Bobby hung up.

It wasn't starting off the way he had hoped, but at least he'd be taking it away from the apartment. Lin Yao would be pissed he wasn't around to massage her shoulders during *Jeopardy,* but he could make up for that later, he was thinking.

He would pick up a fresh piece of the chocolate raspberry cake when he dropped off the sunglasses. He'd serve it to her in bed and let her eat while he massaged her back and legs until she was relaxed again.

And then he would slip her the ring and ask her to marry him.

•◆•

TOMMY AGRO SAID, "Okay, I'm gonna get out the car, walk over to the trailer there, knock on the door, and shoot the guy opens it. I'll go inside and shoot whoever else is in there and come right back out. The thing for you to do is remain calm and not panic. I come back, get in, and you take off. Not too fast and not too slow, either. Just like we stopped to pick up a container of milk. Okay?"

Forzino swallowed hard. "Got it," he managed to say.

Agro screwed a silencer onto the barrel of the Walther. He said, "Turn the thing around so we don't waste time after it's done."

Forzino nodded.

Agro winked. "I'm right back."

Forzino made a U-turn in the used-car lot and pointed the front end of the Lexus toward the exit. He watched Agro in the rearview mirror and saw the wiseguy shoot a man standing inside the trailer doorway.

"Jesus Christ," Forzino said.

He saw Agro step inside the trailer. Less than thirty seconds later Agro was stepping down out of the trailer; he was carrying something out in front of him. He walked to the car and set a pizza box on the backseat before sitting up front.

"Still hot," he said, thumbing over his shoulder.

Forzino turned his head and saw steam coming from the box.

"Okay, let's go," Agro said.

Forzino hit the gas a bit too hard and the car jolted forward.

"Easy does it," Agro said. "We're not in a rush here."

Forzino eased off the gas pedal and turned onto Flatlands Avenue.

Agro opened the glove compartment and removed a pair of latex gloves. He put them on one at a time. He then pulled a roll of black electric tape out from under his seat and removed the silencer from the Walther he had used less than two minutes ago. He used a chamois cloth to wipe down both the weapon and the silencer, then wrapped black electric tape around both separately until they were completely covered.

"Turn right on Rockaway Parkway and take it down the Belt," he told Forzino. "Go around the circle there and head east."

Forzino did as he was told. Fifteen minutes later Agro told him to pull off the parkway and turn off the lights.

"Here?" Forzino asked.

Agro pointed and said, "Yeah, before the bridge there."

Forzino parked the car on the grass alongside the parkway and turned the headlights off. Agro got out of the car and ran up the path on the bridge over Spring Creek. He heaved the taped weapon out over the waters and hustled back to the car.

"Okay, back on the Belt again and get off the Cross Bay exit," Agro said once he was back inside the car. "Turn right on Cross Bay and we'll get rid of this other thing in one of the canals off the boulevard there."

Forzino waited for a break in the right-lane traffic before he pulled back onto the parkway. Agro lit up a cigarette. After a few minutes Forzino reminded him about Bobby Gennaro.

"This was more important," Agro said. "Besides, that one you're doing on your own."

Forzino nearly gasped. "I'm killing him?"

Agro chuckled. "No, not yet, relax. Just give him a message. Nail him in the stomach once or something else that's quiet. Don't mark him up where someone can see it. Not yet."

"Okay, but how will I find him? He was headed to some restaurant in Murray Hill he said."

"Whenever we're finished here tonight, you drop me off and go to his place," Agro said. "It's not like you're gonna make a scene there. He lets you up and you tag him one, stomach or the nuts, whatever you want. Just try and avoid a fistfight that'll make a scene, wake up the neighbors. You know what I'm saying here?"

"Got it," Forzino said.

"Good. Your uncle wanted it done this way, just so you know. It steps you up a helluva lot faster'n than the slow grind of running errands and putting up with somebody's bullshit the next five, ten years. You're now an accessory to a hit, whether you saw something or not. And you're the only one can know I'm the one did it, so anything comes back to me, I know it's you, *capisce*?"

Forzino nodded.

"Good," Agro said. "Not that I'm worried. Like I said, you come from good stocklines."

Forzino's eyebrows furrowed. He was thinking Agro meant to say bloodlines.

"When the time comes, the next thing'll be yours, and you'll be in position to step up to the big leagues," Agro added.

Forzino forced a smile. "Great," he said. "Dynamite."

"Don't be so nervous, kid," Agro said. "You did good. The reason I didn't mention anything before was not to give you time to think. Easiest way to fuck up a hit is to think about it."

"My uncle said you're the guy to learn from."

"And he wasn't jerking your chain. You know how many of these me and him did together? Forgetaboutit."

Forzino smiled again, this time a little less nervously.

"Tomorrow morning, afternoon, whatever, you're gonna read about this thing tonight in the papers, see it on the news," Agro said. "Just forget it ever happened and never discuss it. Never ever."

"Right," Forzino said.

They were approaching Cross Bay Boulevard. Forzino turned onto the exit ramp while Agro fooled with the radio. It had been tuned to a station playing Frank Sinatra. Agro turned the dial until he found something he liked.

"Anita Baker," the wiseguy said. "You can't beat the pipes on this broad."

Forzino smiled.

"These people, say what you want, you can't beat them for music."

"They got soul," Forzino said.

"I'm not talking about that rap shit," Agro said. "I'm talking this here, listen."

Agro turned up the radio's volume and closed his eyes. "Fuckin' beautiful is what that there is. It's like being in heaven."

Forzino turned right onto Cross Bay Boulevard. "How far up do I go?"

Agro still had his eyes closed. "Out past the lights, closer to Rockaway," he said. "There's a bunch of small canals out that way. Just let me know when you see water."

Forzino nodded, although Agro couldn't see him. The wiseguy seemed to be lost in bliss as he hummed the melody on the radio. Forzino wondered if this was how Agro handled killing, if it was his routine after a hit, if the music relaxed him.

Agro said, "Pizza smells good, no?" Forzino didn't answer. Agro added, "The key is to put it out of your mind soon's it's done."

The wiseguy had read his mind, Forzino thought.

"You find something to take the edge off, get a little food in your stomach, some wine, and move on to the next thing," Agro continued. "It is what it is, our thing. You enjoy life while you can and never look back."

Forzino glanced at Agro. This time the wiseguy's eyes were open.

"You don't want that pizza, let me know. I'll dump it with this other thing." He was holding up the taped silencer.

"Right," Forzino said. "I don't really feel like pizza."

"You sure?" Agro asked. "It's a sin to waste food like this." He leaned over the seat, grabbed a slice from the box and took a bite.

"Okay, then," he said after he swallowed. "We'll go to the clam bar after. I'm buying."

CHAPTER 4

Bobby had hung around the restaurant an extra half hour before giving up and leaving the sunglasses with the bartender. He was home before Lin Yao was asleep, but it was long after *Jeopardy* had ended.

She wasn't interested in the fresh piece of cake he'd picked up. In fact, she was still in a bad mood. It took him a full half hour of rubbing her shoulders and neck before she would even talk to him.

He worked the backs of her thighs with both hands until she seemed to give in and moan with pleasure. He alternated between kneading and rubbing her leg muscles and then used his fingertips to lightly brush her skin.

"That's nice," she whispered. "Don't stop."

He didn't. He leaned over in the bed and continued to tease her. He touched her up and down the length of her body, his fingertips lightly brushing the backs of her ankles and then moving up around her hips and back down through the crack of her ass. He leaned over and kissed the backs of her thighs after she lifted herself enough for his hand to slip between her legs and touch her there.

She turned on her side, reached for him, and they made love. It was soft, but passionate, and it reminded Bobby of how much in love he was with her. He forgot about the ring as he brought her to climax again and again. When they were finished, she had come a few times to his once. Afterward he teased her about it.

"You don't sound so tough when you're in the middle of an orgasm," he said.

"Now you wanna talk?" she said.

"You call me baby a lot, too."

"You are a baby."

"Yeah, but you said you loved me."

"I was in the middle of an orgasm. Do you really think I knew what I was saying?"

"I think you meant it."

"Maybe. How was the opera?"

"Huh?"

"The disc I told you to listen to. How was it?"

It was something she had asked him to do so he'd be familiar with the music when they attended an opera later in the week. He remembered it now, but he had only listened to the first act while she was away.

"Oh, okay, I guess. I like the way it started."

"The prelude. You probably heard it a hundred times and don't know it."

Bobby smiled. "What else don't I know?"

"That we have tickets to see it this week."

"Actually I did remember that, just now in fact."

"Yes, well, you should've remembered. I told you a half dozen times."

"Or maybe I was dreaming it. You told me while I was sleeping, right?"

"You're not funny."

"But I'm handsome, in a hard-looking way. You actually said that, too, before. Right before you came, I forget which time."

Lin Yao closed her eyes.

Bobby said, "Handsome in a hard-looking way. I like the sound of that."

"You're not going to stop talking now, are you?" she asked, her eyes still closed.

Bobby tickled her until she rolled over and cocked a fist.

"I'll bust your nose, I swear it," she said.

Bobby stopped. "You want tea?"

"Yes, go make some."

"Want me to spike it?"

"Sure, fine."

"Rum or something else?"

"Rum, I don't care."

"How about Drambuie?"

Lin Yao made another fist. "Anything, I don't care," she said. "I want you to go away and leave me alone for fifteen minutes. Let me close my eyes and enjoy what's left of the moment."

"There were three moments, to be exact. I counted them."

"Well, you can't count either. There were four."

"Think one of them was my kid?"

"You mean our kid?"

"Yeah, what I said."

"No, I used my diaphragm."

"When you gonna lose that thing?"

"When you get a job and get rid of those Mafia assholes."

He could give her the ring now, but he didn't want to argue about the mob again. It had been an issue since before he left the bookmaking business. Bobby wanted to leave the business so they could marry and start a family. Lin Yao wanted him to be stable "in a normal life," what she had called it, before she made the commitment. He had hoped to jump-start the process with the engagement ring.

He got up off the bed and started for the kitchen. He stopped at the bedroom door. "Four, you said? Damn, I must be good."

"You're adequate," Lin Yao said. "Most men are, except others don't talk as much."

Bobby went to the kitchen and took his time preparing the tea. He glanced up at the clock and saw it was nearly midnight. He wondered if Tommy Agro's new muscle had picked up the sunglasses yet. He thought about calling the restaurant to find out when the door buzzer sounded.

"Shit," he said.

He went to the living room windows and looked down. It was Agro's bruiser, Forzino. This time he was alone. Bobby buzzed the lobby door and then stepped outside the apartment to wait in the hallway. If Lin Yao were to wake up and find a mob goon in the apartment, he might as well hock the ring.

He heard the elevator start from the lobby and walked the length of the hallway to wait for it.

•◆•

JOHN FORZINO WAS barely able to hold down the spicy calamari he'd eaten at the clam bar in Howard Beach. He was amazed at Tommy Agro's appetite and how the smaller man had finished two slices of the pizza he'd taken from the used car lot and then an entree at the clam bar before ordering a large slice of tiramisù.

After he dropped Agro off, Forzino had to stop the car twice, because he thought he was about to hurl the late meal he'd just eaten. Somehow he'd managed to keep the food inside his stomach and make the drive back into Manhattan.

The thing of it was, he was now involved in at least one murder, maybe more, and he hadn't done anything but sit in the car and wait. Yet the wiseguy had made a point of telling him he was an accessory. Agro had also mentioned that it was done the way his uncle had wanted it.

Forzino wondered if he would've gone through with it if he had had the time to think about it. He ran the possibilities through his mind a few times while he searched for a parking spot in Little Italy.

"I'm not sure I want to kill somebody yet," he could've told Agro.

"Maybe I can go through the slow grind and take another five years to decide if I really want this."

Yeah, right, and that would've been the end of his new employment situation. He'd be driving a truck all over again, one of the things he had done since he had left college prematurely. It was bad enough that his cheerleader fiancée was quickly getting fed up with his life without prospects since his knee injury had ended his football career. If he blew this gig, he'd probably lose her, too. Lately their discussions about him working for his mobbed-up uncle were the only things that seemed to excite her.

Fuck that shit, Forzino was thinking. He'd learn to get over the queasiness soon enough. Driving a truck and putting up with all the bullshit it entailed, between the prick bosses he had worked for, the traffic, and the tickets they deducted from his salary, he'd learn to kill and keep his stomach soon enough.

And his fiancée wouldn't budge from his side once he was a made guy. In fact, once he went all the way, she'd be the one worried about whether or not he'd hang around to get married.

Forzino smiled as he stepped into the elevator and wondered about some of the trim he'd already sampled at his uncle's strip joint in Brooklyn. The one who had given him a blow job in the men's room two nights ago wasn't the prettiest thing he'd ever seen, but she sure was efficient.

He was still smiling when the elevator door opened on the fifth floor and Bobby Gennaro was standing there. Forzino started to say something when Gennaro's right hand suddenly closed around his windpipe.

"Lesson number one," the retired bookmaker told him through clenched teeth. "You're gonna put the drop on someone, you don't ring his doorbell."

Forzino was having trouble breathing. His mouth was partway open as he sucked what little air he could through his mouth. Gennaro blocked the elevator door from closing with his left foot.

"Lesson number two," he continued. "You don't know what you're up against, learn first. You have me by about eighty pounds, my friend, and maybe a hundred fifty on the bench, but I've been doing this a lot longer'n you. Respect the experience."

Forzino's sucking sounds were louder now. He was worried he might pass out.

Gennaro didn't relax his grip. Instead, he said, "Just hope you never get to lesson number three."

Forzino's eyes started to blink from losing consciousness. Gennaro finally let go. Forzino felt his entire body heave as he struggled to catch his breath.

"Fuck," he whispered a moment before he doubled over and held both knees with his hands.

"Tell Agro whatever you want," Gennaro said. "I'll go along with it because I don't want any more trouble. Tell him you smacked me around and I got the message. Just don't make the mistake of thinking you can come back and try again. You do that, the next time I'll leave you with bruises you have to explain. Trust me, it'll be embarrassing."

Forzino was still bent at the waist. He glanced up at Gennaro.

"Well?" he heard Gennaro ask.

Forzino nodded. "Okay," he said. "Okay."

The elevator door finally closed. Forzino used it to brace himself from falling down.

CHAPTER 5

THE ONE INSIDE the doorway is Avito," Detective John DeNafria said. "The one behind the desk is Furlenatto. The guy in the bathroom doorway is one Ralph Marino. I haven't heard of him before. Could be collateral damage."

DeNafria was briefing his new partner at the Brooklyn crime scene in Canarsie. They had gone inside the trailer for a look earlier. Now they were back outside in the used-car lot going over the sketch DeNafria had labeled with the names of the victims. Sweat drops stained the sketch. It was another hot and humid day. The heat was oppressive.

Ward wiped his forehead with a handkerchief. "We're lucky it was a night kill," he said. "A couple more hours in this heat and the smell would be too much to stand here."

"Avito and Furlenatto were made guys," said DeNafria, ignoring the commentary. "Probably part of the purge. Four of the five made guys with that crew are now dead since D'Angelo flipped. The only one still out there is Fred Panico. Either he's bolted for the Yucatán or he's in some FBI safe house playing cards with the agents."

"And if he hasn't flipped yet, he probably will when he sees this on the news later," Michael Ward said with a slight Irish accent. He yawned loudly before excusing himself.

"Rough night or a lucky one?" asked DeNafria, wiping sweat from his face with a paper napkin.

"I wish," Ward said. "Neither."

Ward had been transferred to the organized crime unit after eight years with narcotics, the last two working undercover infiltrating an Irish gang on the West Side of Manhattan.

"Well, at least you know who Panico is," DeNafria said. "You've been studying."

"Nothing else to do the last two weeks," Ward said. He suppressed another yawn and added, "They give me the book with the names of the players and their idiosyncrasies. I had nothing but time waiting to work with you."

"Idiosyncrasies?" DeNafria said. "I'm impressed. And I appreciate the effort. Not everybody makes one, especially once they come to OC."

"Aye, well, I didn't come here to prepare for my retirement, John. I'm too young for that. We both are."

The detectives shared a chuckle, although DeNafria couldn't help but remember that Ward was at least eight years his junior.

Ward pointed to a stocky man talking on a cell phone. "Kaprowski give you the rundown?" he asked. "He said he would."

DeNafria glanced at the sixty-three-year-old deputy inspector of the organized crime unit, Edward Kaprowski. The twenty-five-year veteran had been promoted through the ranks of the Organized Crime Investigative Division since its inception in 1984. He was a fireplug of a man with broad shoulders, a bull neck, and a flattop haircut. His rugged face turned red as he yelled into his cell phone.

"Something to do with IA," DeNafria said. "I've had my own problems with those rats. Doesn't make you a bad cop you're on their hit list."

Ward was watching Kaprowski's animated conversation. "Guy's gonna bust a blood vessel," he said.

"Why we call him the pleasant Polack," DeNafria said.

Ward turned away from watching the deputy inspector. He said,

"Doesn't make me a bad cop or a bad person. But they did make my life miserable, Internal Affairs. They made it a living hell. My PBA rep advised organized crime. I wasn't too excited about it, tell you the truth, but it has to beat riding a desk."

"Yeah, well, don't let Kaprowski hear you say that," DeNafria said.

"Why's that?"

"The old stump is into this unit. He's been with it from the get-go, Kaprowski. Was one of the first undercover guys working the streets."

"He doesn't look that old."

"He is," DeNafria said. He wiped his face again, then tilted his head at Ward. "I hope you're not an adrenaline junky. I'm not sure I can handle another one of those."

Ward was also wiping his face. "Used to be," he said. "Hurt my back a couple years ago, so I learned the hard way. Can't afford the time off or I would've put in a claim on the back already. My ass is relatively calm these days."

"Relatively?"

"I've learned my lessons. I take deep breaths now before I'm too pissed off."

DeNafria had spent the last ten of his fifteen-year police career with the Organized Crime Unit. Ward had been with the force just under ten years.

The two detectives had been paired up a few days after the start of what appeared to be an internal war going on within the Vignieri crime family. The department wanted to stop the war from escalating. DeNafria was pretty sure they couldn't.

"Who else is vulnerable used to be around D'Angelo?" Ward asked.

"A few associates, we have to assume," DeNafria said. "Anybody who was making money for them, although whoever is ordering these hits will probably try to realign the money guys before whacking them. Word is, unconfirmed right now, the new skipper is Joe Quack. You read up on him?"

"Quastifare," said Ward, suppressing a yawn this time. "He was under a skipper on Staten Island. Old-world as they get, according to his papers."

"Yeah, him and Tommy Agro were close coming up," DeNafria said. "Agro is a cold-blooded killer. So's Joe Quack, except his kills are usually business-related. Agro is known to kill for being in a bad mood."

"The guy in the subway," Ward said. "I read about that."

"It was no joke," DeNafria said. "Poor bastard stepped on the back of Agro's heels getting on a train. Agro warned him not to do it again or he'd kill him. The train started and stopped short, flung the guy into Agro by accident. Agro waits for the guy to get off and follows him, whacks him in front of his house. We got it discussed on two different wires his lawyers had tossed out of court on technicalities. The guys on the wires were both informants, but they got caught in a few dozen lies made their wires and their testimony useless."

"So, he's lucky as well as vicious."

"Something like that, yeah."

Ward stepped aside to let a member of the forensic unit pass. He yawned into a fist this time. "And he's paired up now with Quack you're thinking?"

"Makes sense," DeNafria said. "Maybe we can learn a little more from an associate used to be with D'Angelo's crew. A guy ran book for them until a few months back."

"Follow the money, eh?"

"He's retired since."

"Retired?"

DeNafria winked at his new partner. "And he's even younger than you," he said, "although probably not half as tired."

•◆•

"DID YOU STEAL from those assholes?" Lin Yao wanted to know the next morning at breakfast.

They were sitting in a booth at the Moondance diner on Sixth Avenue. Lin Yao enjoyed the cinnamon-spiked coffee there. Bobby preferred his coffee without designer effects. He made a face after sipping some from his cup.

"Oh, stop it," Lin Yao said. "If you can drink that Italian mud, you can handle a little cinnamon. And answer my question."

"Not technically, no," Bobby said. "I did what everybody running an office does, I booked my own action. But I cultivated those players and I never used office money. They hit, I paid them from my own pocket. I didn't take players from the office."

"English, Bobby, did you steal or not?"

There was no way he could tell her how much money he had stashed in three safe-deposit boxes over the past several years. She wouldn't be able to handle it.

"A few bucks," he said. "But I don't consider it stolen money."

"Do I want to know how much that is, a few bucks?"

"No, you don't. It's not the point anyway."

"So, what, they have a claim? You owe them money, right?"

"No, they don't," Bobby said. "This is bullshit what they're pulling. They don't know what I booked on my own or how much I made. If they did, I'd be dead."

"Jesus Christ," she said.

Bobby waved it off. "Not the point," he said. "They think everybody steals from them because that's what they do is steal. They're greedy cocksuckers at heart, all of them."

Lin Yao made a face.

Bobby said, "I knew they'd try this crap, but that doesn't mean I'm paying them. They come up with something reasonable, I'll consider it. Ten grand, say. Maybe I'll pay that, for peace of mind. Maybe. Not a dime more, though. And I'm not offering them anything either."

"Is that why you left the apartment last night? Because of this?"

"I took out the garbage."

"The garbage was still there this morning," she said. "Don't bullshit me, Bobby."

He had brought the ring to the diner in hope of giving it to her there. Now he was thinking he'd have to wait for a better opportunity.

"You're making it a bigger deal than it is," he told her. "I was just trying to keep it away from our door."

"I don't want those people interfering with our life," Lin Yao said. "You finally got away from that crap, although I didn't know you were stealing from the mob or I would've stopped you. Why don't you just pay them?"

"Because it won't work. You don't understand how they operate."

"No, I don't, but you were supposed to walk away from those morons and here you are, still involved. I was hoping we could make plans soon, that you were finished with this shit, but you're not, are you?"

"We can still make plans."

Bobby had used his last three years of bookmaking to step up his savings and retirement. Now that he had enough money, he couldn't admit it to her, not with the mob trying to shake him down.

"I wish we had made plans to be away again for the feast," Lin Yao said. "I would've if I'd known when the depositions would end."

"So, we'll barricade ourselves inside," Bobby said. "Load up on chocolate cake and ice cream and beer and provolone."

"And this fucking heat. When does it get this humid in September?"

"Just about every September, babe. We're usually down the islands avoiding it and the feast."

The couple sipped their coffees.

"I'm not getting pregnant until you're done with them," Lin Yao said. "I love you, Bobby, but I'm not dealing with this while I'm carrying a child. You promised to take on a straight job when you left that other crap and you haven't yet. What is that supposed to tell me? What, that you stole so much money from the mob you don't have to work?"

"Let's not bring it up again, okay, what you think I stole from the mob," Bobby said. "It's not theirs. It's mine. It's ours. And I will get a straight job. I have some other things I'd like to do too, but you're making it hard, Lin Yao. You're making it impossible, tell you the truth."

Lin Yao had picked up her toasted bagel. "I'm making it impossible?" she said. "Oh, well, just so long as it's my fault."

"I'm not blaming you," Bobby said.

Lin Yao waited a moment while she chewed a piece of bagel. "How much longer before you find a job?" she asked.

"I can work legit tomorrow, I want," Bobby told her. "I can work the feast next week, I want. You know that, but I'm not taking a bullshit job to pass some test. I'm not wasting time doing something I won't like."

"Well, I don't want to wait much longer to start a family."

"We can start one now. What's stopping us?"

"You know what. I also don't want to raise my kid in the city. You know that."

"The kid'll be no more than two years old when we leave, I promise," he said. "He won't know the city from his crib."

Lin Yao shook her head. "You're sure it'll be a boy, huh?"

"Positive, yeah."

She slowly smiled. "You wanna bet?"

He was hoping she'd get around to smiling again. He could tell her about the money another time. He had safely socked away more than five hundred thousand dollars from the private action he had booked on the side. Paying off Agro might take ten thousand, but it would still leave him with more than enough to make the move out of New York when they were ready.

And then he could buy a bar and work for himself. After ten years of running an office for Mafia assholes, he was ready to work for himself.

"What if I said I'd look into running my own business?" he said.

"You mean take a course?"

"Something like that."

"Something like what?"

"Father John from church has a friend'll show me the ropes in his bar," Bobby said. "I'll work tips until I know what I'm doing. Then he'll add shift pay. He said it won't take long before I know the business."

Lin Yao waited for more.

"It's honest money," he said.

She took another bite from her bagel.

Bobby said, "It wouldn't take long, maybe six months to a year before I know what I'm doing. Then we can look for something upstate, a small place."

Lin Yao was listening as she chewed.

"What, that isn't good enough?" he asked. "That's not fair?"

She swallowed and then reached for her coffee.

"Well?" he said. "What's with the silent treatment?"

"If you get me pregnant first."

Bobby nearly choked on a sip of the coffee he didn't like.

"Jesus, where'd that come from?"

"Well?"

"Now?"

"When we get home, doofus."

"Today?"

Lin Yao moved her foot between Bobby's legs under the table.

He tilted his head to one side. "I'm not sure you're gonna tease or kick," he said.

Lin Yao winked. "Makes your answer pretty important, doesn't it?"

CHAPTER 6

SALLY LOOMIS COULDN'T stand the leftover smell of her fiancé's retching from the night before. When she called a housecleaning service to come and disinfect the bathroom, she was told there would be an emergency-service charge.

"No problem," she had said. "How soon can you get here?"

Now she kept the bedroom door closed while the big ape continued to snore on his back. The sounds coming from his mouth disgusted her. When she could still hear them through the door, Sally turned the radio on.

She had almost left him twice since they moved to New York. They had met during her senior year at Michigan, when John was named to the all-conference team and was offered walk-on tryouts to two Canadian football teams. The dope had turned down the offers for a potential paycheck with the NFL, which might've happened had he not blown out his knee during spring ball.

She had been ready to dump him after his injury when she first learned about his connected uncle, Joe Quastifare. A Sunday *New York Times* feature about the New York Mafia had listed Uncle Joe as one of a few rising mob stars. The idea of meeting the gangster someday had excited Sally. When she learned her betrothed was the gangster's godson, she suggested they move to New York.

At first John wasn't anxious to be around his uncle and had turned down an offer to work as a bouncer at one of the strip clubs. Instead, he had taken a job driving a cargo truck at the airport for five hundred dollars a week. It was miserable work for lousy pay. When Sally saw his first paycheck after taxes, she waved it in John's face.

"Are you kidding me?" she had said.

Two weeks later she put her foot down and demanded John talk to his uncle again. The five-hundred-dollar paychecks had completely stifled her dreams of living a good life.

It was immediately after that conversation when John met with his uncle again and asked for new work. After spending a week around his uncle's strip club, John was paired up with one of the men who worked directly under Uncle Joe. It was where he had been the night before.

Now Sally was in the middle of her morning Pilates and was anxious to get to the gym for a facial and body massage before she headed for her afternoon appointment at the beauty parlor. She had seen a couple of Uncle Joe's men getting their nails done at the same beauty parlor. One of them, she knew for fact, was sleeping with one of the married hairdressers. He was a dark-skinned hunk who had flirted with Sally the last few times she saw him there.

Then last week he had slipped her his cell phone number and told her to give him a call when she was bored. At first Sally had wondered if the hunk knew who her fiancé was, but later decided it didn't matter. She was finding Uncle Joe and his mob guys intriguing.

Even though she never explained who she was, Sally had kept the hunk's phone number. She was thinking she might give him a call later today, maybe after she finished at the gym.

Sally had decided she needed a dose of excitement in her life. She certainly needed to get away from the gorilla sounds coming from the bedroom, at least for an afternoon.

•◆•

THE SLIGHT BREEZE blowing off the water on Coney Island offered little relief. The temperature had already hit 90 degrees Fahrenheit. Sunbathers positioned themselves close to the water. Up on the boardwalk, people walked close to the railing facing the beach. They covered their heads with towels, newspapers, or whatever else they carried.

"He's skittish, don't waste time with him," Joe "Quack" Quastifare told Tommy Agro. "My wife begged me for her sister's sake to put him to work. He's my godson, yeah, but he's no blood relative of mine. He can't get it done, who the fuck needs him?"

They were on the boardwalk near the Brooklyn Cyclones' stadium. A group of underlings trailed them by thirty yards. Two federal agents trailed from even further behind. Quastifare was smoking a Cohiba Robusto cigar, a symbolic present he'd bought himself to denote his promotion to skipper. Agro smoked a Marlboro.

"He's a mope," Agro said, "but what do you expect? The kid just come from college, what, a year ago? He wasn't groomed for this like you and me. Give him a few months first, see what happens. Sometimes these guys, the ones have trouble at the start, they turn out all-stars down the road they get the chance. Besides, Joe, what the hell else we gonna use anymore? It's not like the old days we could go down the local pool hall, recruit the kids skipping class."

Quastifare was watching the bubble-assed cheeks on a skinny black woman bounce as she walked directly ahead of him. She wore a brown string bikini that seemed to blend in with her skin color.

"God bless America," he said.

Agro said, "I was gonna send Mickey Nolan to teach him, your nephew, but that crazy mick got himself locked up on Rikers again. I was waiting around for him yesterday until I give up. Today I find out he's back in lockup."

Quastifare's eyes were glued to the bouncing rump ahead of him.

"Started something in one of those mick joints he hangs around, Nolan did," Agro continued. "One of those dives where they serve instant hepatitis to street bums, a Blarney Stone or whatever the fuck they call them. Nolan cracked some guy's head open in one of them and now he's in Rikers until somebody bails him out."

The black woman turned down one of the stairways to the beach. Quastifare blew her ass a kiss.

"Bail who out?" he asked.

"Mickey Nolan," Agro said. "I figure if we need to do anything else, he's the guy to get it done."

"Yeah, except you bail him out too quick, he'll get himself put back in again."

"It's a distinct possibility."

Quastifare leaned against the boardwalk railing and searched for the black woman. When he saw her again, he pointed at her ass and said, "You can't even tell she's wearing anything."

"Or she wipes her ass," Agro said.

Quastifare made a face. "Thanks for the image."

Agro shrugged.

"What about this bookmaker?" Quastifare asked. "What he have to say?"

"He gave us legit numbers, that's for sure, but prolly because we could double-check the work. He said he never stole, so he's not paying anything."

"Yeah, right. He never stole, he's a moron."

"He's no moron."

"Then he's full of shit. You do anything?"

"I sent your nephew back. He called me this morning, sounded sick, the kid. Said he smacked Bobby G around a little soon's he saw him."

"Good," Quastifare said. "Now you can double back and see he wants to negotiate a settlement."

"He might," Agro said. "What's a figure you can live with?"

"I don't know . . . twenty-five grand? Unless you think you can get more, then be my guest."

"He might hem and haw a little before he agrees to that number."

"Then send my nephew again and this time have him do some damage."

"Or I can bail Mickey Nolan out and send him," Agro said.

Quastifare wrinkled his nose. "Bail him out, you want, but I'd save him for something more serious. This bookmaker, his time comes, or my nephew, he doesn't pan out. And then you can take care of Nolan, too, before he's playing cards with the agents someplace in the desert."

Agro tossed his cigarette onto the sand below the boardwalk. He glanced in the direction of the trailing crowd and then looked past them at the pair of federal agents holding binoculars now. Agro turned his back to them.

"Any word on the missing link?" he asked.

Quastifare shook his head no. "Not yet, but after last night, he hears about it, I doubt we'll find Panico before the feds."

"Think he'll flip?"

"He might look to run first, but if they catch up with him, the feds, yeah, he'll probably flip, too. He's gonna be scared after last night. The guy delivering pizza didn't help any."

"Casualty of circumstances," Agro said. "I couldn't leave him."

Quastifare nodded.

"Panico have anybody we can lean on?" Agro asked.

"Just the one sister I know of. She tends bar over in Maspeth in Queens. I used to bang her before I met him."

"She any good?"

"One of the few could handle it, my hose."

Quastifare had a legendary large penis. It had often made him the brunt of jokes when he was coming up.

Agro said, "They close, Panico and his sister?"

"Who knows? It's been fifteen years at least. I couldn't tell you."

"Should I make a visit?"

"Scope the place out first. They might be looking for us there, the feds. You think it's okay, take a look-see."

"She a looker, the sister?"

"She was, but that was what, fifteen years ago now. Who knows anymore? She had an ass on her, I'll give her that. Nice face, too. She was young enough back then, so, yeah, maybe. Why?"

"I'm thinking I bring your nephew," Agro said. "Let him get a workout."

"You gonna bang her or bust her up?"

"Little of both, I was thinking. It's one way to toughen a guy up, let him go to work on a broad. Or maybe you forgot?"

They had come up through the rackets together going back more than thirty years. One of their first muscle jobs, after a madam had run off with a week's worth of receipts from a Vignieri bordello on Park Avenue, was to catch the woman and make her an example of why you didn't steal from the mob. Sheila Cohen had once been a Vegas showgirl. She had aged well and was an attractive forty-five-year-old with world-class legs before Agro and Quastifare used a blowtorch to permanently scar one of her legs.

Quastifare nodded a few times before shaking his head. "Those were the old days," he said. "We can't even think like that anymore. Leave that for the Dominicans."

"Maybe it's why their people don't flip like ours," Agro said.

"I don't like it. I didn't like what we did back then and I still don't to this day. In fact, I wish the fuck you didn't bring it up just now."

"Hey, I won't go near the bitch," Agro said. "Forget it."

"I didn't say that," Quastifare said, eyeballing Agro now. "I said nothing dramatic that'll draw us attention. You knock a couple teeth out, she can get those replaced. You set her on fire and we're on the six o'clock news. I just got upped. Let me enjoy it a few weeks first."

Agro swallowed his pride. "You're right, Joe. Sorry."

Quastifare stepped up to Agro and exchanged a cheek kiss. "Forget about it," he said. "We go back too long for apologies. I'll tell you what, though, you wanna give the kid a workout." He pulled his wallet out and picked through business cards until he found the one he wanted. He handed it to Agro.

"Take the kid and go see this cocksucker tonight, you get a chance," Quastifare said. "His hours there say he works late Wednesdays. The prick likes to hang up on my wife. Some insurance agent. My kid had an accident, my wife calls and the guy has an attitude with her. She's busting my balls two weeks now. I almost went there myself to get her off my back. Let the kid do a number on him."

Agro glanced at the card before slipping it inside his shirt pocket. Then he hugged his boss and patted Quastifare's back after another cheek kiss. "I'll see yous later," he said.

"Later," Quastifare said. He watched Agro walk back through the crowd and away from the two agents. When Agro was finally out of sight, Quastifare adjusted his belt and turned off the recording device he had taped to his leg inside his pants.

CHAPTER 7

THE CLEANING PEOPLE woke Forzino up before they left. He didn't even know they were there until he felt the tiny Hispanic woman shoving the back of his shoulder and heard her voice saying, "Mister. Wake up, mister."

He paid the hundred-dollar bill, although it seemed a little high. Then he dialed Sally's number to find out when she'd be home, but all he got was her voice mail. He left her two messages before he gave up and made himself a pot of coffee.

It had been a tough night he was anxious to forget. Aside from being complicit in at least one murder, he'd been embarrassed by a guy nearly half his size. When he told Tommy Agro that he'd punched the retired bookmaker in the stomach, Forzino was surprised the wiseguy didn't question it.

All he could imagine was that Agro was overly impressed with his ability to bench-press heavy weights.

The problem would come the day Agro decided to step it up with the bookmaker. Forzino was thinking he'd better be carrying something when that day came around, maybe some brass knuckles or an easily concealable handgun.

He had been lucky that Sally was asleep when he came home last night. He had been sick out in the street when he got out of the car and then again as soon as he was inside the apartment. He had just managed to make it to the bathroom the second time.

When she finally did wake up, he blamed his "sour stomach" on bad Chinese food. Sally didn't seem to care what had made him sick, but she was sure pissed off he had thrown up.

He hoped that being an accepted member of his uncle's crew would change things between them. He wasn't so sure he wanted to go all the way and become a made man, but it was critical to his relationship with Sally that he make a lot of money, and soon.

His football injury had been tough on her. The fact he didn't try out for the Canadian teams still bothered her.

"At least you'd be making something respectable if you'd tried out and made it," Sally still told him from time to time. "Now look at you."

Forzino didn't like to admit it, but his fiancée had a point.

He glanced at the clock and saw he had a few hours before he had to pick up Tommy Agro for their trip into the city. He figured he had just enough time for a workout at the gym and to maybe pick up some brass knuckles.

There was no way he could let that bookmaker humble him in front of Agro, not if he wanted to stay out from behind the steering wheel of a truck.

He tried Sally one more time and was surprised to hear music in the background when she answered.

"Sally?"

"Speaking."

"It's John."

"Who?"

"John. What the hell is that? Where are you?"

"Oh, shit," he heard her say.

"Sally?"

The connection was lost.

"Fuck," Forzino said.

He tried dialing again. This time there was no answer. He dialed again and left an emergency 911 page. He waited for a return call, but it never came.

•◆•

THE HEAT INDEX at one o'clock in the afternoon had climbed above one hundred. Tempers were short. Drivers stuck in midday traffic leaned on their horns. A group of homeless huddled under the shade of a restaurant supply store awning on Chrystie Street.

Father Robert John Scavo nudged Bobby with an elbow and motioned toward an Asian woman crossing Stanton Street. She wore gray cotton shorts that exposed too much flesh to ignore and a tight, black Average White Band T-shirt.

The priest winked at Bobby and said, "Pick up the pieces."

The woman smiled. Scavo quickly made the sign of the cross.

"Nice," Bobby said. "Pick up the pieces?"

"Average White Band," the priest said. He put fire to an unfiltered Camel cigarette. "I picked up their best-of CD last week. First-rate funk. Thirty years down the road, they still got it."

Bobby was using a toothpick to dislodge a piece of pastrami from between his teeth. They had picked up sandwiches at Katz's Delicatessen and brought them back to the park. Bobby chewed on the last of a pickle before tossing the wrappings in a trash pail near the bench Scavo was sitting on.

"Gentlemen," a tall black woman wearing a short skirt said as she passed.

"Afternoon," Scavo said. He turned to Bobby when the black woman crossed the street.

"You got balls, I'll give you that," Bobby told his friend.

"It's what I love most about this city," said Scavo, pointing at the woman. "The different people you see everywhere. Chinese, Korean, black, white, Spanish, Russian, everybody and anybody. Must be what heaven is like, all the different souls walking around doing their own thing."

"Yeah, right," Bobby said, "in short skirts showing half their asses."

They had met six years ago in the same park where they were sitting now. They had teamed up in a pickup game of basketball and had become close friends. Bobby was still bookmaking back then. Father Scavo had just become a priest.

"What, you don't approve of short skirts?" Scavo asked. "You're a prude all of a sudden, just because you're about to take the plunge?"

"Speaking of plunges," Bobby said, "you know anything about Tommy Agro, besides he's a first-class asshole?"

Scavo watched two pigeons playing tug of war with a piece of dried bread. "From what I remember, he was an up-and-comer before I went to South America," the priest said. "He used to hang around the neighborhood here when I came back, but then he was gone. Over to Brooklyn, right?"

Scavo had become a priest late in life. He had grown up on the Lower East Side and then moved to Little Italy during his twenties, when he was still pursuing an acting career. After getting involved with drugs, he began robbing cars for a local hood. Eventually he developed a drug habit that had almost cost him his life more than once. A local woman he had fallen in love with managed to convince him to seek help. He kicked his drug habit and they joined the Peace Corps together. They spent several years in South America before the woman died of cancer. Scavo then turned to religion and eventually pursued the priesthood. Ordained at thirty-seven, Scavo had recently turned forty-five.

"That's what I knew about Agro," Bobby said. "Agro was Brooklyn. Bay Ridge, I think."

"Why the interest in him?"

"He showed up at the apartment with muscle. I already handled that, but I figure the next time it won't be so easy."

Scavo sat back on the bench and fanned himself with a piece of cardboard. "Talk to somebody," he said.

"Talk to who?"

"The law."

Bobby squinted at the priest as if he were nuts.

Scavo said, "What, you're above that? Look around you, my friend, nobody is standing up anymore. Even the bosses are making deals now. That last one to go down, he was wearing a wire in the joint. Nothing is sacred with those clowns anymore. Look at your old boss. What it take him to flip? Less than two minutes, I'll bet."

Bobby waved it off. "It's not about that, standing up. I already did that once."

"What's it about then?"

"I don't have anything to deal if I wanted to, which I don't. I didn't hang around those morons. I ran a bookmaking office. I didn't want anything to do with their bullshit. I made them money, and I made myself money, end of story."

Scavo pointed to a tall blonde woman headed their way. "Six-footer?"

Bobby glanced up but ignored the woman. "And I won't go to the cops to try and scare off Tommy Agro," he said. "It wouldn't work anyway."

Scavo said, "How about going to them to save your ass?"

Bobby used the toothpick again when the blonde woman passed. She was wearing tight yellow leggings and a light blue halter. Bobby avoided her eyes when she turned toward him. Scavo nodded hello.

"The thing is," the priest said, "you're probably dealing with a throwback in Agro. One of the dinosaurs won't back down just because you won't. Maybe the law, just the idea of them, will chase him away."

"It's why he came to see me in the first place," Bobby said. "He was feeling me out."

"You try to negotiate?"

"Yeah, of course."

"And?"

"Who knows? He said one thing, I said another. Maybe he'll come back with something I can live with. I doubt it."

"Then you go to the law."

Bobby watched a Porsche try to maneuver through traffic. "What you used to get for one of those?" he asked Scavo.

"Depends," the priest said. "Up to five grand, depending on who I was dealing with. A lot of goodwill, though, I'll tell you that. A lot of goodwill you brought one of those babies into a chop shop."

Both men watched the Porsche race up to the next red light. "Must have a lot of money for gas," Scavo said.

"He's driving one of those, I don't think it matters," Bobby said.

"Oh, yeah? I used to drive one. I drove more than one, come to think of it."

"Yeah, but they were never yours."

They shared a laugh before Scavo tossed the remains of his cigarette into the curb and lit another.

"Your friend still willing to teach me the bar business?" Bobby asked. "I hope so, because that's what I told Lin Yao."

"He's cool with it, yeah. Just say when and I'll bring you to meet him. Not until after the feast, though."

"Soon as I get this thing with Agro settled," Bobby said. "Or they might show up your friend's place and ruin that, too."

"What about the feast. You hanging around this year?"

"Yeah, Lin Yao didn't make plans because of her job, although I wish we could get away right now. Between this heat and the mess the feast usually is, we're both gonna wish we were someplace else come next week."

"Least you can leave," the priest said. "I'm supposed to walk around with a smile on my face, but it's hard when you know half the money from that fiasco winds up in the mob's pockets."

"That's one reason I don't spend a buck at the feast, guys like Agro making money off it."

"Speaking of Agro, that why you didn't give her the ring, because of him?"

Bobby nodded before he winked at Scavo. "Although she might be pregnant now."

"Congratulations."

"I said she might be."

"Well, for getting laid then, congratulations."

"I almost gave her the ring right after, then I decided to take her to the Algonquin. I'll give it to her there."

Scavo shook his head. The hotel had to do with Bobby's childhood. It was where his father used to take him for long weekends after his parents split up. The priest had heard the story one too many times.

"Anyway, I booked a suite there," Bobby said.

"Give it a break already with that place," Scavo said. "If you had her in the throes of lust, you should've slipped the ring on her finger before she knew what was happening. She might've said yes. Besides, your father would be happy you're marrying somebody with twice your brains and ten times your looks."

Bobby stared at the priest until Scavo felt it and turned to him.

"What?" he asked.

Bobby said, "People actually come to you to feel better?"

"When they confess, yeah, it makes them feel better. Care to go a round in the box later?"

"I think I'm washing my hair."

Scavo took a long drag off his Camel and flicked the ash off the end. "Well, I'll say a prayer for you. There's a good chance you'll still blow it, this engagement."

Bobby used the bottom of his T-shirt to wipe sweat from his face. He said, "Do me a favor and say a couple prayers."

•◆•

LIN YAO SMILED now as she examined herself in the bedroom mirror. She turned sideways and wondered if life had started within her womb. She touched her stomach and then felt silly for what she was doing.

It was the first time they had ever had sex without protection. Bobby had wanted to throw the diaphragm out afterward, but Lin Yao had stopped him.

"What are you, a pack rat?" he had asked.

"I'm going to need this again someday. I don't intend to stay pregnant, Bobby."

"What, no playmates for Junior?"

"One at a time, and I'm not naming any child of mine Junior."

"What if we have twins?"

"Then I'm definitely not throwing it out."

"Hey, I was an only child," he had told her. "It's no bargain."

It forced her to think about her own childhood and how hard it had been when her older sister died at age sixteen.

She had been brought up by her mother's older sister, a harsh woman with five sons and no husband. Lin Yao and her sister, Ming Lao, had spent most of their youth looking after their cousins. When Ming Lao died of pneumonia, their aunt had finally let up on Lin Yao and permitted her to attend public school. There had been a lot of catching up to do, but she worked hard and graduated with a college scholarship.

Her aunt had died while Lin Yao was attending Syracuse University. When she came home, she took a paralegal job with a major law firm and lived in a tiny studio apartment on Mott Street. One of the cousins she used to pick up after, Ricky Zhu, had become involved with a local street gang. Two of his brothers had been killed on the streets. Another was in an upstate jail for selling drugs. The youngest had been born with Down syndrome and was looked after by another family member.

Ricky had looked after Lin Yao and made sure the men in the neighborhood didn't bother the attractive young woman. She felt obligated to him for his protection and dated some of the Chinese businessmen he had introduced her to. After a while, when Ricky wanted to know why she didn't get involved with any of them, Lin Yao told her cousin she didn't feel anything.

"What you mean, feel?" he had asked her. "They all rich. I bring you businessman. Stockbrokers, investment bankers. You should feel their wallet next time."

"No spark," she told him. "There has to be a spark."

"You crazy," he told her. He would tell her that a few more times through the years.

She thought about that spark now and how she'd felt it the moment she met Bobby Gennaro a few years later when she was videotaping depositions. He was there with a friend and had just stepped in the room when their eyes met.

She had smiled at him without thinking about it, the initial spark. Later he introduced himself and asked if she'd like to go for coffee. The rest was their history.

Now she put on a robe and remembered there was chocolate raspberry cake in the fridge. She poured herself a glass of milk and brought the snack into the living room. She ate a few bites of the cake before flipping through the channels for the local news.

When she saw the headline at the top of the screen, she set the cake back down. It was a report about three men found murdered in a Brooklyn used car lot the night before. She turned up the volume and learned that two of the murdered men were soldiers with the Vignieri crime family and that both had been under Bobby's old boss, Nicky D'Angelo. The third man had been an innocent bystander, a single parent working a second job delivering pizza.

Then the news report suggested the Vignieri family might be cleaning up the mess associated with Bobby's old boss becoming an informant. A potential mob war was feared.

Lin Yao remembered when the news of Nicky D'Angelo made the front page of the local newspapers. Bobby had said it wasn't good.

"Why? What does that have to do with you?" she had asked him.

"Nothing," Bobby had told her, "except the idiots running things will just assume I knew something before I quit the business. Guilt by association."

It was the first time she had actually heard the term applied to someone she knew.

She had been nervous when it first happened, but then it seemed to go away and Bobby never brought it up again until yesterday when she came home and found the sunglasses on the dining room table.

It bothered her that he had never mentioned the money he had taken, even though he claimed it wasn't stolen. She could understand him trying to protect her from his old life, but now the mob was killing people associated with Bobby's old boss. It wasn't a coincidence she could ignore.

If she had known about the money, Lin Yao would never have let him take it.

She lost her appetite thinking about it, and then set the cake aside and went to meet him at the park.

CHAPTER 8

Bobby could tell they were detectives when he first spotted them standing on the curb. He did his best to ignore them until they blocked his path.

The older and shorter of the two presented his badge. "Detective John DeNafria," he said, "and this is Detective Ward."

The younger one nodded.

Bobby said, "What's it about?"

"We're organized crime," DeNafria said. "You used to run one of Nicky D'Angelo's bookmaking offices. You were his best earner for, what, ten years or so?"

"That's one rumor," Bobby said.

The younger one, Ward, smirked through a yawn.

"We're investigating the purge of Nicky's crew since he flipped," DeNafria said. "Last night another two of his guys were clipped in Brooklyn."

"Not to mention the poor SOB delivering a pizza," Ward added. "I'm sure you already know about it."

Bobby shook his head. "I'm retired," he said. "Whatever happened in Brooklyn is none of my business."

"So, what, they haven't approached you yet?" Ward asked.

Bobby spotted Lin Yao crossing Broome Street and frowned.

"What's the problem?" asked Ward while suppressing another yawn.

Bobby turned to DeNafria. "Not yet," he lied. "But there's nothing to approach me about. I'm out. All I did was run an office. They have a dozen schmucks can do that."

"We're not talking about running it for them," DeNafria said. "I'm thinking maybe they can lean on you a little, especially since you retired so close to Nicky's change of teams. You know, one minute you're a golden boy, Bobby G, then you're history. Since D'Angelo joined Team America and you were one of his guys, you probably lost most-favored-nation status."

Bobby wasn't paying attention. He saw Lin Yao waving. He waved back.

"Look," he said, "what the hell can I give anybody? I ran an office. I hardly ever dealt with those guys."

"Except to hand off their take," Ward said.

"Which I hardly ever did myself, they sent a guy to pick it up. Look, it's no secret how an office runs. Wiseguys can't be directly involved for fear of RICO statutes."

Lin Yao was too close now. He stopped to wait and introduce her. Both detectives were polite.

"You were saying?" Ward asked.

Bobby shot him a dirty look before glancing at Lin Yao. "Contrary to popular myth, bookmakers are nothing more than glorified clerks. The truth of the matter is I'm looking to register for a couple of business courses come the fall. I'm thinking of opening my own place. I have an associate's degree from before I ever got involved with Nicky D'Angelo. And I wasn't his golden boy. Not ever. I used to drive a cab a few years before I ran that office. I'm no mobster. I'm a wannabe businessman."

"Except you did do time," DeNafria said. "You left that out of your résumé."

Bobby said, "I beat up a guy used to slap women around and I got sent up for it. He was a pimp. I'd do it again."

Both detectives smiled.

"He's telling the truth," Lin Yao said.

DeNafria said, "We're not saying D'Angelo shared secrets with you. But the new guys running things might think you shared secrets with us or the federal government since you retired three months prior to your boss's flipping. Coincidence doesn't fly well with the morons running the mob. You went to high school, you can figure that out. You don't need an associate's degree."

"So, what, you're worried about what the mob might think about me because I worked for D'Angelo, so now you stop me in the middle of the street? Why, so they see it and maybe think I'm flipping, too?"

"Being a smart-ass won't help you any," Ward said.

Lin Yao leaned into Bobby. "He's not being a smart-ass," she said. "He's answering your questions."

"They haven't broken my balls," Bobby lied again. "And if they do, I'm not going to run to you guys. Sorry, but that isn't the way I handle my shit."

DeNafria said, "Yeah, well, your shit comes up against Tommy Agro and Joe Quack, the guys we think might be running Nicky's old crew, you'd better have another way out, my friend."

Bobby said, "Sorry, I don't know those guys."

Ward said, "Do you know, by any chance, who it is officially took over for Nicky? Word is Joe Quack. Think about it before you give us another blow-off answer. Remember, we came here in good faith."

Bobby thought about it a moment and, after trying to process the pros and cons of admitting something to two organized crime detectives, shook his head. "I wouldn't know," he said. "Sorry."

DeNafria held his business card out. Bobby ignored it. Lin Yao grabbed it.

•◆•

"HE REALLY WENT away for beating a pimp?" Ward asked DeNafria once Bobby Gennaro and his girlfriend were gone.

The detectives had moved into the shade of a building.

"It's how they first found him, the boys," DeNafria said. "Some broad Nicky D'Angelo used to bang was smacked around by a pimp she used to work for. Gennaro was working as a bouncer in one of D'Angelo's clubs here in Manhattan. They sent him and two other guys to do the job. The other guys watched while Gennaro did the work. The pimp flipped in the hospital. Gennaro took the rap stand-up."

"He beat a pimp, he should've got a medal," Ward said.

"Yeah, probably, but then he come out and D'Angelo was anxious to help him out. Put him to work running his book."

"That where he got the scar, prison?"

"Probably. I didn't know him back then."

Ward yawned loudly.

"You getting any sleep at all?" DeNafria asked.

"It's the schedule change. I'm used to napping this time of the day. I used to work nights mostly."

DeNafria thumbed back at where Bobby Gennaro and his girlfriend had headed. He said, "I think he's been approached and he's keeping quiet until he knows what he's up against. He's playing it smart."

"He could've hinted about Joe Quack, though," Ward said. "The prick, I thought I gave him an out there."

"He figures we'll know soon enough, which we will. A guy says something, it gets repeated, it comes back to haunt him. Remember, Bobby here isn't your average dumbski mob wannabe. He was smart enough, whether he knew D'Angelo was gonna flip or not, to get out."

DeNafria shook his head as his partner yawned one more time.

"What?" Ward asked.

"I hope you don't do that with your wife."

"Never," Ward said. "The woman is half Puerto Rican, half Dominican. She can throw a pot as good as the Big Unit throws a fastball."

DeNafria turned to scan the street. He saw an Asian woman collapse from the heat. A group of Asian men immediately attended to her. At least one was holding a bottle of water.

"The hell you looking for?" Ward asked.

"Feds," DeNafria said. "If Gennaro made a deal, they'll be watching his back."

"You really think he did?"

"I don't know. Then again, I gotta wonder if the boys think so. It's a weird coincidence if the guy just happened to walk away at the right time."

"It's an awfully profitable business to walk away from," Ward agreed.

DeNafria watched as the Asian woman who had collapsed a moment ago was being helped up.

"Things change," he said, "don't get me wrong, but I'd wanna know what prompted his sudden change of heart about the business I was them."

"Them being Joe Quack and so on?"

"We can go rattle those cages later today," DeNafria said. "It's been a while since I had a frank at Nathan's."

"Coney Island, right?"

"Yep, Quack has a social club there. Likes to hold court with the new punks they recruit."

"What about Bobby G?"

"What about him?"

Ward said, "Maybe he's made a deal we don't know about. Maybe we should suggest that to the guys running things now."

"That'd get his legs broken or worse," DeNafria said. He noticed the Asian woman was standing again. Two men helped her walk inside a restaurant. "I don't mind pressuring the guy, but he doesn't deserve being offered up for sacrifice. I'd like to leave him the out, he can come to us. I like the way his girlfriend snatched my card."

Ward started to yawn again. He said, "And I'm thinking fuck 'em. They break his legs he'll come to us anyway."

•◆•

"THEY KILLED THOSE men," Lin Yao said. "I just saw it on the news before I came looking for you. They killed them because they worked for the same animal you worked for."

They had started for home after leaving the two detectives on Grand Street. Lin Yao was still holding the one detective's card. Bobby wanted to take it from her and rip it up.

"Those were made guys," he told her instead. "They killed two of their own. I'm not one of them. I never was."

Lin Yao blocked his path. "And what about the other guy," she said. "The poor bastard delivered pizza. What, his family will feel better today because it was an accident?"

Bobby bit his lower lip. "That's exactly what it was, yes," he said. "I know that won't make his family feel better, but I'm sure they weren't there to kill him."

"Jesus Christ."

"Can we go home now?"

"No."

"No?"

She grabbed his arm and made him walk the other way.

"Let's go see Father," Lin Yao said. "Let's discuss this with him."

"He's probably gone back to the rectory," Bobby said.

"Then let's just walk, okay?"

She took his hand.

It was something he hated trying to explain, the absurd workings of the Mafia. Lin Yao was way too smart to think it was anything more than what it would sound like, except it was also dangerous.

"I'm not in the same danger as those guys were," he told her.

"They're trying to lean on me for a few bucks because it's their way. They see something they think they can take and they go for it. But things have changed, Lin Yao. Nobody takes them half as serious as they used to. Read the papers, they're falling apart from the inside out."

"You read the papers," she said. "They killed three men last night, one of them an innocent bystander, some poor guy working a second job delivering pizza to pay his bills. I hate those fucking animals."

They walked in silence the next few blocks until they were back at Chrystie Street. The heat was intense under the sun. They crossed to the park and sat on a bench under a tree.

"If I go to the police, it might scare them into doing something," Bobby told her. "So long as they know I'm standing my ground, I'm okay. They'll still try to bleed me, but I can handle that. I can back them off."

"And what if you can't? What if they kill you, too?"

Now he took her hand and kissed it. "What if I promise nothing will happen?"

She frowned.

"I mean it," he said. "I'll take care of this thing, pay them if I have to, but you have to let me do it my way."

"And what if they want more than you're willing to give them?"

"You have to let me handle that."

"I'm afraid, Bobby."

"Don't be."

"I can't help it."

"Yes, you can. You need to have some faith, baby, in me."

"You're the only person I ever trusted in my life."

He leaned over and kissed her. They embraced. A passing wino asked for some change. Bobby fished in his pocket without looking and pulled out a dollar bill. He dangled it until the wino took it.

"Thanks," the wino said, then added, "You two should get a room."

Bobby finally broke their embrace. He said, "Man has a point."

Lin Yao said, "I'm still afraid."

•◆•

THE BARTENDER MOTIONED at John Forzino with her head.

"He's a big one," she said.

She was a short woman with a big chest and short black hair. She had a worn look that was accented by the way she dragged on her cigarette. When she turned around, her ass was a size bigger than it should be, Tommy Agro was thinking. He guessed her age to be around forty, and then wondered what she had looked like fifteen years ago when Joe Quack was banging her.

Agro was there with Forzino to learn whatever they could from the woman about her brother, Fred Panico, the missing link to what was left of Nicky D'Angelo's crew.

He thumbed at Forzino. "Bench-presses five hundred pounds."

The woman seemed unimpressed. "Whatever that means," she said.

"Means he can lift small cars," said Agro, turning to Forzino. "Right, kid?"

Forzino smiled.

"He doesn't say much, does he?"

Agro extended a hand across the bar. "Tommy Agro," he said. "I'm a friend of your brother."

Now the woman looked from Forzino to Agro and back again.

"I haven't seen him in weeks," she said. "You want something to drink or is the Q and A over?"

Agro smiled. "Johnny Black, rocks," he said. "The kid is driving, just a Coke for him."

The woman poured the drink first, then the soda. Agro watched her maneuver behind the bar. She had obviously been working one a long time. He wondered if that's all she did. Her brother had been known to move pills in the darker neighborhoods.

Agro set a twenty on the bar. "And your name is?"

"Angela," she said, before turning to make change from the twenty.

Agro winked at Forzino. "Married?" he asked.

"Twice," she said.

"Now?"

"You see a ring?"

"Not everybody wears one."

"I did."

She turned to set his change down. He waved it off.

"Thanks," she said with no emotion.

Agro pulled a pack of Marlboros from the inside pocket of his gray sports jacket.

"I guess it's okay to smoke," he said.

"Knock yourself out," she said. "The inspectors are well greased in Maspeth."

Agro fired up his cigarette.

Angela finished wiping down the bar. She pointed at Forzino. "He breathing?"

Agro chuckled. "Yeah, I think so."

"He didn't touch his soda."

"Gives me gas," Forzino said.

"Gives him gas," Agro said.

"Thanks for the warning," Angela said. "Want something else?"

"Your brother," Forzino said. "And we don't have all fucking day."

They had worked it out in the car while they scoped the place for surveillance earlier. Agro would feed the woman bullshit, even pay for his own drink, then he would light a cigarette and Forzino would come on strong.

"Hey," Angela said. "I don't know where the hell my brother is and I wouldn't fucking tell you if I did, okay? What are you gonna do, break my arms?"

She had started on Forzino but turned to Agro when she asked the question. His face turned red a moment before Forzino stepped up to the bar, reached out, and grabbed a handful of her hair.

"Listen, you worn-out cunt, we came here asking nice," Agro said. "Lose the fucking attitude before I let him show you what he can break."

"Okay, okay," Angela pleaded. "Just let go."

Forzino squeezed her hair a little tighter.

"Ouch!" she yelled.

Agro motioned at Forzino to let go. He did.

Angela took a few moments. She gingerly touched her hair.

"Now, where is Fred these days?" Agro asked.

Angela shook her head. "I don't know," she whispered. "I swear it."

"The cops around yet?"

"Two federal agents," Angela said, "a couple days after Nicky D'Angelo was all over the papers."

"What they want?"

"Same as you," she said. "Where was Freddie, did I know, did I hear from him?"

"Did you?"

"No. I don't know where he is."

Agro stared her down.

"I swear it," she said. "Why would he tell me?"

Agro sipped his drink. "Okay, that's better. There's no reason to get nasty, hon. We're all looking out for each other here."

Angela swallowed hard.

Agro looked her up and down. "Joe Quack said you used to handle his hose pretty good. That true?"

At first she didn't flinch, but when Agro continued staring, Angela managed a slight shrug.

Agro motioned at her crotch. "Must be like a well, that thing."

Angela swallowed again.

"Now we'll go," Agro said. He turned to Forzino. Both men started for the door. Agro glanced back at the woman before he stepped outside. "You have a nice day," he told her.

CHAPTER 9

AFTER HIS PARENTS had divorced, Bobby's father would save for months at a time just to take his son into Manhattan for a long weekend. They would stay at the Algonquin Hotel because, his father had said, there was a lot of interesting history there.

"It's where the Round Table used to meet," Anthony Gennaro used to tell his son. "They were a bunch of writers back in the 1920s. Dorothy Parker, George Kaufman, Heywood Broun, Robert Benchley and some others. Tallulah Bankhead used to come here, too, when she was popular. Tallulah, she was my favorite."

Bobby could remember the twinkle in his father's eye whenever he talked about the controversial actress.

"Oh, she was a wild one, Bobby," Anthony would tell his son. "'I'm as pure as the driven slush,' she used to say."

Bobby had just started high school when his parents divorced. The long weekends with his father were a special time. Anthony Gennaro would bring his son downtown to Greenwich Village, where he had grown up during World War II. He would show Bobby where he used to feed the pigeons at Father Demo Square along what used to be Sixth Avenue before it was renamed the Avenue of the Americas. He would take Bobby for Manhattan Special coffee sodas. They would eat pizza on Bleecker Street before walking east on Houston and turning left onto La Guardia Place to head toward Washington Square Park. It was there Anthony would always stop and make his son take notice of the New York University buildings.

"That's where you want to learn, Bobby," he would say. "It's a great institution, NYU. It's where I had always wanted to go before your mother became pregnant and I had to go to work."

Anthony Gennaro had been a dreamer in his wife's eyes, but his son had always admired his father's optimism. Sometimes, when Anthony lectured his son on Civil War battles, he would get excited and draw maps to illustrate whatever point he was making. Bobby had saved several of the maps his father drew and kept them in one of the safe-deposit boxes where he had stashed some of the money the mob now wanted.

They were times Bobby often thought about. He had felt cheated when his father died. It had left him wanting a family of his own, except he was determined never to have to struggle financially the way his father had. It was why he had taken the risk of booking private bets while running an office for the mob.

If he was lucky, Lin Yao was already carrying the start of the family he wanted so badly.

It was what he was thinking about when Bobby checked in to the Algonquin Hotel in preparation for giving Lin Yao her engagement ring. He had flowers delivered and spread around the room. He ordered a bottle of champagne and a box of Belgian chocolates, Lin Yao's favorites.

He went down to the famous Oak Room for a drink and thought about Tommy Agro and how he would have to deal with the wiseguy again before things spiraled out of control.

He also needed to call Lin Yao and tell her to pack a bag because they were spending the night at a hotel, only he wouldn't tell her the name of the place yet, just give her the address.

Bobby took in the ambiance of the Oak Room and was choked up.

He couldn't help but wish that he'd had the opportunity to share a drink with Anthony Gennaro at least once before his father had died. He swallowed his emotions and pulled his cell phone out. He hit the preprogrammed number for the apartment and was still smiling when Lin Yao answered on the second ring.

"Where are you?" she asked.

"Uptown," Bobby told her.

"Doing what?"

"Waiting for you."

"Waiting for me? Where?"

He gave her the address.

"What's going on?" she asked.

"It's a surprise. Pack a bag. Bring something sexy."

"What?"

"You heard me."

"Bobby, don't do this to me. What's going on?"

"You have the address. Call me before you leave and I'll meet you outside."

"I can't get there for another few hours."

"Just call me before you leave."

"What the hell is going on?"

"You get here you'll find out."

"Get where? Bobby!" she yelled.

"Love you," he said, and then he killed the connection.

He pictured her trying to figure it out while she packed a bag. It felt good to know he could make her happy. He knew he would be luckier with love than his father had been. He knew the reason why, it was all Lin Yao.

He reached down into his front pants pocket and felt the ring he couldn't wait to put on her finger.

•◆•

"WOULD YOU LOOK at this entourage," Detective John DeNafria said.

The late afternoon sun burned hot as DeNafria and his partner sat in a car parked on Surf Avenue in Coney Island. DeNafria sipped a Coke behind the wheel. Ward chewed on the last of a frankfurter he had bought a few minutes earlier across the street at Nathan's.

Joe Quastifare, wearing a blue silk shirt, black slacks, alligator shoes, and lots of gold jewelry, stood in the middle of a pack of his crew across the street from the Luna Park projects. Two men walked ahead and three followed the newly promoted captain of what was once Nicholas D'Angelo's crew as they headed toward Surf Avenue.

"Maybe he thinks he's the pope," Ward said.

"Makes me think he's still running scared," DeNafria said. "So long as Freddie Panico is still out there, I guess Quack thinks he's got something to worry about."

"You going to introduce me?"

"In a minute. I want to see who're the errand boys here."

Ward glanced at a sheet of names of known Vignieri wannabes listed under a makeshift organization chart. "You recognize any of them?" he asked.

"Two," DeNafria said, "but they've been tagging around for years, the two up front. The big one is about to step up. The ones in the back are new blood."

Ward pointed at the crowd when they split up. Quastifare and the two men walking ahead of him crossed Surf Avenue toward Nathan's. The other three turned back towards the social club.

"Let's go," DeNafria said. "Maybe I can get him to spill something on his expensive threads."

They crossed the avenue a dozen yards behind Quastifare and his men. They stood in line behind them at one of the Nathan's counters and made believe they were studying the menus on the wall when one of Quastifare's bodyguards turned to look them over.

DeNafria turned his face toward the street. Ward yawned in the bodyguard's face.

It took a few minutes before Quastifare was holding onto a frankfurter loaded with onions and mustard. DeNafria called to him just before the gangster took a bite.

"Hey, Joe Quack!" he yelled. "Joe!"

Quastifare turned too quickly and spilled a combination of mustard and onions onto his shirt. He slapped at it with his free hand and wound up smearing some onto the waist of his pants.

"Motherfucker," he said through clenched teeth.

The gangster saw it was DeNafria and shook his head. The two knew each other from similar meetings in the past.

"The fuck do you want, besides ruining my lunch?"

"Just coming over to congratulate you," DeNafria said. "I hear you moved up."

The gangster's eyes jumped from DeNafria to Ward and back.

"Who's he?" he asked.

"New guy," DeNafria said.

"He looks Irish."

"He is."

Ward stuck his hand out. "Detective Michael Ward."

Quastifare ignored the gesture.

"That's no way to be," DeNafria said. "You're a skipper now. You're supposed to set a better example for the troops. It's bad enough they're stupid as the day is long. You don't need them insulting officers of the law and making more trouble than they can handle."

"You think I can't handle you?" one of the bodyguards said. "Lose the badge for five minutes and see what happens."

Ward had his badge out. He handed it off to DeNafria.

"Yeah, right," the bodyguard said. "What about your gun?"

Ward kneeled down and pulled his weapon from an ankle holster. He handed it to his still surprised partner and then turned to the bodyguard again. "Let's take a walk around the corner, boyo, and see which one of us comes back with all his teeth."

The bodyguard looked from his boss to DeNafria.

"He serious, this mick?" Quastifare asked.

"Or I can kick your ass right here and now," Ward told the bodyguard. "Unless you want me to take off my pants, too."

DeNafria was still holding the badge and gun. He watched nervously as his partner, leaning in closer, tried to egg the bodyguard on.

"Take a fucking hike, asshole," Quastifare said.

DeNafria stepped in front of his partner. "Easy does it," he whispered.

Ward reluctantly took back his possessions.

DeNafria turned to Quastifare again. "Manners, Joe," he said, thumbing at his partner. "I only know the guy a few days now. I don't know what might set him off. Between this heat and all, I mean."

Ward was standing with the gun in his hand. He continued eyeballing the bodyguard, who was no longer as anxious to return the stare.

"Who're the other three bozos went back to the club?" DeNafria asked. "I would've thought a skipper didn't have to fetch his own food."

"This is starting to sound like harassment, you ask me," Quastifare said.

"Just saying hello, Joe," DeNafria said. "Harassment is when I bust you for jaywalking or spitting in the street."

The gangster tossed the rest of his frankfurter into a garbage pail. "Who can eat now?" he said. "Yeah, right, jaywalking. And maybe I'll call my attorney anyway, just for the hell of it. Between this jerk-off threatening my guys and you ruining my shirt, there should be something he can do about it. I pay him enough."

"That's your prerogative, Joe, calling your lawyer. In the meantime, where's Tommy Agro been lately? Out searching for Freddie Panico?"

"Freddie who?"

"Big waste of time, you ask me. The way you guys flip nowadays, Panico is sure to be playing gin rummy with the agents by now."

"Good for him. I hope he wins."

"You know anything about the three poor bastards found in the car lot in Canarsie? I believe two of them actually deserved what they got."

Quack smirked at his bodyguards. "They're fishing pretty good now, aren't they?"

"Just trying to save time, Joe," DeNafria said. "Rather than make you go through the motions and cuffing you down the road, I mean. You flip now we can all make it home before dinner."

Quastifare gave DeNafria the finger. "Fuck you," he said. "How's that for not wasting time?"

Ward chuckled. "These guys are great for giving hand signals and talking shit," he said. He locked his eyes back on the bodyguard he'd challenged earlier. "Can any of them actually fight is the question?"

DeNafria spoke at Quastifare, "I'll bet Tommy Agro isn't happy they made you boss."

"I don't know what you're talking about," Quastifare said.

"You guys lean on D'Angelo's retired bookmaker yet?" Ward asked.

DeNafria shook his head at his partner.

Quastifare said, "I don't know what you're talking about either."

Ward ignored DeNafria. "The guy quit the bookmaking business about three months ago," he said. "Bobby Gennaro, also goes by Bobby G."

Quastifare forced a yawn. "Never heard of him."

Ward said, "He lives downtown, Little Italy."

Quastifare shrugged. "Don't know him."

"Sure you do."

"No, I don't."

Ward turned to DeNafria. "Then I guess he's home free after all."

DeNafria was seething. He turned to Quastifare and said, "He's just breaking your balls."

Quastifare squinted with rage.

Ward shrugged at DeNafria and turned to the wiseguy. He said, "Good luck with the promotion."

CHAPTER 10

Tommy Agro had told the kid it was a favor for his aunt because the guy in the insurance office next to the Dunkin' Donuts had given her some lip before he hung up on her half a dozen times.

"My uncle know about this?" John Forzino had asked.

"He's the one gimme that," said Agro, pointing at the business card Forzino was holding. "He almost lost his temper, went after the guy himself."

Forzino looked up from the card and across the parking lot at the insurance office. He handed the card to Agro and said he'd be right back.

"I'll pull up soon's I see you," Agro yelled out the window. "I'll be behind the second row of parked cars. It's late enough, maybe he's alone."

As he walked across the parking lot, Forzino understood it was more than just doing a favor for his aunt. This was a test he couldn't afford to fail. He tried to picture what the guy looked like. Then he wondered what he'd do first, because he'd need a game plan in case the guy was sitting behind the desk or standing, or on his way out or whatever. He'd have to take Richard Connors, insurance agent, by surprise. It was a lesson he'd learned from Bobby Gennaro the night before, how important the element of surprise was.

When he stepped inside the office, there were two people sitting at desks on either side of the room. An older woman with eyeglasses hanging from a shoelace sat at one desk. He assumed the blond-haired man, about thirty years old, was Richard Connors. Forzino quickly glanced at the corner of the room to check for security cameras. There weren't any.

"Can I help you?" the woman asked. "We're about to close."

Forzino pointed to the man, who had glanced up briefly but now was looking back down at the papers on his desk, like he couldn't be bothered.

"Richard?" the woman said.

The man turned to her before looking up at Forzino. "Yeah?" he said.

Forzino noticed the metal model of an old Buick roadster being used as a paperweight on the corner of the woman's desk. He picked it up.

"Nice," he said.

"Can I help you?" the man asked.

"You Richard Connors?"

"I am."

Forzino took a quick step to his left as he slammed the Buick model against Connors's right ear. It was a loud smack. Two of the wheels broke off.

Connors grunted as his body nearly toppled out of the chair. His ear and head were cut. Blood flowed freely from both wounds.

The woman gasped loudly before pushing her chair back to stand up. Forzino saw her looking at the phone. He ripped the line out. Then he stepped into a right cross that landed square alongside Connors's jaw. The crack was loud. Unconscious, the insurance agent flew off the chair. Forzino felt pain in his knuckles.

Now the woman was wide-eyed and shaking. Forzino looked back down at Connors and saw his left arm was dangling half off his left leg. He would've preferred to break one of the guy's hands, but he was in a rush. He kicked down hard on the arm, just above the wrist. There was a loud snap and more blood. The woman gasped again before collapsing into her chair. Forzino saw bone protruding from the arm and almost felt queasy. He looked away and quickly headed for the door.

When he was in the car again, Agro quickly pulled out of the parking lot. Forzino looked down and saw his polo shirt was spotted with blood. He unconsciously rubbed at the bruised knuckles on his right hand.

Agro said, "Make sure you get rid of that shirt. They got tests now, can point to you this guy ever finds out who you are."

Forzino flipped down the visor and in the vanity mirror saw he was sweating profusely.

"Your mascara run?" Agro joked.

"There was a woman in there," Forzino said.

"Any cameras?"

"I didn't see any."

"Good. Then you're okay. You bust him up, besides the blood?"

"I think I broke his jaw," Forzino said. "I know I broke his arm. I saw the bone."

Agro was all smiles. He patted Forzino on the back. "Good job," he said. "It'll make your aunt happy, which'll make your uncle even happier, she won't break his balls about it anymore."

"Glad I could help," Forzino said. He wiped at the blood spots on his shirt and was thinking about how it would excite Sally when he told her about it later.

"He's gonna need to feel better about something, your uncle," Agro said.

"Why's that?"

"He called while you were inside there. A couple of OC cops were out to Coney Island breaking his balls before. One of them pushed his buttons about the bookmaker Bobby Gennaro, and ruined a two-hundred-dollar shirt. He went to work on some Chinaman and almost got pinched for it."

"What they say about Gennaro?"

"This and that. They're probing, you know, see what they can learn. They made insinuations about Gennaro maybe cutting a deal, how your uncle saw it. Could be bullshit, though, they're just looking for a reaction."

"What if he did cut a deal?"

"We know that, they're leaving him on the street to get more'n they already have, he's gotta go first chance we get."

Forzino saw it as an opportunity. "I'll do it," he said.

Agro smiled again.

Forzino added, "Just say when."

Agro patted the big man on his huge right arm. "Easy does it there, tiger," he said. "First we gotta make sure he's flipping. There's water to boil in that well. It's a delicate situation."

Forzino almost corrected the wiseguy. Instead, he asked, "How we supposed to know?"

"We apply a little pressure," Agro said. "Something like this afternoon with the broad. Sooner or later, where there's a squeak there's an ocean."

Forzino was sure Agro had meant to say leak. He ignored the mistake and asked about the pressure Agro had mentioned. "You're talking about Gennaro's girlfriend? Going after her?"

Agro said, "I like that idea, too."

Forzino wasn't sure what Agro had meant. He let it go.

Agro noticed the time and realized he was late for another appointment. "We gotta head over and pick up Mickey Nolan," the wiseguy said. "I want him to follow up on that broad from the bar."

Forzino had been hoping their day was over and he could get home early, maybe get laid for a change.

"Tonight?" he asked.

Agro seemed preoccupied. "What's that?"

"We going after her tonight?"

"Oh, not you, no," Agro said. "Mickey Nolan is. You're a good opening act, kid, but you're no closer yet."

Forzino wondered what Agro was talking about, then thought better of it and kept his mouth shut.

"You're my chaperone the rest of the night," Agro continued. "After Nolan we'll grab something to eat, and then I gotta see that wiseass again, Bobby Gennaro. Fact, remind me to give him a call in a little while.

"Then I'm headed to see a girlfriend of mine lives over the old Fort Hamilton House on Fourth Avenue, but I'll need a ride back home afterward. Her, she's got a big mouth sometimes, but she can suck the chrome off a trailer hitch. You want, stop at one of the strip joints while you're waiting and get your knob polished, too."

"You gonna be long?" Forzino asked.

"Long as it takes. She keeps her trap shut, it shouldn't take too long."

Forzino forced a smile.

Agro slapped him on the thigh. "Some day you'll have your own driver," he said. "Just for the record, when I was doing this, what you're doing, driving guys around, running errands, twenty-five, thirty years ago, nobody sent me for a blow job while I waited. Most times they had me picking up their laundry or chauffeuring their kids back and forth to school."

Forzino was thinking about Sally and could care less what Tommy Agro did twenty-five years ago.

"One time me and your uncle spent half the fucking day looking for Angelo Vignieri's Cadillac the night after he went on a bender," Agro continued. "Fat fuck didn't remember where he parked it after getting drunk out of his face. Six fuckin' hours it took us before we found it'd been hooked and was at the pound. Cost us out of our own pocket, too. Every fuckin' dime of the tickets and the tow charge, and he had something like four hundred bucks worth of tickets. You know what that was back then, four hundred dollars?"

Forzino rolled his eyes when Agro wasn't looking.

"Yeah," the wiseguy went on, "the old great bear ain't what it should be."

Whatever, Forzino was thinking. "Right," he said.

•◆•

LIN YAO CALLED a few minutes after seven. It took her half an hour to make it uptown. When she stepped out of the cab, Bobby was waiting outside the hotel with a bouquet of flowers.

He rushed her up to their room where they made love with most of their clothes still on. His cell phone rang a few times, but he ignored it.

He was about to give her the ring when she grabbed one of the small bags she had brought and hustled inside the bathroom. His cell phone rang again. Bobby answered it without looking at the number.

"Hello."

"Yeah, it's me," Tommy Agro said.

Bobby recognized the voice but wasn't about to give the wiseguy the satisfaction. "It's who?"

"Tommy," Agro said.

"Tommy who?"

"Hey, jerk-off, we need to talk."

"I'm busy."

"Tough shit."

Bobby rubbed his crotch with the cell phone. "Where are you?"

"Brooklyn. Where are you?"

"Not there. Let's talk tomorrow."

"We'll talk tonight."

"No can do. I'm busy."

"Tough shit," Agro said. "Gimme a time and place."

Bobby huffed and said, "You know Foley's on Thirty-third, across from the big building?"

"Empire State?"

"You know a bigger building?"

"Okay, wiseass, yeah."

"I'll be there around midnight."

"Around my ass. Be there on the dot."

"Twelve, twelve-thirty," Bobby said.

An uncomfortable pause followed.

"You better be," Agro said and then hung up.

"Jerk-off," Bobby said about the same time Lin Yao opened the bathroom door.

"Wow," he said.

Wearing a black lace garter belt and matching bra, she was standing there in spiked black heels.

He was still holding the cell phone.

"Who was that?" she asked.

"Father John," Bobby lied.

Lin Yao set her hands on her hips. "You called him a jerk-off," she said. "I heard you."

"Because he interrupted this," Bobby said. He lifted the sheets to show her he was getting excited.

Lin Yao smiled. "I hope that's for me."

"It is," Bobby said, and then reached over to the night table where he'd put the ring in the drawer. "And so is this."

•◆•

SALLY LOOMIS WAS relieved to hear the message from her fiancé when she finally made it home. She drew a hot bath and used oils to soften the scent and the water. She was still sore from the pounding Forzino's uncle had given her less than an hour earlier in the backseat of his Mercedes. The pain in her groin forced her to step gingerly into the tub. Uncle Joe had the biggest penis she'd ever seen, much less had inside her.

It was like a scene from a movie, Sally thought, the way her afternoon had gone. After spending the morning getting a facial and a complete body massage at the gym, she headed over to the beauty parlor. She tried the phone number the hunk had given her and was disappointed when no one picked up. Then when she got to the beauty parlor, the commotion across the street from the salon erased the disappointment from her mind.

She recognized her fiancé's uncle as soon as she saw him. Joe Quastifare was standing between two cars kicking at something in the street. It wasn't until Sally stopped to join the small crowd of people watching when she realized it was an Asian man catching the beating.

Someone in the crowd said it was the man who owned the dry cleaning shop directly across the street from the beauty salon. She wondered what it was about when police sirens could be heard and Uncle Joe's men dispersed the crowd.

Sally was about to have her nails done when she saw Joe Quastifare enter the salon. He was friendly with the manager and asked if he could use the bathroom. He didn't notice her when he crossed the length of the shop to the back.

Sally decided to intercept him to say hello when he came out of the bathroom. She headed to the back and was surprised when she saw he'd left the door open a crack. She saw him tucking himself in his underwear in the bathroom mirror's reflection and gasped at the size of his penis. It was huge.

"Oh, Jesus," Uncle Joe said when he heard her. "I'm sorry, miss."

He quickly kicked the door shut. Sally stood there waiting for him to come out. When he did, she said, "Uncle Joe?"

It took a moment for him to recognize her. "Oh, Christ," he said. "You're Johnny-boy's girl, Susan, right?"

Sally had felt her face turning red from blushing.

"Yes, I'm Sally. How are you?"

"Sally, right," Uncle Joe had said, then pointed to the bathroom door. "Jesus, I'm sorry about that."

"No, it's okay," she told him and meant every word of it. "That was my fault. I wanted to say hello."

Uncle Joe's face lit up with a broad smile. "Well, you sure did."

Twenty minutes later he was driving her to one of his clubs for a drink. A car filled with his men followed them. Uncle Joe told her about the Chinaman he had kicked outside the dry cleaning store because he had ruined a two-hundred-dollar silk shirt.

Sally had asked what kind of stain it had been they couldn't get out. Uncle Joe told her "the Monica Lewinsky kind, except without any of the pleasure."

"Really?" Sally had asked.

Uncle Joe had reached across the console to grab her hand. "Nah, not really," he had said. "Just some mustard and onions. I haven't found the woman yet can handle the snake you saw."

Sally had smiled. "It is pretty big."

"It's a curse," Uncle Joe said.

"I wouldn't know," Sally had said. "Johnny's big everywhere but there."

"Big heart, but small where it counts, huh? That's too bad."

"I think he's the one who's cursed."

"While you're the one suffers."

"In more ways than one."

It was then Uncle Joe escorted her into the backseat.

Now she was tender where he'd been earlier. She used a sponge to dab at her vagina, but it was still sore. The problem was he liked having her ride on top. He hadn't even gone all the way inside her, except for when they were into it and her weight forced her down further than she wanted to go. It was something she'd have to adjust to if they were going to meet again. She wondered just how far her vagina could be stretched before he might do damage.

The thought made her wince.

Then she thought about her fiancé possibly coming home horny later and Sally shuddered.

"Fuck that," she whispered, "I'll jerk the ape off before I fuck him now."

CHAPTER 11

BOBBY WAS ALMOST half an hour late when he finally showed up at Foley's to meet with Tommy Agro. He could tell the wiseguy wasn't happy.

"You have an excuse for keeping me waiting?" Agro asked.

"Traffic," Bobby said.

"It's one o'clock in the morning. The fuck traffic you talking about?"

Bobby glanced around the restaurant. "Where's the muscle?"

"Johnny-boy? He's babysitting the car. Not that it's any of your business."

Bobby nodded at the waitress. He asked for a glass of water.

"You talk to Joe?" he asked once the waitress was gone.

"Yeah, I did."

"And?"

"He's willing to be reasonable, even after you were rude the other day."

"I would've thought your muscle showing up last night cancelled that, my being rude."

"You thought wrong, but chalk it up to being late now."

"So?" he said. "What did reasonable Joe say?"

"Fifty thousand."

Bobby chuckled.

"I say something funny?"

"Why not a million?"

"I didn't ask for a million. Maybe I should've."

"I don't have fifty grand."

"Then I'll guess you have to find it."

"Or else?"

"Trust me, you don't wanna know."

"So, now it's outright extortion," Bobby said.

Agro leaned forward. "You wearing a wire?"

"Of course not."

"Let's take a walk to the bathroom and make sure."

Bobby shook his head at Agro, realized the wiseguy was serious, and stood up. Agro stood aside to let Bobby pass. He told the bartender the men's room was off limits until they came back out and then locked the door once they were inside.

Bobby let Agro frisk him. When he thought they were finished, Bobby started for the door. The wiseguy blocked him.

"Step in a stall and drop your pants," Agro said.

"You fucking serious?"

"Just do it."

Bobby went through the motions. When his pants were down around his ankles, he turned around and spread his cheeks for the wiseguy.

"Wanna get closer, you'll have to buy me flowers first."

"Be grateful I don't shove my foot in there," Agro said.

Bobby picked up his pants and adjusted his clothes while Agro unlocked the door and returned to their table. Bobby rolled his eyes at the mirror on his way out.

"Happy?" he asked once he was seated across from Agro again.

"You can't help yourself, can you? With the wisecracks, I mean."

"I don't have a spare fifty grand, Tommy," said Bobby, getting right back to it. "I don't have a spare ten, but that's what I'm willing to pay, if he gives me some time."

Agro cleaned a fingernail with a matchbook. "Sounds like an insult to me, ten grand."

"It's what I might be able to put together," Bobby said. "But it'll take some time."

The waitress brought the water to the table. Bobby sipped at it while looking into Agro's eyes.

"You're telling me to take that number back to a skipper," Agro said. "I'm warning you it's an insult, but if you wanna piss up that tree, be my guest."

"I'm not looking to piss on anybody," Bobby said. "I didn't steal fifty grand. I didn't steal the ten, but if it'll make this square once and for all, it's what I'm willing to pay. I'm not gonna be squeezed, though. Not for fifty and not for eleven. I'm only willing to pay the ten because I understand how these things work and I've been told Quack is a dinosaur when it comes to this bullshit."

Agro leaned forward. "What bullshit?"

"Your world," Bobby said. "Sorry, Tommy, but I never bought into it, not in the past and I still don't. I'll respect it, your thing, but I won't buy into it."

"Nobody's asking you to buy into anything, cocksucker. We're telling you to pay a tax you owe, end of story."

"You're asking for money I don't have."

Agro continued cleaning his fingernails.

"We done?" Bobby asked. "I just got engaged and I'd like to get back to my fiancée."

Agro motioned toward the window facing the street. "The kid outside is engaged, too," he said. "Why I have him sitting the car instead of in here breaking your smart mouth. I don't wanna see him waste his nickels and dimes on parking garages."

"Congratulate him for me," Bobby said. "On his engagement, I mean."

Agro pointed the matchbook at Bobby. "See, that's what I mean," he said. "You got a smart fuckin' mouth. I'm surprised it didn't burn you in the past."

Bobby remained silent.

"In the meantime, it's time you get down to brass taxes," Agro said. "Put your nose in the limestone."

Bobby was confused. He squinted at Agro.

"What, you got something in your eye?" the wiseguy asked.

"I can get him five grand pretty fast," Bobby said. "And the rest over a month or so, but I don't have what you quoted. Not in this life."

"It'd take a sit-down," Agro said. "What you're saying here, if you want Joe to come down on what he already asked for, without breaking you up for refusing." He smiled then. "You got anybody to sit for you?"

"That's rich," Bobby said. "A sit-down? No, I don't have anybody to sit for me. Not that I'd waste my time at one."

"You're talking through your ass now."

"It's the impression I'm getting, Tommy. You're squeezing me. It's a fifth-rate hustle."

Agro's face turned red. Bobby was thinking, here it comes, I went too far.

"You're lucky I'm getting my pipes cleaned later," Agro said. "We wanted to whack you out, it woulda been done already. I got a guy can shoot the tits off a gnat from a hundred places, goes to the range twice a week just to stay sharp, okay?"

Bobby was about to correct the comment when Agro stopped him. "What about Freddie Panico? You got an idea where he's hiding?"

"How would I know that?"

"You tell me."

"I don't know Freddie Panico. Never even met him."

"What about his sister?"

"Never met her either."

"But you know who Freddie is, right? Or you're just jerking me off for the hell of it now?"

"I knew of him, yeah. Nicky mentioned him a few times. I knew of his name, in passing. I never met the guy, though. Not even hello and good-bye."

"You can shave off some of what you owe finding the guy," Agro said. "Maybe Joe'd go for something like that."

"Except I wouldn't know where to look."

Agro gave it a moment. Bobby waited without flinching.

"Then I guess there's no ghost at the dance," Agro said.

"Excuse me?" Bobby said.

"You're fucked," Agro said. "You owe fifty grand."

Bobby didn't see the point in arguing. He waited for the threat instead.

First Agro finished his drink.

"Who you marrying, the Chink?"

"She's Chinese," Bobby said.

"Salute," Agro said.

Bobby wasn't sure if Agro was being polite or sarcastic. He let it go. Agro made him wait.

"You have twenty-four hours to do the right thing here," the wiseguy finally said. "After that it's out of my hands."

"I can get you five in a few days, sooner if I can put it together," Bobby said. "Another five in maybe a few weeks. Like I said, I don't have fifty grand."

"Then maybe you'll pay points," said Agro, before sliding his chair back from the table. "And maybe I should put somebody on your ass to make sure you don't sleep off into the night."

Bobby had had enough. "You mean 'slip off into the night.'"

Agro was standing now. "What's that?"

"You mean 'slip off into the night.' You said 'sleep.'"

"Never mind what I said. Get the fuckin' money or you're the one'll be asleep."

Bobby fully engaged the wiseguy's stare-down.

"Capisce?" Agro said.

"Yeah, I'll do my best," Bobby said in a flat monotone.

"Do better'n that," Agro said. He straightened out his sports coat before smiling at Bobby again. "Or I'll have the kid break your fucking legs before I cap you myself."

•◆•

MICKEY KEVIN NOLAN was arrested twenty-six times since his thirteenth birthday. He had spent eight of his thirty-two years in prison, five of the eight for a manslaughter charge that involved beating a vagrant to death. Except for two assaults on police officers, one undercover, the other in uniform, Nolan had managed to beat fifteen separate assault charges when witnesses and/or the victims refused to testify in court.

Now he was being paid to find and kill a wiseguy before the guy turned up in a criminal court somewhere to testify against members of the Vignieri crime family. Tommy Agro had explained how critical it was that Fred Panico be found and disposed of as soon as possible. He had also given Nolan carte blanche to do whatever was necessary to get Fred Panico's sister to talk.

"What if she don't know?" Nolan had asked Agro.

"Let's put it this way," the wiseguy had told him. "Make damn sure she don't know. Peel her fuckin' skin off you gotta."

It was exactly what Nolan planned on doing once he had Angela Panico in her apartment—using a paring knife to peel back the skin first off her arms, then off her legs, if he had to. Nolan had never tortured a woman before, but he'd gone after men the same way and it had always worked. Either they knew something and told him or they didn't and would beg to be put out of their misery.

Although he'd been convicted of the single manslaughter charge more than ten years ago, Nolan had killed three other men without ever being charged in their murders. Killing was something he did for extra scratch when the jobs were available. It was giving beatings that Nolan preferred.

Agro had taken care of the lawyer when Nolan was bailed out. Now he felt he owed the wiseguy extra. Although he was loyal to one of the Irish gangs in Hell's Kitchen, Nolan's prime jobs usually came from the Italians, Tommy Agro and Joe Quastifare mostly.

He nursed a beer in the back of the Maspeth bar until half an hour before closing time. When he left, there were two drunks chatting with Angela Panico. Nolan waited up the block behind the shadow of a pickup truck to watch the front door. Fifteen minutes later both drunks left the bar. Ten minutes after that Angela Panico stepped out and locked the door behind her.

Nolan, staying within the shadows of cars and trees, followed her to a sports car parked at the end of the block. He waited until she opened the front door before tapping her on the shoulder and showing her a gun.

"Just get in the car and climb over the console like we're best friends," he told her.

Angela Panico froze.

"Do it," Nolan told her.

She did. Nolan sat behind the steering wheel. He grabbed her left wrist and held it while he locked the doors and started the car.

"Okay," he said. "We're going back to your place. You're going to tell me where I can find your brother. You'll probably try to lie. I'll convince you not to. Depending on what you can tell me, I'll either go away or cut your throat. Understand?"

Angela nodded nervously.

"Okay, then, tell me where to go and how to get there. Try and pull your hand away or anything else and I'll kill you and find your brother without your help."

Angela nervously gave him directions back to her apartment. It took Nolan ten minutes to get there and another ten to find a spot. They got out of the car and walked back to the building like dates coming home from a party. Nolan marched her through the lobby, his right arm wrapped around Angela Panico's waist. They took the elevator up two floors and walked the length of the hallway to her apartment door, where Nolan stopped her from using her keys.

"Give it a knock first," he said.

"I have a key."

"Give it a knock."

Angela did as she was told. Nolan heard footsteps behind the door. He stood to the side, out of view of the peephole. Nolan raised the gun when he heard someone behind the door.

He waited for it to open a crack before he grabbed Angela by the hair and rammed her headfirst into the door. He pushed from behind until the person on the other side gave way and they were fully inside the apartment.

Across the living room Fred Panico stood holding a gun of his own. Nolan used Angela as a shield and kicked the apartment door shut behind him.

"Who the fuck're you?" Fred Panico asked.

Nolan used Angela's right shoulder to brace his hand with the gun. The woman was shaking and nearly crumpled to the floor.

"Let her go!" her brother yelled.

"Drop your gun," Nolan said.

"Yeah, right. Fuck you."

Nolan fired first.

Panico caught the bullet in his left shoulder and returned two shots of his own. Both hit his sister in the stomach.

Nolan fired two shots, both catching Panico in the chest. The wiseguy crashed against the wall behind him and slid to the floor. He fired one more shot that lodged in the ceiling. Nolan fired a fourth and fifth time, both head shots. The fourth one killed Panico, the fifth would have killed him.

Nolan let Angela down to the floor and used a T-shirt he found on the couch to pick up her brother's gun. He used it to shoot her in the forehead. He set the gun back in Fred Panico's hand, then quickly went through the dead siblings' pockets and purse for cash.

Nolan was pleasantly surprised when he found a stun gun on the dead wiseguy. He stashed it inside his own pants and got out of there.

CHAPTER 12

Michael Ward parked his green Oldsmobile minivan alongside a blue Ford Mustang in a diner parking lot on Woodhaven Boulevard. A short man with thin red hair and a face laced with freckles nodded at Ward. He adjusted the sunglasses he was wearing so they hung off the end of his nose.

"You'd think it be cooler out now," Jerry Collins said. He looked at his rearview mirror before dropping an envelope out his window between the two cars.

Ward said, "You dropped something."

"Did I?"

Ward checked his rearview and side mirrors.

"It's worth picking up," Collins said.

Ward said, "I tell you what. I don't drive away before you do, I'll consider it."

"I wasn't followed, my man."

"First off, I'm not your man. Second, how would you know you're followed or not?"

Collins shook his head.

Ward had been watching the parking lot for more than forty minutes to make sure neither of them was followed. Now he started a fresh cigarette and motioned at the envelope on the pavement.

"That really worth my effort, picking it up?" he asked.

Collins readjusted the sunglasses he was wearing. He said, "You're looking for an even grand it is."

Ward pointed to the sunglasses. "What's up with those?" he asked. "You auditioning for the dagos?"

Collins flipped the glasses down again. His right eye was black and blue. "Had an incident last night," he said. "Nothing worth discussing, but I am surprised you're driving a minivan. I know you can afford better than that."

"Not lately, I can't," Ward said, "but let's go. I don't have time for small talk. What's up?"

"Ryan is still in Dublin."

"Yeah, so?"

"And Mickey Nolan is off doing work for the dagos."

"Which dagos?"

"Vignieri guys he usually works for. Tommy Agro, another guy, I forget his name. Something like Donald Duck."

Joe Quack, Ward was thinking. He played dumb. "Yeah, so, what's this to me?"

"A hostile takeover comes to mind."

"That's to you," Ward said. "What's it to me?"

Collins motioned at the envelope. "More what's in there, I would think."

Ward took a long drag on his cigarette. "I'll need a more accurate time frame," he said. "Something specific I can plan ahead. If you're gonna take over the West Side, Ryan has to die. Unless you can kill him from here, he's in Dublin, I need to know when you're gonna move. I don't intend to be in town that day. I'm all for it, but I'm up to my ears in dagos now."

"Fair enough," Collins said. "I'll do my best."

Ward pointed his cigarette at the envelope. "Do so with that, too," he said. He waited for Collins to respond. When he didn't, Ward added, "Okay, you can go now. Try not to make noise when you do it."

Collins smiled again. He drove off at a smooth, subtle speed. Ward sat in the car and smoked another five cigarettes before getting out and picking up the envelope.

•◆•

LIN YAO WAS upset when Bobby first left her at the hotel. Now, two hours later, she was close to furious. She sat up in the hotel bed and rang his cell phone a few times before he finally answered.

"Hey," he said.

"Hey? Are you kidding me? Where the hell are you?"

"I'm busy, babe. I'll be back in a couple more hours. I promise."

"Jesus Christ, Bobby. A couple more hours?"

"I'm just taking care of something. I'll be there in a little while. Want me to pick something up? Chocolate raspberry maybe?"

"It's three-thirty in the morning! Where are you going to get chocolate anything? What the hell are you doing?"

"Taking care of that problem. You know."

"I don't know. First you bring me here to this hotel, you give me a beautiful ring, and then you run out on me."

"You forgot making love."

"And now you're making jokes?"

"We can restart our celebration soon as I get back. I promise. Then we'll have the entire day together."

"And when do you intend to sleep? We have the opera tomorrow, too. Tonight actually."

"I'll sleep through that."

"Damn you, Bobby!"

"Look, I'll be there soon as I can. I'm sorry about this, honey, really. Trust me a little longer. I love you, baby."

"You're an asshole."

"Yeah, but I'm your asshole. Gimme a kiss."

"I'll break your teeth."

"Kiss me first."

"No," she said, and then slammed down the telephone.

She saw herself in the large mirror across the room. She had put on the negligee and garters again to surprise him when he came back. Now she felt stupid.

She ate a piece of chocolate candy out of the box before she reached for the remote and turned on the television. She flipped through several cable channels before stopping at one that advertised Manhattan escorts. The girls on the screen were also wearing lingerie.

"I'm the asshole," she said before turning the television off again.

•◆•

TOMMY AGRO'S ARROGANT routine had pissed Bobby off. If he was going to pay the mob shakedown money, he would steal it from them first. Instead of heading back to the hotel after his meeting with Agro, Bobby stopped off at the apartment to pick up a few things he might need to get inside his old bookmaking office.

He changed his clothes and had just put together a bag of tools when Lin Yao called his cell phone. Bobby did his best to avoid a full-scale argument, but it wasn't easy. He had just proposed to the woman less than three hours ago. He had asked for her trust again, but had neglected to tell her he was about to rob money the mob had already accused him of stealing.

He took a cab back uptown to Thirty-fourth Street and Second Avenue, then walked one block north and another east along St. Vartan's Park. Halfway between First and Second Avenues Bobby crossed the street and walked into the apartment building where the bookmaking office was located. He used an old key to gain access to the lobby and then climbed a single flight of stairs to the second floor.

Bobby guessed the locks hadn't been changed since he left the place. He was right. He took one step inside the office and then stopped in his tracks. Somebody was snoring.

A short man was sleeping on his back on the twin-sized bed off to the right. The money drop was in the closet across from the tiny kitchen and was accessible by lifting the coat rack up out of the wall.

Bobby carefully stepped around the two desks covered with telephones and office supplies. He crossed the kitchen area and carefully opened the closet door. A light blue windbreaker hung from a plastic hanger alongside a few empty hangers. Bobby removed the windbreaker and set it on the floor. He removed the empty hangers and set them on the windbreaker. Then he pulled out the coat rack.

Although the clerks who worked the office weren't supposed to bring money there, sometimes they collected on their way to the office and the cash was hidden in the overnight drop inside the closet wall. Bobby had hidden money there himself in the past.

He dipped his hand inside the drop and felt a wad of cash wrapped with a rubber band. He withdrew it carefully, then glanced at the outside bills and saw they were hundreds.

He listened again for the snoring before replacing the rack and hangers. He left the windbreaker on the floor and started for the door when an alarm clock sounded on the windowsill at the opposite end of the bed.

The guy lying on his back stirred a few times before sitting up and turning toward Bobby. The poor bastard barely caught a glimpse of the punch that put him right back to sleep.

Bobby started for the door when he heard a commotion in the hallway outside the apartment. He leaned in close to the peephole and saw a couple embracing on the stairway. He recognized the woman from when he used to run the office. She was a tiny woman in her mid-thirties or so. "Linda Lovelace," he remembered the office clerks had nicknamed her, after catching her giving a guy head in the courtyard. She lived in an apartment on the third floor and had been seen coming and going with several different men, all of them big like the guy out there with her now.

Bobby couldn't leave without her noticing. The disguise he had brought to get inside the building wasn't enough to get him past the woman. When the office clerks showed up to work the next day, they would find the guy Bobby had knocked out and would investigate the robbery by talking to everyone in the building.

He waited a few minutes to see if they would leave, but they didn't. If anything, it looked as if they would make love right there in the hallway. Both appeared to be drunk.

The air conditioner suddenly turned off. Bobby remembered that it had been set on a timer. He looked to the man on the bed, who could regain consciousness at any moment.

Bobby looked through the peephole again. The couple was still going at it. The man had turned the tiny woman around and was groping her from behind. She was giggling.

Bobby tried to scare them off. Muffling his voice, he said, "Knock it off out there."

The woman said, "Mind your own business," and continued to giggle.

Bobby began to sweat profusely. He realized he was stuck until the couple left. He crossed the tiny apartment to where he knew there was rope in one of the drawers. He ripped one of the windbreakers to use as a blindfold and went about tying and gagging the man on the bed.

When he glanced through the peephole again, he saw the couple had stopped mauling one another. Bobby could see the top of the woman's head. He looked up and saw the blissful expression on the big man's face. The guy was getting head.

"Great," Bobby whispered.

He glanced at his watch. It was close to four o'clock in the morning. He wiped sweat from his face and waited for the show outside the apartment door to end.

When he heard the man start to groan, Bobby looked through the peephole again. Before he could see anything, he heard the woman scream. A few loud thumps followed. One or both of them had fallen down the stairs.

Bobby cursed under his breath.

He heard the woman scream for help. It was the man who had taken the fall.

Bobby couldn't believe his luck. Now an ambulance would have to come and take the guy away. The police would probably show as well. They might even knock on some doors and investigate.

It would be at least another hour before he could get out of there. If he had to wait, there was no point in sweating. He crossed the tiny apartment again, turned the air conditioner back on, then sat alongside the poor bastard he had robbed, knocked out, blindfolded, tied, and gagged.

CHAPTER 13

IT WAS FIVE fifteen in the morning when John Forzino finally made it home. He was instantly relieved by the air conditioning inside the apartment. The short walk from the car to the front door had left him sweating. He stood in front of one of the air conditioning vents and cooled off.

Sally was sleeping soundly when he peeked inside the bedroom. He thought about trying to wake her but figured he had a better chance in the morning, after he told her what he'd been up to. Lately she seemed to perk up with interest whenever he told her wiseguy stories. She had been intrigued when he mentioned the "Crazy Joe" Gallo murder at the restaurant that Tommy Agro had told him about. Sally had said she wanted to eat there the next time they went to the city.

It had been a long night made longer because Agro had been drunk when Forzino picked him up from his girlfriend's apartment after the late meeting with the bookmaker on Thirty-third Street. Agro had gotten into an argument with his girlfriend, the wiseguy had said.

"I had to belt her one just to shut her trap."

Forzino had noticed that two of Agro's knuckles were cut. "I hope you didn't hurt her," he had said.

Agro waved the concern off. "It ain't the first time," he had said. "She'll get over it."

Agro had spent the rest of the night rambling about being passed over for skipper and had made a few nasty comments about some of the bosses. Forzino tried to steer Agro's conversation away from remarks about his uncle, but the wiseguy couldn't hold his tongue.

"You know the problem with your uncle?" Agro had asked at one point. "He's got a big dick and small balls."

Forzino ignored the remark at the time, although it still bothered him. Uncle Joe was blood.

Before he finally got out of the car, Agro went on another rant about the Chinese taking over Little Italy. Forzino was pretty sure his new boss had confused whatever he was trying to say one more time.

"Everybody is so concerned about the Russians taking over things," Agro had said. "You ask me, it's the noodles are the real dark force in the palace. Those people, the way they took over Little Italy, they're the ones we gotta watch out for, never mind the Russians."

Forzino had thought he was on his way home after listening to Agro rant about the Chinese, but then the wiseguy brought up going after Bobby Gennaro's girlfriend again.

"He's gonna marry that twat, it might bring him to his senses we can get to her," Agro had said.

The idea of killing Gennaro appealed to Forzino more than having to fight the guy or going after his girlfriend. He wondered if Agro would work Mickey Nolan into the formula. Then he remembered that they had dropped the Irishman off for something else earlier.

"You hear from him, from Nolan?" Forzino had asked.

"Indeed I did," Agro said. "Indeed I did."

Forzino was more than willing to let it go when Agro said, "Just watch the news tomorrow, you wake up. It'll be interesting, to say the least."

At that point Forzino was hopeful that his long night was finally over. He was about to shift into drive, when Agro started in on Bobby Gennaro and his girlfriend again.

"We make it a one-time thing," he said. "Either it gets him to pay off or it don't. Either way, we can whack him, too, the wiseass."

Forzino was all for it now. He kept it to himself, though, still hopeful Agro would say good night.

Instead, Agro said, "I'm sending Nolan downtown tomorrow. I'm supposed to meet your uncle early for breakfast, too, but I have to call the Irishman. Remind me."

Forzino nodded.

"Then we'll know what to do once for all with Bobby fuckin' G," Agro added. "Soon's he shits or gets off the pot, you take over. He pays, you whack him. He don't pay, you whack him. Keeps the math simple that way. Then I'll propose you for a button."

Forzino forced a smile. Agro winked before he finally turned away and headed for his house.

That had been half an hour ago and now Forzino still couldn't get the conversations out of his head.

He stood in the bedroom doorway and looked at Sally. He wished he could wake her up to discuss it. It was one way to turn her on.

Lately it seemed to be the only way.

Instead, Forzino grabbed a cold beer and sat in his recliner in the living room. He was exhausted from the long day. The knuckles on his right hand were still sore. He looked down and realized they were swollen as well as bruised. He started to rub them when he thought the bruising would probably excite Sally in the morning. He made a tight fist until he couldn't stand the pain, then he covered his hand with a towel and punched down on the arm of the recliner to draw blood.

•◆•

"THAT WAS UGLY," Detective Michael Ward said through a long yawn. He stretched his arms down and then out and accidentally nudged DeNafria in the right shoulder.

"Excuse," Ward added.

"The fuck is your problem?" Deputy Inspector Edward Kaprowski said.

"Rough night sleeping," Ward said.

"Take a pill."

"Yes, sir."

Ward and DeNafria had just finished a second walk-through of the crime scene at Angela Panico's apartment. They had been on their way to a diner for breakfast when Kaprowski found them.

"Running away before the feds get here?" Kaprowski asked DeNafria.

"I was hoping to."

"Why, so I have to deal with them?"

"Why they pay you the big bucks."

Kaprowski glanced at his watch. "At six o'clock in the morning they should pay me double time and a half." He turned to Ward and saw him about to yawn again. "You find me boring, detective?"

"No, sir," Ward replied through the yawn.

Kaprowski spoke at DeNafria. "We couldn't find Panico and the feds couldn't, but his own could. How is that, detective?"

"I don't know, sir."

"Yeah, I already know that, what you don't know. Why's the question. Why don't you know?"

DeNafria shrugged.

Kaprowski shook his head and then waved both detectives off. "Get lost," he told them. "Go catch up on your beauty sleep, the botha yous. I'll handle the faggot federalistas. In this fuckin' heat, they're all I need to make the resta my day."

DeNafria nudged Ward to hurry. Both detectives hustled back to the car without looking back. DeNafria waited until they were inside the car and had it started before he spoke again.

"That was lucky," he told Ward. "The old man hates the feds as much as the wiseguys. He must have something to chat about he's letting us walk away from hearing what they have to say. And they'll have a lot to say now. They'll be in a real bad mood they didn't get Panico off the street in time to flip him."

"Yeah, and they'll need a scapegoat, too," Ward said. "Couldn't possibly be their fault the guy didn't survive long enough for them to make a deal."

DeNafria chuckled. "You deal with them much on the West Side, the feds?"

"Not until the hard work was done, once we took apart the crew running the West Side. After that, yeah, you bet your ass we did. They came in gangbusters after that, took all the glory."

"Not all of it. You did okay."

"Except for the Internal Affairs fiasco, I did. And it's my humble and accurate opinion that was the feds looking to shoot down the only credit us locals had left, the greedy bastards, what they tried to do to me."

"Well, the work you guys did on that crew was great. Splintered them down to nothing the way I hear it."

"Yeah, well, big deal. They'll be back, same as the Italians will once we break them up. There's always a new boss waiting in the wings somewhere. I know of at least two guys looking to run the West Side again. One's got the old world behind him, the boyos overseas, Kenneth Ryan. The one here is a renegade from Boston, Jerry Collins. They'll fight it out on the streets and the local slobs like you and me'll sit the hours watching and waiting and doing the dirty work of nailing them, and then you wait and see what happens after that."

"Headline federal organized crime bust?"

"Like fucking clockwork," Ward said. "Only that's not the worst of it. Every time we took somebody down, and I'm talking genuine pieces of shit, they stepped right in and offered some deal put the bastards right back out on the street. Either that or they took them away to Arkansas. Defeats the purpose of law enforcement, you ask me. What's the point of taking bullets to put them away if the feds are gonna turn around and let them go?"

"I forgot you were shot," DeNafria said. "And I agree, although there's no denying the deals work. Look what's become of the mob. They're in tatters."

"Yeah, well, you were shot at, too," Ward said. "Didn't it make you nuts, the grief they gave you over that, defending yourself, while they turn around and let some piece of human garbage like Sammy the Bull walk away from nineteen murders?"

DeNafria had almost lost his job for fatally shooting a black teenager during an armed robbery prior to working organized crime. The kid had fired three times and hit a duffle bag DeNafria was carrying before the off-duty detective returned fire.

"What are you gonna do?" DeNafria said.

"Where the hell is Arkansas, anyway?" Ward asked.

"Home of Hillary and Bill Clinton."

Ward looked confused. "I thought they're from New York."

DeNafria said, "What about that routine you pulled back at the Nathan's yesterday? I hope that wasn't real? It looked it."

"He got under my skin."

"I'm not talking about the punk you almost got into it with," DeNafria said. "That last bit there about Bobby G, shoving him down Quastifare's throat. You can get a guy killed like that."

"You make him sound like a saint, Bobby G."

"I didn't say that, except the guy isn't involved anymore."

"Not that we know of."

An uncomfortable moment passed. DeNafria decided to end it.

"Look, the fastest way to a headache with the powers that be in this unit is to blow a case by losing your temper," he told his partner. "I had another partner couple years back, great guy with a very short fuse. He banged up some rat the feds were protecting and was forced into retirement."

"Alex Pavlik, I heard."

"Good man, but he let them get to him. You can't on this detail. And you gotta learn to live with the frustrations of the FBI. They're fuckups, some of them, but they usually hold the cards."

"I just don't like it when some meathead mob muscle thinks he can talk shit like we're not standing there," Ward said. "I had an incident on the West Side a couple years ago with one of the Corelli people from the Bronx. He was working with the Irish lads I was infiltrating, moving electronic equipment off the docks and so on, and he came off like an asshole with me one night we were waiting on something."

DeNafria waited for more. Ward lit a cigarette and seemed to forget he was telling a story.

"And?" DeNafria said.

"Huh? Oh, I kicked him square in the solar plexus so hard I had to revive the bastard on the spot. Had to get down on all fours and put my mouth to his to get him breathing again."

DeNafria was smiling ear to ear.

"Wasn't funny," Ward said. "I was never so scared in all my life. Thought I'd killed the fucker and would have to spend twenty years in the joint for it."

DeNafria laughed. "How'd he taste?"

Ward flipped him the bird.

"Serious," DeNafria said. "Did you at least get his number?"

Ward said, "I thought I'd share that with you to be up-front with each other, not so you could break my balls."

"I'm sorry," said DeNafria, still laughing.

"Yeah, I can tell."

"I can't help it."

"Obviously."

"I'm sorry, man. Really."

Ward puffed on his cigarette as DeNafria laughed hysterically.

Five minutes later, once DeNafria was able to compose himself again, they pulled into a diner parking lot on Queens Boulevard.

Ward said, "Could be a good time to shake up things with Bobby G about now."

"Because of Panico?"

"What I'm thinking, yeah."

"What about sitting on him? Maybe we catch them making a move on Gennaro."

"We might, you let me talk some more trash about the guy to the wiseguys."

"That's too dangerous."

"At least push them further along in Gennaro's direction," Ward said. "Maybe stop and talk to Tommy Agro, drop another hint or two. I'll bet Quack mentioned our talk with Bobby G to Agro already."

"I'm not keen on that," DeNafria said. "Nudging is one thing. Like I said, you can get a guy killed."

Ward raised his hands in submission.

"Gennaro is clean now," DeNafria said. "I'd rather give him the benefit of the doubt."

"No problem, but Agro is Quack's enforcer, right?"

"He's a real piece of work, too. Big balls and a bigger mouth. You might want me to do the talking, though. He's the kind of guy that likes to push buttons."

"Fine with me," said Ward, yawning again. "I'll stand quiet."

"Yeah, I think so," DeNafria said. "Because the other thing I hear is Agro's breath can smell pretty bad. It might be tough to resuscitate the guy you lost your temper again."

"You're gonna be a genuine asshole about this, huh?" Ward said.

DeNafria winked at his partner and said, "Just for the rest of the day."

•◆•

"THIS BROAD, I'M telling you, I never felt like this before," Joe Quastifare told Tommy Agro. "She's got that sweet face thing going on, you know? I never noticed it before yesterday, but she's got it."

They had met for an early breakfast at a diner in Canarsie. Quastifare had chosen a booth alongside a window. Agro shielded his eyes from the sunlight. He was still feeling the effects of a hangover from the night before. He was there to discuss their plans for Bobby Gennaro. Quastifare continued to obsess over his nephew's fiancée.

Both men had already discussed the news about Freddie and Angela Panico and had agreed to forget the brother and sister forever.

"This could be bad, this thing with this twat," Quastifare continued. "I mean with my nephew and all. It could get ugly."

"Considering the guy can bench-press five hundred pounds, yeah, I guess so," Agro said.

"Fuck his bench press. I'll put two behind his ear."

Agro had to clear his throat. "Hey, Joe, the kid did the right thing yesterday," he said. "He passed that test with flying colors, broke the guy's arm and his jaw."

Quastifare wasn't anxious to give his nephew any credit yet. "He's fucking big enough," he said, "except where it counts. Poor broad is suffering, his fiancée."

They had been friends a long time and had come up through the ranks together. They were both made in the same ceremony more than twenty-five years ago, although Agro had always been a little jealous of Quastifare's close relationship to Gene Vignieri, the acting boss of the family still serving time in Greenhaven on federal RICO violations.

Agro also knew that he had more than double the kills on his mob résumé than his longtime friend, but Quastifare had that extra juice with the acting boss. It seemed to have made the difference when it was time to name a replacement captain for Nicky D'Angelo.

Now Agro was trying to get his new boss to focus on Bobby Gennaro instead of a piece of tail.

"The bookmaker," he said. "I frisked him last night, but that doesn't mean anything, he wasn't wired then. We want to give him the time to cut a deal?"

Quastifare smiled at a waitress across the floor.

"Joe?" Agro said.

"I'd rather we squeeze him first," Quastifare said. "Get whatever we can."

"Unless he's already cooperating," Agro said. "I don't wanna be the one squeezing him he's wired up."

Quastifare smiled.

Agro squinted. "I must be a comedian."

"I'm thinking about the lug, my nephew," Quastifare said. "It's one way to get him out the way, he leans on Gennaro."

The idea didn't sit well with Agro. His face showed it.

"What, I should shoot the kid I can avoid it?" Quastifare said.

"You shouldn't be banging his fiancée," Agro said.

"It's one of them things, Tommy. And it's not like he's made. It's not like he's off-limits."

"Not technically, no," Agro said. "But it's still not right. I mean, Jesus Christ, Joe, he's your fuckin' nephew. He's out there giving it his best shot."

"It's her face," Quastifare said, "his girl, there, Susan, Sally, whatever the fuck. She's got that innocent face thing going on. It's hard for me to ignore that."

Agro shook his head. Both men remained silent a while until Agro chuckled.

Quastifare narrowed his eyes. "Now I'm a comedian?"

"I'm thinking back to the bank job we did upstate twenty years ago," Agro said. "You and that hose of yours. You saw something you liked and took her phone number."

Quastifare smiled as he remembered it. "Yeah, well, I would've used it, too, the papers didn't say she was the local chief of police's daughter, that one. And she was interested, too. The smile she gave me handing over that number. I asked, but she gave. I didn't have to force her."

Agro said, "Well, I'm glad you never used it."

Both men shared a hearty laugh. Quastifare said, "Okay, you want, send the Irishman over to shake things up with this retired bookmaker. Keep my nephew in the loop, but out of the action until something goes down. I want him in the game at some point, to school him if nothing else. In the meantime, I'll keep in touch with you so I know he don't walk in on me and his fiancée. That, I'm not giving up yet. I probably will down the road, but not yet. She's got that look."

Agro nodded. "We'll probably catch a lot of heat the rest of the week now, the task forces and whoever else they got watching us, after this other thing last night. And then there's the feast, they'll be climbing all over us again this year, the feds."

"Why you should keep close tabs on the Irishman," Quastifare said. "Because I don't trust them any more'n our own. He starts to look rattled, let my nephew do the work with you."

Agro agreed. "That works, too," he said.

Quastifare was back to smiling at the waitress again. "She's got nice eyes," he said. "Tits, too."

CHAPTER 14

When he finally returned to the hotel room, it was almost time for checkout. Lin Yao was packed and ready to leave. First she wanted to know where he had been and what was inside the bag he was carrying.

"I had to see a guy," Bobby told her. "To get some of what I'm paying them. About half."

He set the money in two piles at the foot of the bed. One pile was large bills and totaled five thousand dollars; the other pile consisted of smaller bills and came to one thousand.

"That's more than half," she said.

"I said about half." He pointed to the five thousand. "That's for Agro," he said, then pointed at the thousand. "That's gravy."

She waited for more.

"Father John is helping me get that job," Bobby said. "Maybe I'll donate it in good faith."

Lin Yao said, "Where did you get all that money in the middle of the night?"

"Same guy helping me with the job," Bobby lied. "He lent it to me."

"Another Mafia asshole?"

"No, somebody else. A friend of Father John's."

Lin Yao didn't believe him. "Another few hours and it's checkout time," she said. "I spent most of the night alone."

"You never did say you'd marry me," he said. "I mean, you got horny and everything, but I could've gotten that with a piece of chocolate cake."

"I can't believe you're still cracking jokes."

He went to hold her. She took a step back.

"I'm sorry," he told her. "I just need to drop this off later and then we're on vacation. For real this time."

Lin Yao set her hands on her hips. "Now it's a vacation," she said. "Are you fucking kidding me?"

Bobby said, "What time's the opera?"

"Eight o'clock. Think you can make dinner, too, or should I expect you at intermission?"

"I'll be there, I promise."

"You're promising a lot lately."

"I'm trying to get these guys out of our life, Lin Yao. Until I do, I have to take care of a few things. You have to cut me a little more slack."

He sat on the end of the bed and yawned from exhaustion. He had spent more than six hours sitting in a dark studio apartment waiting for a guy who had fallen down the stairs and killed himself to be pronounced dead and removed from the building. He had spent the last hour sitting in the sweltering heat when he realized the police were knocking on doors. Bobby had been forced to turn off the air conditioner and keep his victim pinned to the floor for fear of the police hearing them.

When he was finally able to escape, he had to drop off his tools back at the apartment as well as take a shower. He had brought the money back to the hotel to prove to Lin Yao that he intended to pay Tommy Agro. Now he was thinking he should have tossed the tools out along the way and come straight back to the hotel.

"Cut you more slack?" she said. "I'd like to cut something else right now."

Bobby couldn't suppress another yawn.

"And now you'll fall asleep and what am I supposed to do the rest of the day?"

She picked up her bags and started for the door.

Bobby said, "Jesus Christ, give it a break."

Lin Yao turned to him. "Excuse me?"

"I just need to do one more thing and we're off the hook. Can't you just look at the good side of this? Go shopping in the meantime. Get another one of those outfits."

"God damn you, Bobby."

"I just need a quick nap. Then I have to drop this off and we'll go to dinner. How's that?"

Lin Yao said, "Did you take the room for two days, because checkout is at noon."

"I'll make a call."

"You do that, make your call, and then take a nap and run your errands. I'm going back to the apartment in the meantime. I don't need to stay here and watch you sleep."

He got up off the bed. "Forget it. I'll come home with you now."

She was at the door. "No, I don't want you to," she said. "I'll go home and you stay here. We'll meet at the fountain in front of the Met tonight. Six o'clock."

Bobby stepped up to her. "Six is fine," he said.

Lin Yao shook her head. "We'll eat before the opera," she said.

"It's a date," he said. He stepped forward to kiss her.

She stepped back. "No."

"You still gonna marry me?"

"I never said I would."

She opened the door. He reached out to grab her. She smacked his hands away.

"Go to sleep, Bobby," she said. "And make sure you're there at six tonight, in front of the fountain."

He was yawning again. He waved. She mumbled something he couldn't hear. He was pretty sure she had called him an asshole again.

•◆•

"THAT FUCKER WORKING out?" Deputy Inspector Kaprowski wanted to know.

DeNafria and Ward had just pulled to the curb for coffee. Ward was standing on a short line at a wagon on the corner. DeNafria had answered his cell phone without checking the caller I.D.

"Ah, yeah, I guess," he said. "Why?"

"You guess?"

"It's just been a couple days."

"The fuck's he so tired for?"

"I don't know. Says it's the hours."

"Bullshit, the hours," Kaprowski said. "He worked the same shift undercover for five years."

DeNafria was uncomfortable talking over the phone with his partner so close. "Why, what do you think?" he asked the Deputy Inspector.

"I don't know, but he pissed me off this morning," Kaprowski said. "I don't like it one of my detectives yawns in my face."

DeNafria attempted to deflect the conversation. "What the feds have to say?"

"Nothing worth the time I spent with them. They thought Panico was hiding upstate. Apparently he was, right after D'Angelo flipped. He stopped down here for money his sister was holding in some safe-deposit box."

"They knew about the box before or after?"

"That's what I asked. They didn't answer. Fuck them. Where yous headed now?"

"Tommy Agro."

"Yeah, well, he's got some new guy riding shotgun. Quastifare's godson."

"Keeping it in the family, I guess."

"Don't guess," Kaprowski said. "See what the story is. I got that bit about the godson from our people watching the Corelli crew."

"Right," DeNafria said.

"Right, balls," the chief said. "If I got it from our people, so can you. Biggest problem with you guys is you don't talk to one another."

"Right," DeNafria repeated, then quickly added, "I got it."

Kaprowski huffed on his end of the line. "And find out why your partner isn't sleeping nights."

DeNafria made a face. "You want me to tail him?

"Jesus Christ, I didn't say that. Try asking."

"Right, okay."

"Have a nice day."

"You, too," DeNafria said, but the chief had already killed the connection.

•◆•

"YOU DID WHAT?" Father John Scavo asked Bobby.

They were having espresso in the priest's office at the church rectory. Bobby had just told his friend how he had stolen money from his old office. Scavo was seated behind his desk. He petted a large gray cat sitting comfortably on his lap. Bobby sat in an armchair across from the priest. His eyes were still red from the few hours' sleep.

"I took it from the drop in their office," Bobby repeated. He twisted to one side and pulled a folded envelope from a pants pocket, then tossed it on the desk.

"And that's what, blood money?" the priest asked.

"Bookmaking money," Bobby said, "but it buys just as good as blood money."

"Drop it in one of the poor boxes on your way out later," Scavo said.

"Fair enough," Bobby said. He picked the envelope up and stashed it back inside his pocket.

"You're sure you got away with this stunt?" Scavo asked. "Is there any new danger after this last brilliant move?"

"You don't know the half of it," Bobby said. "I won't tell you what happened because you wouldn't believe it if I did, but, no, nobody saw me."

Scavo shook his head.

"Agro had me meet him at a bar last night, one in the morning," he said. "I had to leave Lin Yao at the hotel. Needless to say, she's still pissed off. She went back to the apartment soon as I got back to the hotel. I told her I borrowed it from your friend is gonna put me to work. I took the room for another day and caught a few hours' sleep." He looked at his watch. "Three hours' sleep before I came here. Lin Yao doesn't know I'm here."

"It gets complicated, all the lying," the priest said.

"You don't know the half of it."

After Lin Yao had left the hotel, Bobby had called the front desk and extended his stay another night. He'd asked for a wake-up call at two thirty to make a meeting with Tommy Agro later in the afternoon. He had left himself just enough time to get that done and make it to Lincoln Center before six. He told Scavo about it.

The priest held up the front page of a late-edition local newspaper. It was a picture of the apartment building in Maspeth where Fred Panico and his sister were found murdered.

"They're not playing," Scavo said. "They find out you robbed their office, you could be putting Lin Yao in jeopardy. I guess they're finally desperate enough to kill women."

Bobby took the paper from the priest and quickly turned to the page with the story. He read quickly and set it back down on the desk.

"Panico was a wiseguy," he said. "He was somebody could do damage if he flipped."

Scavo said, "And what about his sister? Wrong place at the wrong time? Like the poor bastard delivering the pizza in Brooklyn the other night?"

"Probably."

"Bullshit, but isn't that enough?"

"They want money, John, nothing more than that," Bobby said. "It's the way these guys operate, from greed. Panico was dangerous to them because of what he was. I'm a nobody."

"Will you at least consider going to the law?"

"Please, those assholes, no thanks," Bobby said. He pointed to his scar. "I got this from the law. I made the mistake of breaking up a beating a few guards were giving a kid in prison and they pinned me to the floor and cut me with a key."

"Corrections are a different breed of cop," Scavo said.

"Yeah, sure," Bobby said. "Yesterday two detectives approached me on the way home from the park. Right out in the middle of the street so anyone looking could see."

The priest was confused. "I don't get it."

"They come to me asking if the boys are leaning on me yet, because of D'Angelo flipping, like it's from concern for my safety, but what they're really doing is setting me up. Agro or any of his people see me talking to cops, they don't hear what's being said, what're they going to think but the worst? Like I said, no thanks. The cops are just in this for a bust. I don't need their help."

"Well, you need somebody's help. At least Lin Yao does."

"I'd never endanger Lin Yao. I'm trying to end this thing without letting those leeches bleed me dry. If I thought fifty grand would guarantee they go away, I'd give it to them, but it won't. I give them fifty, they'll want a hundred. It's the way they are. They can't help themselves."

"They're treacherous bastards is what they are," said the priest as he scratched under the cat's chin. "And they aren't above hurting women, not anymore. You might not intend for Lin Yao to be in danger, but she is. So long as this is going on, she is."

"Lin Yao is fine," Bobby said defensively. "I'd kill myself if anything ever happened to her."

The priest sipped his coffee.

Bobby was uncomfortable about getting loud with his friend. He shrugged and said, "If this doesn't work, what I'm doing now, then I'll go to the law. I promise."

"I hope so," the priest said. "In the meantime, you and Lin Yao okay for dinner tomorrow night? My treat. An engagement present."

Bobby fidgeted in his chair. "I'm not sure."

"Why's that?"

"She didn't say yes yet."

The priest smiled.

"The hell's so funny about that?"

"Saves me some coin," Scavo said.

CHAPTER 15

"WHO'S THE YOUNG'UN?" Detective DeNafria asked Tommy Agro.

He was looking at John Forzino through the passenger window of the black Cadillac Eldorado. Agro quickly lit a cigarette. DeNafria backed away from the window before the gangster could blow the smoke his way.

"Friend of mine," Agro said. "Why?"

"I like to know the players," DeNafria said. "For the scorecard."

"You fuckin' guys," Agro said. "You got nothing better to do, huh?"

Detective Ward was standing alongside DeNafria. He presented Agro with a card. "Actually, this is our job," he said. "We're with the organized crime unit. We get paid and everything."

Agro didn't take the card. Ward tossed it through the window onto the gangster's lap. Agro tore it in half and dropped the pieces on the floor of the car.

"You wanna take off?" Forzino asked Agro.

"Why, because of them? No. It's a public street. Fuck these two."

"He mean us?" Ward asked DeNafria.

"I think so," DeNafria said. "You mean us?"

Agro said, "What's the matter, Bobby Gennaro couldn't come out to play today?"

Ward winked at DeNafria. He said, "Sounds like the man is nervous."

"Yeah, right," Agro said. "I read about one of your rats this morning. It didn't work out for him, your witness protection bullshit."

"He talking about Freddie Panico?" Ward said. He bent at the waist and spoke directly at Agro. "You kill the woman, too?"

Agro looked at DeNafria and thumbed at Ward. "He for real?"

"I think so," DeNafria said. "It's the feds giving out deals, Tommy. It was up to us, you would all do the time you deserve."

"Not to mention how manly that move was yesterday," Ward added, "killing the woman. Must make you feel strong."

"I got a friend says she used to take a flagpole up her ass," Agro said. "He claims she was anything but innocent."

DeNafria said, "Still, you gotta admit, whacking a broad . . . I mean, that's supposed to be a no-no, no?"

"What can I say," Agro said. "Whoever did this thing, it was like an abbreviation."

Both detectives looked at one another. "Huh?" they said.

"Hey, the paper said it looked like they shot each other, the brother and sister there," Agro said. "Take it up with them, whatever beef yous got."

DeNafria shook his head. He'd known Tommy Agro had a reputation for mixing idioms and saying stupid shit, but he'd never actually heard the man do it up close before. DeNafria stared at the gangster's eyes.

"The hell is your problem?" Agro asked.

"Intelligence," DeNafria said. "That's it."

"What, you'd like some?"

DeNafria shook his head again. "It's what's missing from your eyes," he said. "You're like brain-dead, I think. Or maybe it's just some of your brain cells."

"Like a retard," Ward said.

"Fuck yous both," Agro said, "and your mothers."

Ward started toward the car. DeNafria held him back. He looked both ways on the sidewalk before stepping toward the car himself. "You know, if it was dark enough outside right now, or if there weren't so many people on the street, I might have to take a piss."

Agro brought up his window.

Ward spoke out the side of his mouth at his partner. He said, "I'm carrying a knife can cut through those tires like butter, you can keep them occupied for two seconds."

DeNafria did a double take at Ward. "No."

"Just one'd do the trick," Ward said. "Take me two seconds. I'll drop my pen in the gutter."

DeNafria put a hand across Ward's chest. "No," he repeated.

Ward stared until DeNafria removed his hand.

"Fine, okay," Ward said. "I'm cool."

"Let's go see if we can find his boss," DeNafria said. He tried to guide Ward to turn around.

"I said I'm cool," said Ward, pushing DeNafria's arm away.

DeNafria did another double take at his partner. Ward didn't acknowledge it.

•◆•

MICKEY NOLAN WAS supposed to get it over with as quick as possible, and most important, what Tommy Agro had told him, without making a mess.

Agro had sounded pissed off on the phone earlier, something about the cops breaking his balls and then getting stiffed by the retired bookmaker, the guy whose girlfriend he was supposed to terrorize now.

"Just don't go half-cocked on this one," Agro had told Nolan. "Scare her some, yeah, but don't get stupid and break her up. Whatever you do, make sure you don't kill her."

The past twenty-four hours had been good for Nolan. He was determined to keep his luck alive. Maybe he'd just punch the broad in the mouth once she answered her door. Maybe, if she was good-looking, he'd cop a feel or two before slapping her around some. According to Agro, that seemed about right, either a punch in the chops or a couple of slaps.

When he stepped off the elevator, Nolan was surprised to see a Chinese woman in tight shorts and a tight half T-shirt taking out the garbage. Or maybe it was one of those athletic bras she was wearing. He couldn't be sure. She had long dark hair, though, and she was pretty, too. He wondered if she was the one and decided to ask before she made it back to her apartment.

"You Bobby Gennaro's girlfriend?" he asked.

The woman turned. "Who're you?"

Nolan smiled. "Friend of your boyfriend's," he said, exactly what Agro had told him to say.

"Excuse me?" the woman said.

It was then Nolan started for her and was surprised with a kick square in the stomach. He hadn't even seen her leg move it had happened so fast. He dropped to his knees and immediately sucked wind.

"Oh, shit," he managed to gasp.

"Who sent you?" the woman asked.

Nolan could do nothing but shake his head.

"Who?" she asked again.

"I can't breathe," he gasped.

"Tough shit."

"I need water."

"Yeah, right, I'm running for it."

"Please."

"Who sent you? Tell me first."

He was trying to get up now. The woman cocked her right foot.

He held up a hand. "Don't, please," he said.

She seemed ready to spring at him the moment before he pulled the stun gun from his pants pocket. He feigned another step and her leg went up like a piston. Her right foot caught him under his left arm and he was lifted a few inches off the ground, but he managed to jab her right thigh with the stun gun. The woman's eyes rolled before she crumbled to the floor.

Then Nolan finished catching his breath, grabbed her by the feet, and dragged her inside the apartment.

CHAPTER 16

THE FRENCH HAVE a word for it, but I can't think of it right now," Sally told Uncle Joe. "It's something like enjenue. Something like that."

They were lying in bed in Sally's apartment. They had just finished trying to have sex, but Sally was still too sore from the day before. Uncle Joe had to settle for a two-fisted hand job. He lay on his back with a pillow half covering his head.

"Well, whatever it is, I think I'm falling for you, kid," he told her. "I couldn't stop thinking about you all last night and this morning. You're clouding my judgment."

"I couldn't stop thinking about you, too," Sally said. "I was so glad you stopped by. Are you sure John won't come home early, though?"

"Yeah, he's with that other moron, Tommy."

Sally had been nervous since she found John sitting in the recliner earlier in the day. She had faked having a headache to avoid talking with him. He had tried to tell her about something he did the day before, beating some guy up for his uncle or something, but she had gone into the bathroom and turned the shower on so as not to hear him.

She had almost felt guilty until she got the call from Uncle Joe saying he was in the neighborhood.

Now that she'd taken care of him, she wanted to go out someplace. She was hoping he'd take her to dinner, maybe someplace in the city.

"I could look at that face all day," he told her.

She saw he had propped his head on the pillows and was staring at her.

"You must've had a hundred boyfriends back in Wisconsin," he added.

"Michigan," said Sally. "And I really didn't. I had a few, that's all. I met John during his junior year. He really had potential. I thought he was going to make it. He could've tried out for the Canadian league but he wanted the NFL."

"I know my wife was really disappointed for him when he got hurt. I guess he didn't take the school part of college too serious, huh?"

It was the first time he'd mentioned his wife. Sally felt instant disappointment. She tried to talk over it.

"Most of those guys don't worry about school, the athletes. John isn't a dummy like some of them, but he's too shy. He doesn't go after things. Frankly, he's not very exciting anymore."

Uncle Joe held one of her hands. "I can fix that, hon, you're looking for excitement."

She wiggled closer to him on the bed. "I hope so," she said, giving him a half-frown, half-smile.

Uncle Joe started to get hard again. Sally said, "I wish I could get the whole thing in my mouth for you."

"You'd have to be a sword swallower t'do that."

"Yeah, but I wish. I really do."

She thought about telling him her idea to stretch herself with a dildo when he surprised her and suggested it himself.

"There are things you can do, you know, make it easier to handle that thing of mine. I had a girlfriend once, she was able to stretch her box with a kielbasa."

Sally smiled. "Really?"

Uncle Joe made the sign of the cross. "Swear to God."

"Okay, because I was actually thinking about that. Getting something, you know."

She was afraid to say dildo.

"How about them dildo things?" he suggested.

"I guess so. Sure."

"I got girls at the club do routines with them all the time," Uncle Joe said. "You know, the double-sided ones, or the ones with the flat bases they squat on the stage there for private customers, they're not supposed to do that shit, not on stage, but they all do it for guys pay to see it in the private rooms, the ones with money."

"Sure," Sally repeated. She was already picturing what he had described. "I'll pick one up."

"I'll leave you the cash before I leave," he said. "But we gotta be careful with my nephew here, know what I mean? Don't get sloppy and leave it someplace he can find it. You don't want to get him thinking about this, you and me. Don't forget his mother's my sister-in-law, the bitch. Make sure you take care of him every once in a while. Don't turn the faucet off all the way."

She frowned at the thought and made sure Uncle Joe saw it. This was okay for now, and she knew he couldn't or wouldn't leave his wife, but she didn't intend to stay with John forever. Not after being with a real man.

Then he said, "At least not yet don't turn it off."

Sally smiled as he pulled her to him for a kiss. She climbed on top of him to grind against his huge penis. She worked it hard until she could feel herself coming. Her release was long and loud. She hugged him tight when it was over.

"That was incredible," she whispered. "God, that was great."

"Imagine what it'll feel like inside you again?"

Sally sat up on his lap. "Imagine nothing," she said. "We can start the stretching right now."

"Just so long's I can look at that face," Uncle Joe said. "That jenue thing. I fuckin' love it."

•◆•

HE HAD ONLY dropped off forty-five hundred dollars at the restaurant for Tommy Agro. It still pissed Bobby off that he had to give Agro and Quastifare anything, but he figured it would look better if he was a little short. He'd have to hear another lecture or two, maybe some more threats, but so long as he was paying, the wiseguys would probably let him slide a little while longer.

Then Agro had called and given him more shit than he had expected.

"You think you're real cute," Agro had said. "I got a way to handle cute."

"I'll have more in a couple weeks," Bobby had told him.

"Couple weeks, huh? I don't think so, pal. I think maybe you need a lesson sooner rather than later. Something to make the point that this isn't going away, what you owe."

"Give me another few days and I'll get you more," Bobby had forced himself to say.

"Nervous now?" Agro had said. "You should be."

Bobby was about to tell Tommy Agro to go fuck himself when the wiseguy killed the connection.

Now he was waiting in front of the fountain at Lincoln Center. They had agreed to meet there at six in order to grab dinner before the opera. It was already six fifteen and there was no sign of Lin Yao. The humidity was still thick. Bobby wiped his forehead with his wrist, then wiped his wrist on his pants. He flipped open his cell phone and dialed the apartment. When she didn't answer, he figured she must be in transit and didn't leave a message.

At six thirty, he started to wonder if she was purposely making him wait because of all the running around he'd done the last two days. At six forty-five, he dialed the apartment again. This time he spoke to the answering machine.

"Is this some kind of a joke?" he asked. "You're forty-five minutes late. You wanted me to go to the opera and here I am. I'm going inside for a cup of coffee and then I'll wait near the box office. This isn't right, Lin Yao. I'm starving over here."

He killed the connection, lit up a cigarette, and stood staring at the fountain. A heavyset man wearing a brown fedora waved at the smoke from Bobby's cigarette.

Bobby told him, "Go chase yourself."

He finished two cigarettes before going for coffee inside the lobby of Avery Fisher Hall. When he saw how long the line was, he decided to skip the coffee until later. When Bobby glanced at his watch again, he saw it was already a few minutes past seven.

"The fuck is she?" he said.

He crossed to the Met lobby. The crowd was still fairly thin. He grabbed one of the opera schedules hanging from a plastic sleeve on a column and found a seat on the bench against the wall. He tried to kill time by reading through the schedule. He guessed at which operas were Lin Yao's favorites.

A woman sat next to him and smiled. Bobby was polite and smiled back.

"You have tickets?" she asked.

"Ah, yeah, we do. My fiancée has them."

"Where are they?"

"I'm not sure, tell you the truth. This is her thing, the opera. She's an opera snob, though, so they're probably pretty good."

The woman held her smile and said, "If she doesn't show, I'll buy her ticket."

"Oh, okay, but she's the one has the tickets. I'm waiting for her. I don't have them."

"Oh, okay. Sorry."

"No problem."

He looked up and realized the crowd around him had grown. He glanced at his watch and saw it was seven fifteen.

"Shit," he said.

He stood up and walked outside to call the apartment again. There was no answer. He left another message.

"If you're doing this to piss me off, it's working. I'm here and I'll wait you out, but I'm not happy about it. This is really dumb. You made your point an hour ago."

He smoked another cigarette. He saw two guys holding up tickets for sale and wondered if the woman he'd sat next to had found one yet. He searched for her, but the crowd had grown too thick. He heard the chimes signaling last call for seating and saw it was now seven forty.

"God damn it," he said.

"Need a ticket?" a short man with a thin mustache asked.

"No," Bobby said.

"I got center orchestra I can let you have for face value," the short man said.

"No," Bobby repeated.

"How about a center balcony for face?"

"I don't need a ticket."

"Grand tier, left side, twenty under face," the short man said.

Bobby wheeled on him. "How many times you wanna hear me say it?"

The short man quickly walked away.

Bobby waited the rest of the time in front of the revolving doors. At eight ten, a full fifteen minutes after the crowd was comfortably seated inside the opera house, he finally gave up and headed across the plaza toward Columbus Avenue. He called the apartment one more time.

"One for you," he said into his cell phone. "I stood out here like a moron for two hours. Next opera I go to is in your dreams."

He killed the connection and decided to walk a few blocks and let her wait on him now. He was furious. He used the walk to physically vent his frustration and bumped shoulders with anybody refusing to yield walking space on the sidewalk. He cursed under his breath a half dozen times before a cab cut the corner he was crossing a bit too close for comfort; Bobby slammed the hood with an open hand.

"Asshole!" he yelled.

He reached Fifty-seventh Street before he remembered Tommy Agro's threat earlier. Then he started to panic.

•◆•

BEFORE HE LEFT DeNafria, after their visit with Tommy Agro, Ward had taken a call from the woman he'd been seeing on the side the last few years. Margaret O'Donnell told the detective that she was anxious to see him and that she would cook him dinner if he stopped up at the apartment. Ward was thinking he could use a little action, for the sake of relaxation if nothing else, but knew he couldn't make it for dinner. He told her he'd see her after nine o'clock. Then he warned her about not drinking beforehand. Lately, she'd been drinking too much.

Afterward, he told DeNafria that he needed to stop home before they went looking for Joe Quastifare, and that he'd try to catch up with him later. DeNafria didn't seem happy about it, but it could've been what had transpired between them earlier, after their meeting with Tommy Agro. Ward knew his partner was pissed off about getting his hand smacked.

On his way home Ward had stopped to pick up a silencer from an Israeli gun dealer he'd used in the past. The piece cost him two thousand dollars. He would later sell it to Jerry Collins for four thousand.

When he walked in the house through the backyard entrance, Ward saw his wife sewing a patch on another pair of his older son's pants. He immediately felt guilty for not leaving her the money for a new pair. He pulled a twenty from his wallet and was about to set it on the kitchen table when Nellie Ward stuck her finger with the needle and cursed.

"Bastard," she said.

Ward frowned. "What's that?"

"I stuck my finger with the needle."

"The cursing help it any?"

Nellie turned to her husband. "A little, yes," she said.

Ward put the twenty back inside his wallet. It was something he didn't tolerate in his house, his wife cursing. He had been brought up the same way back in Ireland. When his parents first moved to America, the rule had applied here as well. Although he didn't follow all the rules of the house he'd been brought up in, there were a few he had strictly adhered to. Women and children weren't permitted to curse, the boys weren't allowed to roam the house in their underwear, and money was to be saved whenever it could be.

It was how the Ward household had been run from the time he married Nellie five years ago. She took care of the house and the children while he earned and saved the money.

"You coming home for dinner?" his wife asked.

Ward shrugged.

"You were up early again this morning," she said.

"Work," he said.

Nellie frowned.

"What?" he asked.

"You don't wake me."

"For what?"

She smiled coyly. "You know."

"For sex?"

She continued to blush.

Ward kissed her forehead before patting her on the ass. "I have to go," he said.

"I have to pick up a few things," Nellie reminded her husband.

Ward reached into his wallet and pulled the twenty. He saw she wasn't watching and gave her a ten instead.

"See you later," he said before kissing her forehead again.

She hugged herself against him. "Be careful," she told him.

CHAPTER 17

JOE QUASTIFARE HAD gone up to take a shower when he realized he didn't have his microrecorder. He stomach dropped at the idea it was lost.

He quickly stepped out of the shower and ran into his bedroom to check his pants. He turned them inside out two times before dropping them on the floor and grabbing his hair.

"Jesus fuck!" he growled.

He slipped on a pair of shorts and ran out to the car to check if the recorder was there. It wasn't. He went through the car three times but still couldn't find it. He cursed aloud again and started to dial his nephew's apartment when he realized it was best to check with Tommy Agro first. He waited three rings before Agro picked up.

"Tommy?" said Quastifare with a desperate voice.

"Yeah, Joe, what's up?"

"Thank God I got you. Where's my nephew?"

"Home or on his way."

"Fuck!"

"Why, what's the problem?"

"I need you to get him out of that apartment."

"Where he lives?"

"Yeah, right now. I left something there I'm afraid he finds."

"Jesus Christ, Joe. What the fuck?"

"Yeah, yeah, you can lecture me later, okay? Just get that kid out of that apartment soon's you can."

"Hey, I'll do my best. I'll call him nine-one-one right now."

"Thanks, Tommy. Then call me back when he's with you again."

"Right, soon's I see him."

Quastifare hung up and tried to remember where the hell he might've left the wire. He was thinking it had to be under the bed when Sally had first tried to blow him and he pushed his pants down. He tried to remember if he had kicked them off to one side or not.

Or maybe it had come off and gotten mixed up in the sheets when she climbed on top of him.

Or maybe she'd found it.

"Fuck," he gasped. "God damn it to hell, fuck."

•◆•

SHE COULD HEAR Bobby talking into the answering machine while the animal made a pig of himself in her kitchen. Lin Yao had been tied and gagged twice since she was caught by surprise with the stun gun. The first time she had tried to yell something the animal had removed the gag. When he leaned down to ask her what she had said, she spit on him and screamed as loud as she could.

That was the first time he slapped her. It had hurt. Then he had stuffed the gag back inside her mouth and slapped her again. She was sure she had at least one bruise somewhere on her face.

Now the animal was using her sink to urinate and she had to watch from the dining room chair she was tied to. She tried to yell through the gag.

He turned to her and smiled. "If I take the gag out again, you gonna behave?" he asked.

Lin Yao growled through the gag.

"I'm asking because I'll do it if you say yes."

She hated this man and wished she weren't tied. She wouldn't make the same mistake twice. She wouldn't miss with another kick.

"Well?" he said.

Lin Yao forced herself to nod.

The animal put himself back in his pants and walked across the dining room. He pulled the towel out of her mouth and then pushed it down to her chin with one hand. He cocked a fist with the other. She could see each finger had been tattooed with an Irish shamrock.

"I won't scream," she said.

"Good, because I'd have to break your face you did it again. You know, I didn't plan on hanging around here, but you had to pull that Bruce Lee bullshit before."

"You were going to attack me."

He held up the stun gun and she flinched.

"Not with this," he said. "This was your fault."

He stuck the stun gun back inside his pocket.

"Just don't ruin my apartment," she said. "Can you please use the bathroom next time?"

"Maybe," he said. "I guess you're lucky I don't have the runs, though, huh?"

"You're disgusting," she said.

"Yeah, and you're a Chink."

Lin Yao rolled her eyes.

"An uppity Chink," he added.

"What do you want here?"

"Originally just you, Miss Saigon. Now I want your boyfriend, too. Where is he?"

"I'm Chinese, not Vietnamese."

"Same shit. Where is he?"

"Duh, he isn't here. You heard the phone calls. He's at the opera."

This time the animal was annoyed at her sarcasm. He said, "Duh," and slapped her across the face again.

Lin Yao clenched her teeth. "God, I'm gonna kick your ass when I'm out of this," she swore.

"You think so, huh?"

"You didn't have that stun gun your nuts would be where your eyeballs are now."

"Says you."

Lin Yao stared bullets at him.

He took a bite from a sandwich he had made earlier. "What's your problem?" he said.

"You know he's not here," she said. "You know he went to the opera."

"Right, and so now he'll come back here. I feel I owe him something for that kick you gave me before."

"Asshole, we split up. That's what this is all about. We were meeting there because we split up."

The animal put his feet up on one of the chairs. "I tell you what," he said. "The next time you call me an asshole, I'll rip some of the hairs off your twat. How's that?"

Lin Yao shook her head.

"Come to think of it, they sideways, slope twats?"

"Do you have any fucking idea who my cousin is?" she asked.

"One of them delivery boys on the bikes?"

"No, he's the head of the Mott Street Shadows."

"Chinky gang?"

She nodded.

"That supposed to make me shit my pants? In case you didn't notice, you people, you're all tiny."

"God, you're a jerk."

He reached across the space between them and smacked her left breast hard.

"Motherfucker!" she gasped.

"Not too loud," he warned.

"Keep your hands off me."

"Or what?"

"Just keep your hands off."

She was staring him down again. It seemed to be pissing him off even more when the phone rang one more time.

"Your guy is one pussy-whipped motherfucker," the animal said.

It was Bobby's voice again when the answering machine kicked in. "I just called my friend with the feds," he said. "They're sending a car over now to see what's wrong. I realized something had to be wrong."

"Finally," Lin Yao said.

The animal was already up and looking for things to take with him. Searching for jewelry and cash he had already gone through her purse and a few of the drawers in the bedroom. Now she realized her ring was missing.

"Hey, you took my ring?"

"What ring?" he said.

He glanced down at the street through the living room windows and bolted for the door.

"He's gonna be pissed about that ring," she said.

The animal stopped at the door and put an open hand to his ear. "I'll give you a call."

•◆•

THAT BULLSHIT WITH the cops had pissed Tommy Agro off again. Forzino had been grateful when his boss cut him loose for the day. He thought about stopping at the gym to get a few reps in before heading home and then decided he was too tired. He hadn't had much sleep the last few nights, hardly any the night before, and he was anxious to take a shower and relax.

He was especially anxious to have sex again with Sally since it had been a few weeks since the last time. He was hoping she was in a better mood tonight. Maybe when she heard a few more mob stories she would perk up. He was planning to take her to the feast in Little Italy the next week.

He had called from the car as soon as he dropped off Agro. Sally sounded okay, except she was yawning and said she felt tired from a long day. Forzino couldn't think of anything Sally did during the day that would tire her, except maybe the gym. He hoped she wasn't getting her period.

She was in the bath when he came home. He knocked on the door and she told him she had just stepped in the bath and would be a few minutes. Then she turned a radio on, and he had to use an empty water bottle to take a piss. Sally had gone crazy in the past when he walked in on her showering or bathing just to use the toilet.

He undressed in the bedroom. He tossed his shirt in the hamper and hung up his slacks. When he turned from the closet, he saw something on the floor alongside the night table on his side of the bed. He kneeled down to pick it up and was shocked to see a wire attached to a recorder with a small Velcro strap.

He looked in the direction of the bathroom. "Jesus Christ," he whispered.

He looked back at the tape recorder. "Holy shit," he said.

He looked back toward the bathroom and his cell phone rang. He saw the number displayed was Tommy Agro's. He swallowed hard, then looked back at the bathroom.

CHAPTER 18

Bobby swore to himself that if anything had happened to Lin Yao he'd grab the Mossberg he kept in the second bedroom closet upstairs and blow Tommy Agro's head off.

It took him another fifteen minutes to get home after he'd made the call. When he was finally inside the building, he ran up the stairs rather than wait for the elevator. He had his keys out to open the door when he stepped into the hallway from the stairwell. He saw one of his neighbors, another Chinese woman, peeking out from behind her apartment door. He ignored her and ran to his own door. His eyes opened wide when he was inside the apartment. Lin Yao was tied and gagged in a chair. He didn't even notice his neighbor standing behind him until she gasped.

Five minutes later, he examined Lin Yao's bruises up close on the couch. He was showing teeth without realizing it.

"I'm okay," Lin Yao told him. "He didn't hurt me."

Bobby pointed at the bruise on the left side of her face. "He did this," he said. He pointed to another bruise on the inside of her right thigh. "He did this, the motherfucker."

"I'm okay," she said.

Bobby said, "Anything else?"

"No."

"You sure?"

"Positive."

"He didn't touch you?"

"I would've killed myself as soon as you untied me. No, he didn't touch me."

Bobby punched the back of the couch hard.

"Motherfucker!" he growled.

Lin Yao reached up to him. Bobby looked into her eyes.

"What he look like?" he asked.

Lin Yao shook her head.

"I need to know," he said. "What he look like?"

"Ugly," she said. "He had scars. And a beard. He was disheveled, disgusting. He peed in the kitchen sink."

Bobby's jaw tightened.

"He had Irish shamrocks on his fingers. Tattoos."

"Nolan," Bobby said.

"Who?"

"An Irishman works for Tommy Agro."

Lin Yao swallowed hard.

"What?" he asked her.

"He took my ring," she said, and then she began to sob.

He cradled her head against his chest and did his best to suppress the rage tensing every muscle in his body. He had left the phony message about a federal agent friend just in case Agro had sent someone. He knew whoever might be there would back off. He also knew he'd be marking himself as an informant if there was somebody there. Once he thought Lin Yao might be in danger, he didn't care.

She had been embarrassed that their neighbor had seen her tied in the chair. They had spoken Chinese to one another afterward, but Bobby could tell Lin Yao was upset. When he asked her why, she told him because the entire neighborhood would know what happened as soon as their neighbor reached her telephone. She told Bobby once word hit the street of what had happened, her cousin would show up and try to save face.

"Just what I need now," Bobby said.

Her sobbing had turned to anger again. She stood in the center of the living room with her hands on her hips. "Now what happens?" she asked him. "If you know the animal who did this, you can call the police, right?"

"No," Bobby said, "but he'll wish the fuck I did."

"What do you mean, no? Why not?"

Bobby held both hands up. "Not now, please."

Lin Yao was furious. "Excuse me? Not now? Jesus Christ, Bobby, I was the one tied up here. I don't need you to call the police."

She started for the phone. He got up to stop her. She pulled away from him.

Bobby said, "The police can't do what I'll do to this cocksucker. They won't do it. Let me handle it. Please, Lin Yao. I'll take care of it."

"You haven't taken care of a single fucking thing. Not once yet. Every time you say that, something else happens."

"I can't call the police. You can't. I know how to get this prick. I know where to find him. And I know how to deal with Tommy Agro after this."

"Deal with him? Are you kidding me? If you're not going to call the cops on the animal who assaulted me, what about the other ones? You gonna go after them, too, the Mafia?"

"If they don't back down now, I'll bring the police in. I promise."

"And what if they kill you first? Or me?"

"They won't. I know they won't. They fucked up and now they have to back down. It's the way it works."

"Jesus Christ, Bobby, I wish you could hear yourself. The way what works? Those assholes don't have rules. They're fucking animals. They don't have honor. I thought you paid them."

"I did."

"And? What, it wasn't enough?"

Bobby remained silent. He was picturing Tommy Agro and wanted to smash his face with a baseball bat.

"Well?"

"I tried to take care of it," he said. "Agro thinks he can get fifty grand from me, that's what this is about."

"Fifty grand? And, what, you have it? You have that much money?"

He wasn't about to go into how much money he had.

"No," he said. "That's what he was looking for. Now he'll have to live with what I offered in the first place. He knows that."

Lin Yao held her face with both hands. "My God, I wish you could hear yourself."

"I want you to stay with somebody," he said.

"What? Why? Where are you going?"

"I'm going to find Nolan first, then I'll get somebody to sit down for me with Tommy Agro, if I don't break his fucking neck first."

Lin Yao shook her head. "No. What sit-down? What are you talking about? I'll go to the police myself."

"You do and I'm a dead man," he told her. "That what you want?"

"God damn you!" she yelled.

"I'll call Father John and you can either stay there with him or I'll ask him to come here."

"No, leave him out of this."

"I'll call him from downstairs."

"No, I said. Leave him out of it. It's embarrassing enough."

"I'm sorry," he said. He grabbed a pair of brass knuckles from the junk drawer in the kitchen and started for the door.

"And what if I'm pregnant?" she asked.

"Don't do this now."

"What if I'm pregnant and you get killed?"

"I'm not getting killed."

"Pay them the money," Lin Yao said. "Forget this Nolan animal and let's move away."

"I can't forget Nolan. Don't ask me to."

"I'm afraid," she said.

He started for her. She stepped back.

"I love you," he told her.

"I don't want you to leave."

He reached for his cell phone.

"Please?" she said.

"I'll call Father John," he said, and then he left.

•◆•

JOHN DENAFRIA WAS uncomfortable when his partner didn't return. He drove to Canarsie to have dinner with his son before driving out to Massapequa, Long Island, to sit surveillance in front of Joe Quastifare's house. He was there less than an hour when he saw the wiseguy leave in an apparent rush.

He tried to follow on his own, but it didn't take long before Quastifare spotted the tail and gave DeNafria the finger out the window.

DeNafria replied in kind before Quastifare suddenly cut through an exit to a Wendy's parking lot and exited out the entrance onto another street.

"Son of a bitch," said DeNafria, when he tried to follow through the lot and was blocked by a minivan.

By the time DeNafria was out of the lot again, Quastifare was gone. DeNafria pulled over to the curb instead of driving blind.

His resentment for his new partner quickly turned to anger. For one thing, it wouldn't have been so easy for Quastifare to shake the tail if he were being followed by two cars instead of one. The other issue had to do with trust. Ward had said he would be back, but he never showed. He hadn't even bothered to call.

DeNafria assumed it was their contentious exchange after their talk with Tommy Agro that had caused the rift. Ward had clearly been pissed and had wanted to slash the wiseguy's tires. DeNafria had been looking out for them both when he stopped his partner.

Ward's behavior bothered him now. He called his ex-partner to ask if she had ever heard of his new partner. DeNafria and Arlene Belzinger had been lovers once but rarely spoke anymore. After a pleasant exchange Belzinger told him that Ward's name seemed familiar, but she couldn't place it.

"Maybe from when I worked narcotics," she said. "I can ask around, you want."

"Nah, it's probably just ego bullshit," DeNafria said. "He's got a temper and I'm not anxious to deal with that again."

"You talk to Greene? Maybe he knows something."

Detective Dexter Greene had been partnered with both DeNafria and Belzinger in the past.

"No, I called you."

"I'm honored."

"Yeah, I guess you should be."

"How are you?"

"Good, except for this. You?"

"Thinking about moving."

"Really? Where to, undercover again?"

"No, moving moving. The Southwest. Arizona, New Mexico, like that."

DeNafria was surprised. "You serious?"

"Yeah, I am. I'm making sure it's not just a whim and looking into things for now. I could probably get a job there with the state police, though."

"That's a big move, kiddo. Make sure before you leap."

"I will. How's your son?"

He was disappointed she didn't remember Jack's name. "Growing, and way too fast," DeNafria said. "He's into girls now."

Belzinger chuckled. "Oh, yuck," she joked.

DeNafria smiled on his end of the line. Belzinger was bisexual. He wasn't sure which sex she was dating now and was afraid to ask.

"Anyway, Jack's at that age, so I have to be a little more diligent."

"Anything going on with the ex?"

He was surprised she was asking. "She's serious with some guy, that's about it."

"I meant with you, John."

"Nope, we don't talk unless she's giving me shit about something."

"Are you seeing someone?"

"Outside of the wiseguys I watch, I'm not."

"We should get together sometime, for lunch or dinner or just drinks."

It was another pleasant surprise. When things hadn't worked out between them and their relationship ended a few years ago, Belzinger had kept her distance from him.

"Sure, I'd like that," he said. "Say when."

"I'll call you. Same number?"

"Same old, same old."

"Okay, and I'll look into this Ward guy if I can."

"Without ruffling feathers, okay?"

"You got it."

DeNafria's day seemed to take a turn for the better. He hadn't been serious with anyone since his brief fling with Belzinger a few years ago. When she broke it up, he was hurt pretty bad. Because it had come on the heels of his wife filing for divorce, it had helped push him toward alcohol.

Suddenly he wasn't as upset with his partner as he had been earlier. Tomorrow was another day and it was to start extra early with sitting surveillance at Tommy Agro's place in Valley Stream. DeNafria decided to call it a night and head home.

CHAPTER 19

JOE QUASTIFARE HAD never considered taping his business conversations until the string of made guys who had flipped crippled the Gambino family a few years ago. The world of organized crime had become more like a tribe of cannibals than a brotherhood since the day Sammy Gravano dealt away nineteen murders. Nothing was sacred anymore. It had become deal or be dealt away.

So the recordings he had been making the last few months were nothing more than insurance in the event one of his own crew flipped and turned rat first. Quastifare had no intention of using the tapes he was making without having his back against the wall. Currently, the fifty or sixty tapes he had recorded were safe in a strongbox he kept under the floor of his office in the basement of his home. They were there for when he needed them.

Giving up his friends without a good reason was the last thing he had planned on until he realized he had lost his recorder. Now, if he couldn't find the thing before his nephew or the girl, Sally, did, he just might have to play it safe and flip before he was killed. He still had the tapes in the strong box if push came to shove.

The thing of it was, he didn't know for sure that he had lost the recorder there. It might've fallen down his leg after he left the house. It might be anywhere.

He had checked his car a few times after he realized it was missing. When he called Tommy Agro, it was from pure desperation. If he could get his nephew out of the apartment, he could search the place himself. If Sally had found it, he'd have to learn whether or not she had listened to it.

Quastifare thought about how the recorder was voice-activated and started to sweat profusely. What if the fucking thing was working when he was in the bed?

As soon as Tommy Agro called back that the kid had picked him up, Quastifare rang Sally's apartment over and over until she finally answered.

"Uncle Joe?" she said.

"Yeah, it's me. Listen, I left something at your house. It's important. It's very important."

"What is it?"

"Just something," he said. "I'm coming over to look for it."

"You're coming here? Now?"

"Yeah, don't worry about it. I had Tommy pick up John and take him someplace. He won't get back until I call them first."

"Are you okay? You sound weird."

"I'll be right there."

"Okay. I'll leave the door unlocked."

Quastifare hung the phone up and ran to his car. He was less than half a block away when he realized he was being tailed by one of the organized crime cops. He gave the cop the finger out the window and the cop responded in kind. Then Quastifare cut through a Wendy's parking lot out onto the boulevard.

•◆•

"WHERE'S MY COUSIN, white boy?" Ricky Zhu asked Bobby.

Bobby had just come downstairs. Ricky was waiting for him in front of the apartment building with six of his gang.

"She doesn't need your help," Bobby told Lin Yao's cousin.

"Fuck you," Zhu said. "She my cousin."

"She doesn't need your help."

Zhu was all of 160 pounds on a five-eight frame. He wore a white muscle T-shirt and black dungarees. A Marlboro dangled from his lips.

"Some guy break in and smack her around?" he said more than asked. "Where the fuck are you?"

"I'm here now," Bobby told Zhu. "I'll take care of it."

"Where Lin Yao?"

"Upstairs. A friend of mine is coming over now. A priest."

Zhu smirked. "What he gonna do, say prayer?"

Two of Zhu's gang laughed. Bobby figured the other three didn't understand English.

"You're a funny guy, but you're wasting my time," Bobby said. "Why don't you take your boys to a movie?"

Zhu looked Bobby up and down. "I cut your fuckin' balls off, stuff them in your mouth."

Bobby started to step around Zhu. "I don't have time for this," he said. He was cut off by two of Zhu's gang. The rest surrounded Bobby.

Bobby eyeballed Lin Yao's cousin. "You're smart to bring your posse along," he said. "You'll need them you wanna fight me."

"I cut your dick off and mail it to you mother," Zhu said.

"Yeah, you keep telling me about it."

"You afraid, white boy? Go upstairs and say prayer when your priest get here."

Zhu's cellular telephone rang. He turned his back on Bobby to answer it. Zhu listened at first, then walked away as he spoke into the phone. When he turned around and came back, Bobby was staring down one of the gang that had laughed earlier.

"That was my cousin," Zhu said. "We take care of this now."

Bobby turned and looked up at the apartment. He saw Lin Yao at one of the windows. He shook his head.

"You go upstairs now," Zhu said. "Go hide behind couch."

Bobby glared at the gang leader. "You're in over your head," he said. "This isn't some punk street gang you're up against."

Zhu smirked. "Fuckin' Irish pussy assholes," he said. "We kick Irish and Italian ass both."

Bobby bit his lower lip. "She tell you who the guy was?"

Zhu pointed up at the building. "Go upstairs, hide under couch," he said.

Bobby watched Zhu and his gang head north on Baxter. He saw them pile into a car parked off the corner of Grand Street. He glanced up at the apartment windows again and saw Lin Yao was still there. He ignored her and headed south toward Hester.

CHAPTER 20

SHE MUST HATE me," Forzino told Tommy Agro. "She's doing this, taping me, she must."

The kid was sure it was his fiancée's recorder. Agro was thinking something else.

"I found it alongside my night table on the floor," Forzino continued. "I can't believe she'd do this. It must've been hooked up to the phone, too. We have a portable on my night table. And I thought she was into this, the mob."

They had gone down to Agro's basement and locked the door to listen to the tape.

Sally's voice said, "The French have a word for it, but I can't think of it right now. It's something like enjenue. Something like that."

Then Joe Quastifare's voice said, "Well, whatever it is, I think I'm falling for you, kid. I couldn't stop thinking about you all last night and this morning. You're clouding my judgment."

Agro looked to Forzino. The kid was stunned.

Sally said, "I couldn't stop thinking about you, too. I was so glad you stopped by. Are you sure John won't come home early, though?"

Agro saw the kid was pale. He was about to stop the recorder when he heard Quastifare's voice say, "Yeah, he's with that other moron, Tommy."

Agro bit down hard on his lower lip.

A few seconds passed before Quastifare continued, "I could look at that face all day. You must've had a hundred boyfriends back in Wisconsin."

Sally said, "Michigan. And I really didn't. I had a few, that's all. I met John during his junior year. He really had potential. I thought he was going to make it. He could've tried out for the Canadian league but he wanted the NFL."

Agro saw the kid was heaving. He stopped the tape.

"You okay? You don't have to listen to this."

Forzino nodded. "I have to," he whispered. "It's okay."

Agro hit PLAY again.

Quastifare said, "I know my wife was really disappointed for him when he got hurt. I guess he didn't take the school part of college too serious, huh?"

Sally said, "Most of those guys don't worry about school, the athletes. John isn't a dummy like some of them, but he's too shy. He doesn't go after things. Frankly, he's not very exciting anymore."

Quastifare said, "I can fix that, hon, you're looking for excitement."

Agro saw Forzino's eyes were tearing.

Sally said, "I hope so. I wish I could get the whole thing in my mouth for you."

Quastifare said, "You'd have to be a sword swallower t'do that."

Sally said, "Yeah, but I wish. I really do."

Agro stopped the tape again. The kid had started to bawl.

"It's not your fault," Agro told him. "This is your uncle's fault, and the broad's."

"I'm gonna be sick," Forzino said.

Agro helped him to the bathroom. "Take your time," he said. "I'm gonna listen in a little more."

Agro rewound the tape to the beginning. He pressed PLAY after the tape was rewound. He waited a few seconds for the recording to play back and then opened his eyes wide when he heard his own voice.

"Cocksucker, motherfucker," he yelled.

He was listening to a conversation between himself and Quastifare that had taken place at the diner that same morning. He was lucky the kid was using the bathroom when Quack started talking about Forzino's fiancée.

When he stopped the tape again, Agro realized why his old friend had been so frantic about getting the kid out of the apartment. The tape recorder Quastifare had been wearing was his death sentence.

And now Agro had it.

He wondered how many other tapes there were.

Then he heard the kid retching in the bathroom. The poor bastard had been humiliated in the worst possible way. Agro called the underboss of the family and told him it was urgent they meet.

•◆•

BOBBY DISTURBED A few friends from his bookmaking days with telephone calls and eventually learned that Mickey Nolan hung out in one of three bars on the West Side. He gave the cab driver the addresses and showed him a fifty-dollar bill through the Plexiglas divider.

It wouldn't take Ricky Zhu and his gang very long to find Nolan, either. Bobby needed to get to the Irishman first or he might be blamed for something he wouldn't get the pleasure of handling himself.

The closest bar was an O'Shaughnessy's on Tenth Avenue and Forty-fifth Street. Bobby tried to read the driver's name off the license, but it was a Russian one he couldn't pronounce. He slid the fifty-dollar bill through the money slot and asked him to wait.

"If I'm not out in ten minutes, it's yours," Bobby told him.

He walked inside the bar and quickly glanced around the tables. No Mickey Nolan. He slapped a buck on the bar and went into the men's room. It was empty.

The next bar was three blocks up and one avenue east. Bobby had the cabbie stop in front of The Two Clovers. He added an extra twenty to the fifty he'd already greased the driver with. The Russian was more than willing to wait again.

This time he was lucky. Bobby recognized Mickey Nolan as soon as he saw him. The thug was hunched over at the far end of the bar with two shot glasses in front of him. Bobby's rage took control. He grabbed a pool stick from the rack.

"Hey, hey!" the bartender yelled, but it was too late.

Bobby smashed the thick end of the pool stick across Nolan's mouth. The Irishman was knocked off his stool onto the floor. He spit up at least two teeth before Bobby cracked the stick over the center of Nolan's head.

The only customers in the place beside Nolan were a few barflies waiting for it to close. All of them were too old or too drunk to stop what was going on. Even the bartender backed off when he realized the beating was going to be serious. He tried to threaten calling the police, but Bobby gave him a death look and the bartender set the phone back down.

"Gimme a pitcher of water," Bobby told him.

The bartender did as he was told. Bobby turned it upside down on Nolan's head. The water washed some of the blood from Nolan's face and he tried to stand. Bobby threw a right from way back and sent the Irishman over a table.

The stun gun Nolan was carrying fell out of his jacket pocket. Bobby kicked it back toward the entrance of the bar with his left foot. He grabbed a beer bottle off a table, broke off the bottom end on the floor, and held the broken edge against Nolan's throat.

"Where's the ring?" he asked.

Nolan remained silent.

Bobby moved the bottle up alongside Nolan's left cheek and pressed until the skin broke. The Irishman gasped.

"Where's the fuckin' ring?" Bobby asked again.

Nolan motioned toward his front pants pocket. Bobby turned the pocket inside out and the ring rolled onto the sawdust floor. Bobby grabbed it, then tossed the broken bottle aside.

Nolan was slow in moving. He struggled to make it to his knees.

Bobby waited for the beaten man to look up before kicking him full force in the center of his face. Nolan's nose flatted on contact. This time he was unconscious.

"You're gonna kill the man, you haven't already," the bartender said.

"Yeah, I know," Bobby said.

"Well, leave him be now, you've done enough."

"Maybe," Bobby said. He was still looking for a sign of movement from Nolan. There was none.

Suddenly he heard footsteps behind him. Bobby turned and saw Ricky Zhu standing in the doorway.

"Hey, white boy, good job," Zhu said as a few of his gang stepped inside the bar.

"Christ, this is going to get worse, isn't it?" the bartender asked.

"Everybody go home," Zhu told the rest of the bar.

The few patrons began filing out quickly.

Zhu said something in Cantonese to his gang. Four of them went to where Nolan lay on the floor and grabbed him.

Zhu walked up to Bobby. "You think this is enough, what you do?"

"Fuck you," Bobby said.

Tommy's gang dragged Nolan out of the bar and tossed him in a Chinese produce truck parked at the curb.

"You kill him and you'll start a war," Bobby told Zhu. "With his people and the Italians."

"You give your people too much credit," Zhu said. "They nobody anymore. All rats. We taking over, white boy."

Bobby smirked. "Taking over what?"

Zhu turned and left. Bobby saw the truck pull away from the curb and immediately looked for his taxi. It was gone. The driver must've been scared off.

Bobby turned to the bartender and tossed a fifty on the bar.

"Sorry for the trouble," he said. "One Jameson and I'm gone."

The bartender set a bottle down and said, "Feel free to take it with you."

CHAPTER 21

HE WAS CAREFUL after leaving the bar on the West Side. He switched cabs two times before getting out at Pennsylvania Station. He went down the long escalator at the Thirty-fourth Street entrance and came back up in front of Madison Square Garden at Seventh Avenue. There, Bobby grabbed a cab at the stand and headed downtown.

Word would spread quickly about what he'd done to Mickey Nolan. Aside from the bartender, there had been several patrons there before Ricky Zhu and his gang arrived and emptied the place. The bigger issue would come after Ricky Zhu's gang asked for a ransom or if they killed Nolan just for the hell of it. Either way, Bobby was guilty by association.

He knew a few people he could go to for help, but only one he fully trusted, Father John Scavo. The priest would at least offer him temporary sanctuary. He called Scavo's cell phone from the cab as it headed south on Seventh Avenue.

"It's me," Bobby said when his friend answered.

"I figured," Scavo said.

"She there?"

"Yep."

"Right there?"

"Yep."

"I can't talk to her. Not yet."

"Right."

"I need to stay someplace, but not there."

"I can give you a room in the rectory."

"You sure it's not a problem?"

"Where are you?"

"In the twenties somewhere. I can be there in ten minutes."

"And then I'll come back here."

"I'd appreciate that."

"But I'll have to leave again for morning mass."

"I understand."

"Okay, then. Ten minutes."

"Right," Bobby told his friend, and then he killed the connection.

The cab picked up speed and Bobby leaned toward the window to catch some of the breeze. His head was sweating from the humidity. The air was still thick with the threat of a rain that wouldn't come.

As they turned east on Twenty-third Street, Bobby wondered if Lin Yao was giving Scavo a hard time about the phone call. He wondered if she would make the trip to the rectory with the priest. He knew there would be no placating her again. Once she understood the danger he was in, she would demand he go to the police. It would only lead to another argument he couldn't win.

At some point he knew he would have to get in touch with Lin Yao and try to make her understand why he couldn't come home yet. He would also have to deal with Tommy Agro again. Bobby knew the wiseguy had sent Nolan to the apartment to scare Lin Yao. It wouldn't be easy sitting across from Agro without wanting to strangle the wiseguy.

This time he would have to clear things up for real before returning home. The West Side gang would send spotters downtown to look for him. In the meantime Bobby needed to remain under the radar.

He switched cabs again at Union Square Park. He gave the next driver the rectory address in Little Italy. The cab headed east to Third Avenue and then south. Bobby slid down low in the backseat when the cab turned west on Houston Street. It was an awkward and uncomfortable feeling to be hiding in his neighborhood. He ducked his head from embarrassment.

•◆•

"YOU DON'T HAVE to come back, Father," Lin Yao told Scavo. "I'm fine."

"I gave my word," he said.

"You're going to meet Bobby now?"

"I'm sorry about all this."

"I'm the one who should apologize."

"Don't be silly," Scavo said. He stood up from the couch.

Lin Yao said, "He didn't want to talk to me, right?"

"He's trying to avoid a fight with you, hon. He knows he's been wrong about a few things. He still can't forgive himself for that guy showing up here."

"Why won't he go to the police?" she asked. "If he's trying to protect us, he has to know he can't do it alone."

The priest said, "He's not a Mafioso, Lin Yao. Bobby is just a guy who got caught up with the wrong people at the wrong time in his life. You changed that for him. He's never been one of those people and he never will be. He doesn't respect them any more than you or I do, but he's also done time and there is a culture on the streets that some people, people like Bobby, can't ignore. It's like he gave his word or something. He's giving them one last chance to do the right thing. He needs to have his back against the wall to go to the law. So long as he thinks he can straighten it out without the police, he'll try."

Lin Yao shook her head. "That's insane," she said. "Those people are animals. He'll get killed."

Scavo glanced at his watch. "I have to get going," he said. "I'll try to talk to him, I promise. And I'll be back as soon as possible. Don't let me in without seeing me through the peephole first, okay?"

"You don't have to come back," she said.

The priest shrugged. "I gave my word," he said.

•◆•

MARGARET O'DONNELL WAS a worn-looking forty-year-old with fair skin and red hair. She was also the former wife of an undercover New York City cop who was killed during a drug bust in Washington Heights. Michael Ward had known John O'Donnell briefly before his death and had met Margaret at the funeral. They had seen each other on and off over the next five years.

The latest tragedy in the widow's life had occurred six months earlier when her only child, a nineteen-year-old son, was killed in action in Afghanistan. Her sudden loss had started Margaret O'Donnell drinking regularly. It was her drinking that had kept Ward away the last few months.

He had visited her immediately before he was reassigned to the organized crime division and was surprised when he learned she was about to be evicted for not paying rent. Ward took care of the three months owed. It was the only time he had ever used any of the dirty money he had stashed away for his own retirement.

Today he thought himself lucky to find her sober when he first showed up before nine o'clock. He did his best to keep her that way, but Margaret managed to spike her own coffee with scotch after they had sex and while Ward napped in the bedroom.

Now that she was waking him up, he could smell the alcohol on her breath.

"What you drink?" he asked.

"It was just a taste, Michael. Just a taste."

"Bullshit. The least you could do was let me sleep you're gonna drink."

"There's someone here for you."

Ward didn't think he had heard her. "What?"

"Kenneth Ryan," Margaret said.

Ward immediately sat up in the bed. "Who?"

"Kenneth Ryan," she repeated. "He's in the kitchen with two other men."

Ward grabbed Margaret by the arm. "The fuck you know Ryan from?"

"I didn't until yesterday. He said he was a friend of yours. He asked me to call you. He wanted to surprise you."

Ward turned toward the chair across the room where his pants, holster, and Glock were. He was about to get up when the bedroom door opened. Three men entered the bedroom. Two were holding handguns. The third, a slight man with a thick head of red hair, stepped between the other two. He nodded at Margaret before stepping aside to let her pass.

"Thank you," she said. "I'll be in the kitchen if you need anything."

The slight man waited until she closed the door behind her. He turned to Ward and said, "I'm Ryan."

Ward looked to the two men holding guns on him.

"You don't need to know their names," said Ryan with an Irish accent.

"I heard you were in Ireland," Ward said.

"I was."

"How do you know Margaret?"

"Same way I know you're the wanker helping Jerry Collins. Friendlies."

"Friendlies?"

"Don't play idiot and I won't have them kill you," Ryan said. "You know the term as well as I do. You had friends on the street. I have friends on the force. It all works out in the end. Consider this your big chance to bet the right horse. Up till now, you're backing a loser."

Ward swallowed hard. "You're a friend of Phalen? That it?"

"What's the difference who my friends are? I'm here and there are two guns pointed at your chest."

"Does Margaret . . . is she . . ."

"The woman doesn't know a thing. I approached her yesterday, and that was a long time before I learned about Mickey Nolan. That I got a little while ago."

Ward shook his head. "Excuse me?"

"That stupefied look on your face better be genuine."

"Look, you have me at a distinct disadvantage here, my pants across the floor and all, but I've been here since nine and I don't know what the fuck you're talking about regarding Mickey Nolan."

Ryan crossed the room to where the chair was. He tossed Ward's clothes and gun off the chair and sat.

He said, "Then I guess we have a few things to discuss, boyo, you and me."

Ward took a moment to think about it, then nodded.

CHAPTER 22

FATHER JOHN SCAVO shook his head after listening to what Bobby had to say. He lit a Camel and took a few drags on the cigarette before pouring himself a half glass of brandy.

"I didn't think her cousin would walk in there with his gang or I never would've hit the piece of shit," Bobby said. "I knew he was out looking for Nolan, but I didn't think he'd find him that fast."

"And now he took him and you don't know what happens next," the priest said, "except whatever it is, by all appearances, you're complicit."

"To Nolan's crew," Bobby said. "You're forgetting that other whack job, Tommy Agro. Nolan was working for him. That stunt he pulled at the apartment was something Agro put him up to."

Scavo downed the brandy. He poured himself another, then offered the bottle to Bobby.

"No, thanks," Bobby said. "You need to get back to Lin Yao."

"I was hoping you might spell me," the priest said. "It is where you belong."

"We'll just argue and fight more than we already have," Bobby said. "If she hadn't called her cousin in the first place, this never would've happened."

"She said she didn't call him. She said it was your neighbor."

"I don't mean that, about what happened to her. I'm talking about when I was in the street and Ricky showed up with his punks. Lin Yao called him because we were about to go at it. I know she thought she was helping, but it didn't. It made things worse."

Scavo pointed at Bobby. "You're the one made things worse, my friend. First, by not going straight to the law, and second, by chasing down that asshole her cousin grabbed from the bar."

Bobby said, "I have to get Agro to sit down and talk this out."

"Yeah, right, that'll solve everything now. Tommy Agro, that's the answer."

"I can do without the sarcasm, okay?"

"You can do with a fucking psychiatrist."

Bobby remained silent. Scavo downed his second brandy and capped the bottle.

"You've got a woman who still manages to love you worried sick back at the apartment," the priest said. "You've got other options as well. I think it's time to fold your hand, kid."

"I won't be able to back down the Irish without Agro," Bobby said. "It became a lot more complicated tonight."

"It's only complicated if you try to reason it out. The jerks you're dealing with can't reason. They're either caught up in their own bullshit or too stupid to see the forest for the trees. You're smarter than that. It's time to use your head."

Bobby sat in silence.

"If it's what you've been waiting for, you're back is against the wall now," Scavo added. "You don't have another way out of this thing, except to go to the law. Right now all you did was give a guy a beating. From what you said, I doubt he'll press charges."

"And what the fuck'm I supposed to tell the law?" Bobby said in frustration. "Tommy Agro leaned on me a little? I think some Irish crew on the West Side is gonna try and whack me because the guy I beat up is a friend of theirs and it was just a big coincidence that the same guy beat up my girlfriend and her cousin is the leader of the Chinese gang that grabbed him?

"Or am I supposed to go and tell them mob secrets I don't know, because that's all they'll be interested in anyway, the law. In case you don't know, the cops don't give a fuck about me or Lin Yao, or anything else that don't make a case for them. It's as simple as that, John. Everybody is playing their own angle in this, including the law."

Scavo had heard enough. He stood up to leave. "I have to get back," he said.

"Tell her I love her," Bobby said.

"She knows," Scavo said.

Bobby said, "Tell her anyway."

•◆•

DENAFRIA WAS AWAKE extra early but couldn't figure out why until he realized he was covered in sweat. Then he noticed the silence.

No air conditioner.

He tried the light switch. Nothing happened.

"Fuck me," he said.

He glanced at his watch and saw it was one fifty in the morning. He had another two hours before he was to meet with Michael Ward at Tommy Agro's place, another two hours of sitting in a sauna with no electricity.

He saw he had messages on his cell phone and played them back. The first was from his partner. It was an apology for not making it back. Ward's son had fallen off his bike and needed stitches.

The next message was from his boss, Deputy Inspector Kaprowski. Tommy Agro had given one of his girlfriends a beating and a broken nose the night before. She had called the police and was willing to wear a wire. Kaprowski said she was currently being interviewed by federal agents of the "Fuck-Bee-Eye." They were trying to convince her to let them wire her apartment.

DeNafria glanced at his watch again and decided it would be a lot cooler sitting in his car with the air conditioner running than in the trapped heat of the apartment.

He took a quick shower. He grabbed what was left of the ice cubes in his freezer and dropped them into a plastic container. He poured day-old coffee over the ice and added four spoonfuls of sugar. By the time he left the apartment he was sweating all over again.

Five minutes later, sitting in the Ford Taurus with the air conditioner blowing full blast, the detective felt a lot better.

He listened to a few minutes of news radio and learned that the current heat wave was expected to last another few days at least.

DeNafria decided to head to Valley Stream and pick up his partner instead of meeting in front of Tommy Agro's home. He had plenty of time to grab a fresh coffee along the way.

The drive took him twenty-five minutes. When he was about to turn onto the street where Michael Ward lived, DeNafria realized he had passed a Dunkin' Donuts in the middle of a small strip mall across the avenue. He made a quick U-turn and drove to the parking lot.

He had just pulled into the lot when he spotted his partner with another man he didn't recognize. DeNafria checked the time and saw it was two fifty in the morning. He slipped a Jets baseball cap on his head, pulled into a spot at the opposite end of the parking lot, and then slumped down low in his seat.

He wasn't sure what was going on, but like a few other incidents involving his new partner the past few days, it made him uneasy. The guy Ward had been talking with didn't look right. It would bother DeNafria the rest of the day.

•◆•

"THE FUCK HAPPENED to Mickey Nolan?" Michael Ward asked Jerry Collins. He was cranky from the heat and from the scare Kenneth Ryan had put into him earlier. Now he took it out on Collins.

"I get a call from some frantic bartender," Ward lied, "and I couldn't make heads or tails what the fuck it was about."

The two men were heading out of the local Dunkin' Donuts close to Ward's house. It was two fifty-five in the morning. Ward had called Collins for the emergency meeting less than an hour ago. He glared at the street thug waiting for an answer.

Collins sipped his iced coffee laced with milk before wiping his mouth on his shirt sleeve. "He was working for the dagos," he said. "What he usually does. One of them come looking for Nolan, found him in one of his hangouts and broke him up. Nobody seems to know what it's about. A gang of Chinks came in after that and dragged him out to a van. He's freelance muscle, Nolan. Why Ryan's been able to keep him so loyal, because of the dagos. They keep him out of jail and in booze money. Frankly, if Nolan disappears, it's one for our side."

Ward was looking for an answer that was a lot less ambiguous. Collins had been Ward's best source of information and was the person most responsible for the arrest of a former leader of the West Side gang on heroin trafficking. The gang had since splintered into two factions. Collins was maneuvering to take control and had recruited Ward's help for cash compensation. Ward had been a willing supporter until the impromptu meeting with Kenneth Ryan in Margaret O'Donnell's bedroom earlier.

"You want my assistance you're gonna need to tell me what Nolan did to get scooped up like that," Ward said. "I'm working with OC for Christ sakes. I'm watching dagos all fuckin' day. Christ, I'm working with them. Mickey Nolan's involved in something can surface to bite me, I gotta know when and where so I can duck. And if you're gonna make a move, it can't be under my nose. Not while Ryan is still breathing."

"Ryan's a dead man," Collins said.

Ward smirked. "Yeah, so you keep telling me."

They walked to the curb and stood there awhile before Collins opened the trunk of a sports car parked there. Ward handed Collins a silencer wrapped in chamois cloth. Collins pointed to an envelope under a rag in the trunk.

"I can't kill a man he isn't here," Collins said.

"Spare me another war story," Ward said.

"He's dead as soon as he gets back."

"I said spare me."

Collins finally got in his car and drove off.

Ward glanced at his watch and saw it was getting close to the time he was to meet his partner. DeNafria had planned on getting an early start on surveillance, but Ward was hot, sweaty, and tired, and in no mood for sitting in a car all day.

He had new money to stash at the house. While he was home, he might even manage an extra couple hours of sleep.

He made the drive back to the house in under five minutes. He checked his mirrors at the curb for a tail before pulling into his driveway. When he finally turned the engine off, Ward sat in the minivan a few extra minutes wondering what would happen if he didn't make it another three months to his retirement.

What if he were busted with the money he'd already stashed?

What if Kenneth Ryan wasn't bluffing on the threats he'd made before leaving the apartment?

Ward couldn't get the threats out of his head.

"And should things become the Chinese fire drill they sometimes do," Ryan had told him, "should I find myself standing in a police lineup someday because of anything to do with you or Jerry Collins, understand it'll be your family who pay the price, boyo. I'll have each one of their throats cut. Your wife and two sons up here, and then Mom and Dad down in Florida."

Ward shuddered at the thought.

After a few more minutes of thinking the worst, he forced himself to shake it off. It had been tough enough trying to sleep the past two years with the knowledge that Internal Affairs had been looking to take him down. Now that he'd been transferred to a tit detail with organized crime, his life should've become easy. He was still close to walking away from it, except he was too close to play it safe.

Kenneth Ryan would obviously win the street war against Jerry Collins. There was no point in backing a loser at this late stage of the game.

Ward's father had brought the family to America almost thirty years ago. The United States had offered everything his father had always desired for his family. Ward had been a good son to his father's dream, except early into his police career, he had taken a bite of forbidden fruit. The easy cash he made as a dirty cop had tasted too good to ignore.

Greed had steered him to where he was now, hiding the cash he'd just picked up for the sale of a silencer.

CHAPTER 23

"FAT TONY" GANGI finished listening to the tape and pushed a book of matches across the dining room table. Tommy Agro grabbed the matches without hesitation. He called to John Forzino to come up from the basement and then introduced him to the underboss of the Vignieri crime family.

Gangi was a short, squat man with a thick head of dark, curly hair. He stood up to exchange a cheek kiss with Forzino before leading him into the living room. Agro remained in the dining room.

"I heard the tape and I'm sorry for what the woman did to you," Gangi told Forzino. "Now you have to redeem yourself as a man for this family. What you do about the girl is your business, but your uncle is lost. I hope that won't be a problem for you."

Forzino, without hesitation, said, "He's nothing to me now."

"Good," Gangi said. "Tommy will explain to you what happens next. As of now, you're with Tommy. Do you know what that means?"

Forzino nodded.

"Good," Gangi said. "He's now in charge of your uncle's crew, although nobody should know about that until your uncle is dealt with."

Forzino nodded again.

Gangi said, "When this is done, Tommy is going to submit your name through me. You understand?"

Forzino nodded one more time.

"Good," Gangi said. "Tommy is your boss now. When this is done, what you have to do, the next time we meet will be under better circumstances."

Forzino waited for more.

Gangi smiled. He said, "Hopefully you'll be one of us in this thing of ours."

Forzino forced his own smile. Gangi pulled him in close to hug. The two men exchanged another cheek kiss. Gangi told Forzino to wait in the living room while he got Agro.

The newly promoted skipper was hustling beer down to other members of the crime family waiting in the basement. When Agro was back up the stairs, Gangi was waiting.

"We okay?" Agro asked.

"Tell him what to do," Gangi said. "And send backup in case he can't get it done. Quack can't leave that house alive."

"Right," Agro said.

"Turn the place upside down and find whatever other tapes he has."

"Will do."

"Because if he had this one, he's got more."

"I understand."

"He's still home?"

"I told him we're in Atlantic City, me and the kid," Agro said. "I told him I'm sending the kid back early to collect."

"Okay," Gangi said. He leaned closer to Agro to whisper in his left ear. "And if he can't get it done, the kid, get rid of him, too."

"Right," Agro said. "Of course."

•◆•

LIN YAO HAD spent most of the night wondering whether she had made it worse by calling her cousin. After the priest left for the rectory, she sat up waiting for Bobby to come home. When Father Scavo returned alone forty-five minutes after he had left, she was reluctant to press him for information.

It was close to five o'clock in the morning when exhaustion finally took over and she fell asleep. Lin Yao dreamed about the last deposition she had filmed in Texas, how the guy, the CEO of an energy company, had smiled for the camera before answering each and every question. In her dream he was smiling at her, like he was daring her to ask the direct questions she had been waiting to hear all during his deposition.

"Did you cook the books?"

"Did you steal from the company?"

"Did you defraud your investors?"

Then her sister appeared. Ming Lao said, "Did you steal money from the mob?"

Lin Yao woke up from the bright sunlight cascading through the bedroom windows. She was sweating. It would be another hot, humid day. The image of her sister asking that last question had shaken her.

She glanced at the time and saw it was after six in the morning. She didn't know if Bobby had come home or not. She remembered Father Scavo had come back after meeting Bobby, but that had been a while ago. She was anxious when she heard footsteps outside the bedroom. She quickly got out of bed to put a robe on.

"I have to leave in a few minutes to say mass," Scavo told her through the bedroom door.

"I'll be right out," she said.

"He's okay," said Scavo when Lin Yao joined him. He was headed for the kitchen. "I have to clean up a little. I made coffee."

"I'll take care of that," she told him. "Please."

"It's no bother," he said.

She followed him across the apartment. "Did he find that guy?" she asked.

Scavo glanced toward the kitchen window. The sun was bright. "It's already another hot one," he said.

"Did he?"

"I'd rather you two talk to each other."

"I didn't know if he was alive until he called you," she said. "I purposely didn't ask you last night. Please, Father."

"Bobby found the guy who was here and he beat him up," Scavo said. "Then your cousin was there and he took the guy out."

"Ricky?"

"And his gang."

"What do you mean, took him out?"

"Please, Lin Yao, I have to get back to say mass. I'd rather you discuss this with Bobby."

"Where is he?"

"At my office, but I have to go now."

"Why won't he come home?"

"He can't do that right now. He wants to, though. I know he does."

"I'm afraid for him, Father."

"Try not to worry," Scavo said. "He's okay. And he'll call you as soon as he's ready."

An uncomfortable pause ensued. The priest finally gathered his things and then kissed Lin Yao on the cheek.

"Give me a call if you need anything," he told her. "I have an early mass and then a meeting about the feast later this morning. I'll call in the afternoon and see how you're doing."

Lin Yao thanked him again before seeing him out. After she heard the elevator door close down the hall, she walked to the living room windows and looked down at the street. She watched Father Scavo leave the building and head north up Baxter Street. Another forty minutes she stood there looking for Bobby before she finally gave up.

CHAPTER 24

FORZINO PICKED UP his fiancée a few minutes after seven in the morning. He had called half an hour earlier and told Sally to be ready when he got there because he was in a rush. She had given him a hard time until he explained how she was going to try on the fur and leather jackets he was getting swag.

"We got a van meeting us in Queens," he had told her. "You want a few you'll be ready when I get there."

She was smiling when she sat in the car. Forzino told her she looked tired.

"I was up late," Sally said.

"Oh, yeah? What for?"

"Once you called and said you were going to Atlantic City, I wound up watching television most of the night," she lied. She had spent most of the night cleaning up the mess Uncle Joe had left behind. "Did you win?"

"I didn't play," he told her. "It was business with some people from Baltimore. How we wound up with this van this morning."

Sally seemed excited. "Is it real fur, the jackets?"

"Fur and leather both, yeah," Forzino lied.

He took the Belt Parkway to Springfield Boulevard. Tommy Agro had given him an address that was an empty warehouse on 141st Avenue.

He would take the parkway back east to his uncle's house in Rockville Centre afterward.

When he saw Sally fidgeting with the radio, he asked, "You hungry?"

"A little."

"We can stop at a diner on the way back."

"Okay."

She leaned toward him and reached out to stroke his right hand. She noticed his knuckles were bruised.

"What happened to your hand?"

"Huh? Oh, nothing. I scraped it."

Sally half smiled. "Sure," she said.

"What, you'd rather I tell you I banged somebody out?"

"You do what you have to," she said, flirting now.

Forzino felt his teeth clenching.

"But this is a nice surprise," Sally added, "a fur jacket."

Forzino's tension turned to a smirk. "Like I said, might be some leather, too. I know how much you like surprises."

"Yes, I do," she said. "This is so cool."

He pulled into an empty lot alongside the warehouse and then drove around to the back. He glanced at all four mirrors before getting out of the car. He waved at Sally to wait in the car while he did a quick search inside the building for any dopeheads or vagrants.

Five minutes later the van pulled around the back of the warehouse. Forzino opened the door for Sally and helped her out of the car.

"This is so exciting," she said. "That the van?"

"Yeah," Forzino said. "Come on."

He guided her through an open doorway, then down a long hallway.

"Where we going?" she asked.

"Out of view from any nosy fucks," he told her.

They walked the length of the hallway until they reached a stairwell off to the right. Forzino guided Sally inside the stairwell. "One minute," he said.

She was uncomfortable in the dark space. She was careful not to touch the walls.

Forzino pulled a 9 mm Beretta from inside the waist of his pants. Sally didn't see it until he pointed the gun at her. She gasped before leaning her back flush against the wall.

"Think you can get your mouth all the way down on this?" he asked a moment before he shot her in the face.

He waited until her body crumpled to the floor and then shot her two more times, both in the back of the head.

•◆•

AFTER SAYING MORNING mass, Father Scavo found his friend asleep on the couch in his office at the rectory. He poured an extra cup of coffee and set it on the edge of his desk before he woke Bobby up.

"I smell coffee," Bobby said.

"On the desk."

"What's it doing there?"

"You want it, you'll get off the couch."

Bobby yawned before sitting up. He stretched his arms out wide and yawned a second time.

"Back hurt?" Scavo asked.

"A little, yeah."

"How long you asleep?"

Bobby sat across from the desk and grabbed the cup of coffee. "Since two minutes after you left," he said.

The priest sipped his own coffee. "Anybody come looking for me?"

"No, but that fat cat of yours was looking to get out. I opened the door for it."

"General Lee," Scavo said. "I found him the day I moved in. Nobody knew his name or where he had come from. I named it General Lee because of its color."

Bobby sipped at the coffee. "Not bad," he said. "How was Lin Yao?"

"How do you think? She's upset."

"I can't go to the law."

"You can, but you won't. There's a difference."

"It isn't that simple."

Scavo wiped sweat from his forehead before turning the air conditioner up to high.

"This heat is killing me," he said. "We're up to two meetings a day about this damn feast and it's the same thing over and over. Half want to know how we can accept blood money donations from the mob, and the other half wants a bigger cut. And all I'm wondering is how anybody can pay six dollars for a half a sausage sandwich."

"Or three-fifty for a soda," Bobby said.

"They're your friends."

"Not anymore, they're not."

"Yeah, I know," Scavo said. "You have a plan or you intend to live here the rest of your life?"

"I'm waiting on a call from Tommy Agro," Bobby said.

"And why's that?"

"Because of last night. Nolan works for Agro. If Ricky is looking for money, Nolan will tell him to call Agro. Then Agro will call me."

"And if he doesn't?"

"Then I'll call Ricky myself. I'll work something out."

"You make it sound easy."

"Sometimes it is when you don't have a choice. Easier, I mean."

Scavo put his feet up on the desk and leaned back in his chair. "You mind if I catch an hour or two sleep?" he asked.

"Knock yourself out."

"There's stuff in the fridge, you're hungry."

"I'll find it."

Scavo yawned. "Wake me before noon," he said. "I have those meetings."

"Buona sera," Bobby said.

"Yeah," Scavo said. "I wish."

•◆•

AFTER TURNING HIS nephew's apartment upside down in his search for the recorder, Joe Quastifare had returned home determined not to leave the house again until he knew it was safe. The first thing he did was turn off the ringer on his home telephone so the machine would have to pick up.

A nervous hour had passed before Tommy Agro finally called. He told Quastifare that he was heading down to Atlantic City and that he was taking Forzino with him. Quastifare immediately called his nephew's fiancée to check on Agro's story. When Sally told him it was true, that his nephew had called to tell her he was going to Atlantic City, Quastifare was temporarily relieved.

After several drinks he was finally relaxed enough to fall asleep. When he woke up, it was just after eight o'clock in the morning. He saw there were two messages on the phone machine. The first was from his wife.

"Miami is too hot, even in September," she had said. "I'll never go there before winter again. Never, ever—"

Quastifare deleted the rest of her message to get to the next one. It was from Tommy Agro.

"Your nephew was good for me down here," Agro's voice said. "Had a beginner's luck roll at the craps table. I'm gonna spend the rest of the day here and come home later tonight. I'm sending the kid to pick up in Brooklyn on his way home. He'll drop it off, you don't mind. I'll call you when I'm home. My cell's on, you need me."

The situation seemed pretty normal. Tommy Agro became the degenerate gambler he was whenever he won a few dollars. Quastifare wasn't too crazy about seeing his nephew so soon after what had happened the day before, but the kid was dropping off money.

He looked at the time of Agro's phone call and saw it had registered at four thirty in the morning. If the kid had left around the same time as the call, he would have picked up the money and would be at the house soon.

Quastifare had gone through the sequence of events leading to the missing recorder two dozen times and it still made him crazy to think he could've lost it. If he hadn't gone through his nephew's apartment the night before, turning it upside down, even going through the dirty laundry—he'd forced Sally to empty every drawer and cabinet in the place—Quastifare might've called an FBI emergency phone number and cut a deal right there and then.

Sally had been scared shitless the night before. She had sworn that his nephew was only in the apartment a few minutes before the phone rang and John told her he was leaving to go with Tommy Agro. He was sure she didn't know anything.

He watched the clock above the fireplace and tried to remain calm. If he received a call from any of his men or if any of the family bosses summoned him, he would grab the tapes he still had in the basement and drive to the nearest FBI safe house.

There was no way he could meet anyone until he located the recorder. Not without fear of losing his life.

He thought about the times he had been on jobs when a fellow wiseguy was sent for. It was always in the most relaxed atmosphere when a hit went down. He and Tommy Agro had been involved in at least three such kills.

After another half hour Quastifare's nerves were getting the best of him. He poured a tall highball and drank it way too fast. He poured himself another two when his paranoia took full control.

He decided he would have to be ready in case he was going to turn himself in. He went down to the basement and unlocked the strong box under the floor in his office. He pulled out all the tapes and put them in a small leather bag. He was about to add a Browning .380 when the doorbell rang upstairs.

"Fuck," he said. He shoved the gun inside the bag and slid it under the desk.

The doorbell rang a second time as he reached the top of the basement stairs. He looked through the kitchen blinds and saw his nephew standing on the stoop in the back of the house. He could see the kid was holding a thick envelope.

At least he'd make one last score, Quastifare was thinking.

He opened the kitchen door leading to the pantry, then opened the back door to the house. His nephew held up the envelope.

"Can I use your toilet?" he asked.

Quastifare frowned at the request. "Yeah, sure, come in," he said. He pulled the door open to let his nephew in and saw the gun a moment too late.

The impact of the first two bullets forced him to the floor. He tried to sit up but immediately started to choke on the blood in his mouth.

"Maybe she can blow you in hell," he heard his nephew say.

Quastifare saw the door close at the exact same time he realized what his nephew was talking about. He tried to reach up with both hands when the first of the next two bullets entered his forehead and everything went black.

CHAPTER 25

"TOP OF THE morning," Michael Ward told his partner. He had picked up two large cups of coffee and a half box of donuts on his way. He handed DeNafria one of the coffees and set the box on the console.

DeNafria pointed at his watch. "More like end of the morning," he said. "It's noon, where the hell were you?"

"Catching up on some sleep," Ward said. "Sorry, I passed out."

DeNafria knew his partner was lying. The exchange he'd witnessed back at the strip mall was fresh on his mind. He didn't know what had been passed between the two men, except here was Ward lying about sleeping again.

"Get enough this time?" he asked.

"Tons," Ward said, "at least I dreamed I did." He picked a chocolate donut with sprinkles from the box. "I saw Demi Moore bare-assed naked standing in my kitchen so I'm pretty sure it was in my head."

"Well, there's been a lot of activity here," DeNafria said. He motioned at two cars parked in Tommy Agro's driveway. "Guys coming and going since before I'm here. Tony Gangi, the underboss, and a couple of skippers."

"A peace conference?"

"I doubt it."

Ward was waiting to see if his partner knew anything about what had happened to Mickey Nolan the night before.

"I could've used you yesterday, though," DeNafria said. "I lost Joe Quack when he cut through a parking lot."

"You lost him or he lost you?"

DeNafria ignored the jab. "He seemed in a hurry. Now I'm wondering it had something to do with all this, except Quack is the only one missing. None of his guys are here, at least none of his goons."

"I had that thing with my kid yesterday," Ward said, "which I've got to get back to later today. Sorry."

DeNafria peeled the lid back and sipped at his coffee. "Later today?"

"Few hours, actually, so I can't stay long."

DeNafria let out a long breath of frustration.

"Anything more on Panico?" Ward asked.

DeNafria remembered what Kaprowski had mentioned the day before and told his partner.

Ward said, "Day late and a dollar short, aren't they? They knew he had money stashed in banks down here, they should've staked them out."

"Not enough manpower," DeNafria said, then decided to add a dig. "Like Quack giving me the slip yesterday."

Ward could tell his partner was still pissed off, but he wasn't about to apologize again. He went silent instead.

DeNafria pointed toward Agro's house. "And there's Tommy giving us a noonday salute."

Ward turned just in time to see the wiseguy close the front door.

Five minutes passed before DeNafria spoke again. When he did, he still wasn't looking at Ward.

"There might be a break from one of Agro's girlfriends," he said. "The one lives over the Fort Hamilton House."

"What he do to her?"

"Broke her nose, apparently. The feds wanna wire the apartment."

Ward was impressed. He was surprised at his partner's lack of enthusiasm. "That's a big deal, no?"

"It is for the feds," DeNafria said. "It'll be their case."

"That's fucked," Ward said.

DeNafria said, "You want to split the shift a few days, rotate through the night?"

Ward shook his head. "No can do. Not without more notice. The way I'm going now, I'm liable to sleep through a night shift. 'Specially sitting in a car like this. Not to mention I'll put on a dozen pounds within a week."

"The bad guys seem to be playing at night again. Wherever Quack rushed off to yesterday, it wasn't like him to go without one of his goons."

"You said."

"I had a patrol unit pass his house. His car is there, but he wasn't answering his phone when I had them call. I don't know he went back out again or not. And these guys were already in motion when I got here this morning, which means they were up and around before six o'clock, if they went to sleep at all last night."

"I can't work through the night without changing my hours," Ward said. "I can try, but I can't guarantee I'll stay awake. What about getting some help? With all this activity, it shouldn't be a big deal."

"It is," DeNafria said. "We're on this solo for now."

"Well, is it a problem I don't change my hours?" Ward asked.

DeNafria took his time answering. "We'll work it out," he finally said.

"Good."

Ward was staring at his partner. DeNafria looked as though he was about to say something, then turned away. A car had pulled up in front of Agro's house. It was a young Chinese man making a delivery.

"Makes me hungry, seeing other people about to eat," Ward said. He grabbed the last donut.

•◆•

TOMMY AGRO GLANCED out his living room window to see if the cop was still parked in front of his house. The crowd of wiseguys he had hosted had left an hour ago. When Agro couldn't see from the window, he went to the front door and opened it. He noticed a second cop sitting surveillance and gave them the finger before slamming the door shut.

He turned to John Forzino and said, "I've got some very good news for you, my friend."

Forzino knew it had to do with his uncle. If killing his uncle had been a test, he'd passed with flying colors. Killing his fiancée was a bonus. Still, there was a moment when he was driving back to Agro's house after killing his uncle and finding the bag of tapes in the basement that Forzino thought he might be killed himself.

When he was back at Agro's house and the underboss of the family called him a "man's man," Forzino knew he had been accepted.

Now Tommy Agro handed him a shot glass filled with whiskey.

"You're going to be straightened out," the wiseguy told Forzino. *"Salute."*

The two men touched shot glasses and downed their drinks. Agro quickly poured another two shots. He raised his glass. Forzino did the same.

"And I'm your new boss," Agro said.

"Salute," Forzino said.

Half an hour and a few shots later, Agro explained how it would happen.

"I'll give you a call one night, tell you to be ready in an hour or so and to get dressed in your best suit," the wiseguy said. "I'll pick you up, take you to an undisclosed location, and there you'll meet with the same people were here today. You'll be asked a few questions, go through the ceremony, and you'll be a made man with this family."

Forzino nodded without expression.

"Everybody appreciates what you just went through," Agro said. "I can't imagine what it felt like to hear the shit on that tape. But I also know you can't blame yourself. No man can blame himself when a woman goes bad. As for your uncle, well, women were always his Italy's heel.

"Again, it's not your fault what happened between them. And now you've made them pay the way they should've paid. You turned a horrible thing into a blessing. And that's how I explained it to the underboss of this family. That what happened when you found that tape, as horrible as it was, it was a blessing in disguise. Because you're the kind of man we need in this thing of ours today. It used to be a thing of honor until people like your uncle lost their way. Now we can look forward to turning it back around."

"I appreciate it," Forzino said, still without expression.

Both men downed another drink. An uncomfortable silence ensued. Then the doorbell rang and the kid offered to answer it. Two minutes later he returned to the living room carrying a brown shopping bag filled with Chinese food.

"The hell is that?" Agro asked.

"I figured you ordered it," Forzino said. "There's a menu attached, this address. Cost eighteen bucks."

Agro was squinting at the bag. "I didn't order anything."

"You don't mind, I'm a little hungry," Forzino said. "Might as well eat, it's here."

"Good for you," Agro said. "Sure, what the hell. I'll get some plates."

He went to the kitchen to grab a few plates and silverware from the cabinets. When he returned, the kid had already set the cartons of food out on the flat cardboard squares used to stack the food inside the delivery bag. Agro set a plate, knife, and fork in front of Forzino. Forzino opened the first carton and pushed his chair away from the table.

"What the fuck?" he said.

Agro glanced at the carton and dropped his plate and utensils. He was staring at half an index finger lying on a bed of lo mein. An Irish shamrock tattoo was clearly visible.

"Jesus Christ," he said. "What the fuck is this?"

CHAPTER 26

Bobby was confused when Tommy Agro mentioned an unwanted delivery of Chinese food he had just received at his house.

"To my house!" Agro yelled.

Bobby wasn't sure what the hell Agro was talking about, but he was still pissed off the wiseguy had sent Mickey Nolan after Lin Yao in the first place.

He said, "Yeah, so now you know how it feels somebody pulls shit where you live."

"You telling me that was you sent that delivery?" Agro asked.

"I don't even know what you're talking about. Was it you sent Nolan to my place?"

"No way. Of course not."

"Bullshit."

"Bullshit you. And fuck you!"

Bobby hung up. His cell phone rang again a few seconds later.

"Yeah?" Bobby answered.

"A guy you had an issue with the other day on the West Side, he went missing right after that, right? I just got something a his in a food delivery. Can you figure that out?"

"The hell are you talking about?" Bobby asked.

"You know who I'm talking about," Agro said. "And somebody delivered one of his fingers in a carton of lo mein."

"Creative, but it wasn't me," Bobby said.

He could hear the wiseguy trying to control his breathing.

"We need to meet," Agro said. "Someplace I know you're not wired."

Father Scavo had already offered his office for a meeting between Bobby and Tommy Agro when the two discussed it earlier. Bobby told Agro, but the wiseguy insisted it be somewhere more public.

"The guy is a priest," Bobby said. "How much more public you want it?"

"The church," Agro said. "You got God on your side, a priest friend, he won't mind that."

"I don't know he'll go for that," Bobby said. "Think what you're asking here."

"It's the church or you come to me," Agro said.

"Hold on."

Scavo had just stepped inside the office. Bobby relayed the message.

The priest huffed once before reaching for the cell phone. Bobby let him have it.

"Tommy?" the priest asked.

"Who's this?"

"Father Scavo."

"Are you kidding me?"

"No, I'm not. What time do you want to meet Bobby?"

"Excuse me, pal, but how do I know you're a priest over the phone?"

"You don't, but if you want, I'll give you the number to the rectory, or you can get it yourself and call back."

"Right, like that'll prove you're not a cop."

"Look, you can either have your meeting or not have it. I've had a long enough day already. It's hot and I'm tired. If you want to use the church, I suggest you get over here soon. There's a late-afternoon funeral.

You can't use it then. You can use it before if you want. Until four o'clock, if that's enough time."

"Put Gennaro back on."

Scavo rolled his eyes as he handed the phone back to Bobby.

"Yeah," Bobby said.

"I'll be there three o'clock," Agro said. "I'll meet you out front. I see a cop anywhere near the area, I'll just drive away and that'll be that. You can answer to the people over on the West Side for yourself."

Bobby was about to respond when the line went dead.

"We using the church?" Scavo asked.

"Yeah," Bobby said. "Three o'clock. You sure that's okay?"

"So long as you're out before four o'clock." The priest wiped his forehead with a towel. "It's like soup out there."

"Thanks for this," Bobby said.

"Just get it over with," Scavo said. "Hopefully, you'll go straight to the police afterward. I know I would."

•◆•

LIN YAO TOLD the gangbanger standing guard outside the restaurant that she needed to see her cousin. The stocky youth blocking the restaurant door told her Ricky Zhu was busy and to come back later. Lin Yao stood her ground. Yelling in Cantonese, the two went back and forth until she threatened to kick him in the balls.

"Please go away now," the gangbanger told her. "Your cousin is busy."

Lin Yao kicked him in the right shin and watched his leg buckle. She stepped around him and slipped inside the restaurant. She spotted her cousin talking on a cell phone and called to him. Ricky Zhu waved at her to be quiet.

The stocky guard limped inside the restaurant. Ricky waved him off, then finished his conversation on the cell phone. When he was through talking, he approached Lin Yao with both hands open.

"What you doing here?" he asked.

"What did you do with that guy?" she said.

Ricky put a finger to his lips. "I don't know what you talking about. Come downstairs."

He led her down the stairs to his basement office. He slammed the door shut when they were alone.

"What's wrong with you, coming here?" he said. "Talking out loud upstairs. You crazy?"

"What did you do to that animal?"

"None of your business. Who sent you here, your boyfriend?"

"Bobby didn't come home last night. I know he beat the guy up. And I know you took him. What are you going to do?"

"Don't ask me questions. Go home. This is none of your business now."

"It is if it involves Bobby."

"Fuck Bobby. Okay? I don't care about your boyfriend."

"God damn you, Ricky! What did you do?"

Zhu looked at his watch. "I going to meet somebody now about Irishman, okay? I going to meet somebody and then I release him."

"When?"

"Soon. I have to go now. You making me late."

"I want to come."

"You fucking crazy, you know that? Go home. I going now." He opened the door.

Lin Yao stood in his face. "I'm coming," she declared.

Ricky said, "You try and follow me, I have my guys take you down here and tie you up until I get back."

Lin Yao didn't answer.

"I mean it," Ricky said.

They stood staring at one another until Ricky tried to take her by the hand. Lin Yao pushed his hand away and walked out ahead of him.

•◆•

BOBBY WAS SURPRISED to see Ricky Zhu sitting in the back pew of the church. He responded to Zhu's smirk by flipping the Chinese gang-banger the bird.

He saw that Tommy Agro had the big guy with him again. Forzino frisked Bobby before joining Agro in the row ahead of Zhu. Bobby directed Father Scavo to sit across the aisle. The priest ignored the directive and moved into the row with Agro. Bobby sat a few feet from Ricky Zhu.

Agro motioned at the priest. "The fuck is this?" he asked Bobby.

"Try and watch your mouth," said Bobby, motioning up and around with his head.

"Well?" Agro said.

"I'm here to make sure Bobby isn't harmed," Scavo said.

Agro pointed across the aisle. "You can do that from over there," he said. "We didn't frisk you, how do I know you're not wearing a wire? Go sit there or we're out of here."

Bobby nodded at his friend. The priest stood up and crossed the aisle. Bobby looked at Agro. He said, "Come to think of it, we didn't frisk you."

"You not touching me," Ricky Zhu said.

Agro glared at Bobby. "Don't push your luck," he said. "Let's just avoid being specific."

Bobby motioned at Zhu. "Where'd you find this clown?"

Zhu said, "I cut your fucking throat, white boy."

Bobby said, "Careful, your punks aren't around."

Agro said, "Knock if off, the two a yous. We're in a church here."

Bobby winked at Zhu. The Chinaman seethed.

"What's it about?" Bobby asked Agro.

"He's got somebody," Agro said. "What I mentioned to you earlier. He already did something he shouldn't have. Then he did something else he shouldn't have, sent something to my house."

"What's it got to do with me?"

"I was forced to forward the delivery to where I think it was meant inna first place," said Agro, turning toward Zhu again. "You know, wrong address and all, how it got to my place."

"What, you sent it to his people, the piece of garbage you sent to my apartment to terrorize my fiancée?" Bobby said. "I'm really supposed to care?"

Agro said, "I didn't send anybody anywhere. Like I said, maybe you said something to piss somebody else off. You got a big enough mouth."

Bobby stroked the air with his right fist.

Agro huffed. "Anyway, you beat the living shhhh—crap out of this person, there's no denying that." He pointed at Zhu. "And then this guy and his crew picked him up and tossed him in the back of a van. There were several witnesses, in case yous don't remember."

"The guy is lucky I left him breathing," Bobby said. "He assaulted my girlfriend. Tied her up and slapped her around. They know about that, his friends?"

"That doesn't change what happened," Agro said. "And these other people aren't gonna appreciate it, what happened after. Some friends on the West Side, I'm talking about. This person did work for us more than a few times. You know that."

"How I know you sent him," Bobby said. "And if you think I owe you an explanation for kicking his ass, you're smoking dope, because I'm not."

Agro gripped the top of a pew with both hands and took a deep breath. Bobby could tell the wiseguy was trying to keep his cool.

"Look, you think what you want about me and this guy is missing now. And whatever happened to her, your girlfriend, I had nothing to do with it, okay? The bottom line is the people want their boy back. This other jamoke over here took him. They way it looks, you helped him. Somebody's gotta answer, especially now something happened to the guy." At this point Agro turned to Ricky Zhu. "Which if anything else happens, you'll be the one responsible, nobody else."

Zhu gave Tommy the finger. "I say fuck you and fuck him."

Agro forced a smile. "A regular conversationalist, huh?"

"He doesn't speak the mother tongue very well," Bobby said. "But he isn't stupid. Not always." He turned to Zhu. "What is it you intend to do with the guy?"

Zhu rubbed two fingers together. He said, "Cash, white boy."

Bobby turned to Agro. "He says he wants cash."

Agro's eyes narrowed. "Don't get too cute yet," he told Bobby. "He wants cash he'll be getting it from you."

Bobby smiled. "You're smoking something, you think that. Where's it end, Tommy?"

"It ends when I say it ends."

Bobby shook his head. "I'm not paying ransom money for the guy assaulted my girlfriend," he said. "You're gonna threaten me over that, you might as well go all the way and whack me."

"The thought has crossed my mind."

"Yeah, well, that type of threat won't fly with this, okay? The guy slapped my fiancée around. Fuck him. I'm not paying anything on his behalf. This clown thinks he's worth something, let him take it to somebody gives a shit."

"Language," Agro said.

Zhu turned to Bobby and dragged a finger across his own throat.

Bobby grabbed his crotch.

Agro said, "You kids finished?"

Bobby said, "What's the deal, Tommy? What do you want?"

"We come up with a figure for the Irishman your friend here can live with," Agro said. "Then we discuss the unfinished business between me and you."

Bobby turned to Zhu. "Well?"

Zhu gave Bobby the finger. Bobby laughed in his face.

"I'll shoot your fuckin' eyes out," Zhu said.

"Jesus Christ," Agro said. "You guys fight half as good as you talk about it, we could send you two to Iraq, clean up the whole mess there in two weeks."

Bobby turned away from Zhu. "How much?" he asked.

"Hundred thousand," Zhu said.

Bobby looked at Agro. "Okay? You still wanna jerk yourself off, knock yourself out."

"It can't be that much money," Agro told Zhu. "Let's get real here."

"Fifty thousand," Zhu said.

"He said real," Bobby said. "I might go three figures for the guy who assaulted your cousin, like a hundred bucks, but only so I can break his face all over again."

"They'll be none of that," Agro said. "Not ever again."

"Chinese honor was insulted," Zhu told Agro in as sarcastic a tone as he could muster. "White boy's girlfriend is my cousin."

"I understand that," Agro said. He turned to Bobby. "So should you."

Bobby said, "White boy's girlfriend is ashamed of her cousin, and the Chinaman should understand that."

"I can't wait to kill you," Zhu said.

"Jesus Christ," Agro said. "You two are worse'n kids."

Bobby said. "Last time, how much?"

Agro opened his hands to Zhu.

"Ten thousand," Zhu said.

Bobby shook his head. "Too high."

"I don't go lower."

"It's too high."

"What if I sweeten the pot?" Agro asked Bobby.

"How you gonna do that, offer to kill this asshole afterward?"

"Faggot motherfucker," Zhu said.

"Shhh!" Agro said to Zhu. "You can take it off the top of what you owe me," he told Bobby. "Bring that figure down ten to forty."

"I already told you I'm not paying fifty grand in shakedown money," Bobby said. "I'm not paying forty, either. I already left you something, and you got greedy and sent that other punk to my apartment. I'll give you the balance of ten and that's it. And I don't have it now, whether you or Joe Quack accept that or not. As far as this clown, you can give him what I owe you on the ten, but I'm not giving him a dime."

Zhu said, "Ten thousand or no deal."

Bobby ignored Zhu. "How long we gonna do this?" he asked Agro.

"Fuck you," Zhu said. "I don't come here to get insulted." He pointed at Bobby and Agro. "Fuck you and fuck you. I deliver more food container."

Both Agro and Bobby watched as Zhu got up and left the church.

"Now what?" Bobby asked when Zhu was gone.

"Now I know why our people left Little Italy," Agro said. "Those roaches have absolutely no class whatsoever."

•◆•

FATHER SCAVO WARNED them they had another five minutes before they had to leave and Agro said, "Now, the real reason I'm here, put you back to work."

Bobby laughed. "What, running the office?"

"Exactamundo."

"I'm retired, Tommy. I'm out."

"What, you're saying it's not negotiable? The guy Quack had running the office just got caught short six large, which means he's either an idiot can't count or he's skimming. I don't need that in my life now. At least with you, I know you'll do the right thing."

"What, you trust me now?"

"I didn't say I trusted you. I said you'll do the right thing."

Bobby was confused. "What is this? I don't get it."

Agro motioned at Forzino. "We're in a good way," he said. "Let's just say the worm has burned in our favor."

"You mean 'turned,'" Bobby said.

"Huh?"

"Forget it. What's going on?"

Agro leaned over to whisper. "The kid is getting straightened out, for one thing," he said. "Congratulate him."

Bobby turned to Forzino and said, "Good luck. You'll need it."

"I'll make believe that was sincere," Agro said.

Bobby waited for more.

"Anyway," Agro continued, "this Chink was here a minute ago, I know he's somebody to your girl, and he's got his dick in his zipper over whatever the other guy did to her, but frankly, all it does is give my life extra constipation. I'd like to get the Irishman back, but I'm not paying for it. The problem becomes what happens when his people learn this half-assed gang from Mott Street kidnapped him and nobody paid the note? See, then it comes back to me, and I can't have that."

Bobby shook his head. "I'm getting confused, Tommy. What is it you want from me?"

"A little of this and a little of that," Agro said. "Some money for these Chinks to take care of the one problem and you can work off what you owe me running the office. I don't know, what, a grand a week knockdown? You're done end of a year."

Bobby couldn't believe what he was hearing. Agro had fucked up by sending the Irishman in the first place, things had spiraled out of control and become dangerous for everybody, and the wiseguy still couldn't contain his greed.

"How about I give you what I said before and we make believe we don't know each other," Bobby said.

Agro said, "I had to smack around some broad the other night to get her to pay attention. Maybe I should do that with you, too."

"Not in here," Father Scavo said.

Agro smiled at the priest. He turned to Forzino. "How's this sit with you?"

The big man opened his jacket so Bobby could see the handgun jammed inside the waist of his pants. Then Forzino leaned forward and counted off his fingers. "The balance of what you still owe tomorrow, that'll keep you alive, but you still owe the balance on the forty. Forty because we're taking the ten off the top for the Chink to save some face and not kill the other guy. You don't wanna run the office, you can still take the year to pay it, but we juice you two points a week, an insider rate. That's eight hundred in vig starting one week from today. You find the balance, you wanna whack it down all at once, knock yourself out, but the money for the noodle we'll need tomorrow."

"I'm impressed," Bobby said. He turned to Agro. "He learns fast."

"Why he's where he is," Agro said. "And don't forget he benches five hundred pounds."

Bobby thought about mentioning the pause again, then glanced back at the gun and decided to let it go.

CHAPTER 27

IT WAS FOUR thirty when Tommy Agro met Ricky Zhu at the Chinese restaurant on Bayard Street. Agro handed Zhu the envelope Bobby Gennaro had left him the day before.

"Here's a down payment," Agro said. "The rest is coming."

"How much is here?"

"Count it."

Fingering through the bills in the envelope, Zhu counted as he did so.

"Forty-five hundred," he said when he was done. He folded the envelope in half and stashed it in a front pants pocket. "When I get rest?"

"Soon's your future brother-in-law gives it to me or drops it off here," Agro said. "Tomorrow, the next day, no longer'n that."

"Lin Yao is cousin, not sister," Zhu said. "If she were, I kill that white boy three years ago."

"Whatever," Agro said. "But I need to know you're not gonna do something stupid with that Irishman you're holding. Not unless you wanna start a war you can't win."

"I get the money, I let the mick go. Not before."

"Fair enough. Just don't get stupid. He's not alone. He's got friends, too."

"Drunk micks, I know," Zhu said. "I no worry."

"Yeah, good for you, but I do worry. You're not the first group to start kidnapping people, my friend. The guy you're holding, his people perfected it a couple dozen years ago. Don't think they forgot how."

Zhu smirked. "Now you threaten me?"

"You got a serious chip on your shoulder, you know that?"

Zhu didn't understand the remark.

"Anyway, just do the right thing here," Agro said. "You get the money, let the guy go."

"I think about it."

"You do that."

Zhu pointed to the front door. Agro had to bite his tongue until he and Forzino were out on the street again.

"You see what that noodle did?" Agro said. "Dismissed us, the cocksucker. Pointed at the door like we're the hired help. No fuckin' respect."

Forzino opened the passenger door for Agro. He said, "He's a punk feeling his oats."

Agro saw a Chinese woman spit off the curb and waved it off. "I think I hate these people," he said. "Let's get out of here before I have to shoot one of them."

Forzino got behind the wheel and started the engine. "You think Nolan is okay?" he asked.

"He better be. Figure the noodle waits another day or two, at least until he sees he gets paid or not. It's the smart move."

"What if he doesn't get the money?"

"Bobby G isn't that stupid. At least I don't think he is. The micks on the West Side are gonna want his ass for the beating he gave Nolan. Technically, I would've had to eat some crow and maybe knock down his note with us because of Nolan going to the apartment there, roughing up the Chink broad, but once the noodle and his gang got involved, all those witnesses in the bar saw them, it looks like Gennaro and the Chinks were working together. If the Irish don't think he had something to do with the kidnapping, it'll be a surprise to me."

Forzino smiled. "So, it's Gennaro's headache either way?"

"Now that I interceded, tried to straighten things out, the Irish got no beef with us," Agro said. "Why I met with this noodle now. Playing the middle against both ends is a skill you'll have to learn fast you wanna survive this game. Far as we're concerned, this bullshit with Mickey Nolan and Bobby Gennaro and everybody else, it's a win-win."

Forzino nodded, taking it all in.

"The thing we're gonna have to deal with sooner or later is the missing people we used to know," Agro said. "That police escort sitting outside my house all morning was just the start. They'll be looking at you, too, now."

"When you think I should mention she's missing?" Forzino asked. "I mean, to her family."

"Give it another day," Agro said, "Call her people, whatever family she got. Leave a message they're not home. Then call the police, but after you call her family. Just don't say too much. Don't put your foot in your face. They're not complete idiots, the cops. Even a broken clock has a bad day."

Forzino was pretty sure Agro had misspoken again, but now he was getting used to it.

•◆•

THEY HAD HUNG around Tommy Agro's place until the Chinese food delivery. Then Ward had said it looked like the boys were staying in at least through lunch and that he had that thing to take care of for his kid.

DeNafria had said, "You're leaving?"

"What I mentioned before, yeah," Ward had said. Then he held up the empty box of donuts. "Besides, we're all out."

DeNafria had sat surveillance another few minutes after Ward left before he called Arlene Belzinger and asked if she was free for dinner. He was pleasantly surprised when she said she was and that she had something to show him.

DeNafria called it a day a few minutes later and drove back to Bay Ridge to shower, change his clothes, and catch a quick nap. A few minutes after five o'clock he was sitting across from Belzinger in a small Mexican restaurant on Third Avenue off Seventy-fifth Street in Bay Ridge, three blocks from her apartment.

She handed him a copy of an organizational chart that depicted the structure of the West Side Irish gang. DeNafria noticed there were two boxes side by side representing the top slot.

"Ryan and Collins," he said. "This the split it appears to be?"

Belzinger sipped her margarita. "I couldn't get pictures without pushing it," she said. "Yes, it is a split. Ryan was the heir apparent. Collins is the one challenging it. Ryan is believed to be away right now."

"Prison?"

"Ireland."

DeNafria reached for a tortilla chip. "As in the country?"

"He's got connections to the IRA. Collins is a rogue. American-born, from Boston originally. Came here a few years back. Did a small stretch on Rikers for assault."

"Where'd you get this?"

"Don't ask and I won't tell."

"Fair enough. What about Ward? Anything?"

"Not really. People aren't anxious to discuss him. That's what my source said, although your new partner was intrinsic in bringing down the old leadership. He had an insider, though, an informant."

"Your source with Internal Affairs?"

"He asked to remain anonymous."

DeNafria nodded.

"What's it about?" Belzinger asked.

"What I mentioned on the phone. The guy doesn't feel right. He's got an agenda of his own. He prepared better than most for the transition, learned all the players and so on, and then he kind of drifted. He's not getting enough sleep, for one thing. He gets into it every chance, too. Went nose to nose with one of Joe Quack's goons. Then he almost slashed some tires. I stopped him."

Belzinger made a face. "He's not getting enough sleep?"

"No, I'm not his mother, I'm just saying. He's always tired, exhausted really. Then he takes off middle of the day, doesn't come back. Or he comes late, like today, and leaves early. Claims something happened to his kid. Now he doesn't want to work nights."

"Doing surveillance? You gotta be kidding."

"No, he made a point of it today. Doesn't want to change his hours."

"Tension in the car?"

"Oh, yeah. And then today I was up early, my power went out, I sat in the car for the air conditioning. I decided to head over early and pick him up, I saw him talking with some guy on the boulevard near his house. Didn't look right. When he finally showed up, he gave me some bullshit story for being tired. Said he was home and couldn't sleep."

"When you saw him meeting someone?"

"I didn't tell him, but, yeah."

Belzinger sipped more of her drink. DeNafria reached for his water.

"Don't get me wrong," he said. "I'm starting to feel sleazy myself doing this, asking after him, watching him. Then again, I don't appreciate the bullshit, or the lack of effort."

"Ask for a transfer."

"Yeah, maybe. It keeps up, I will. I'm not comfortable with the guy."

Belzinger reached across the table to grab his hand. "How about me?"

"What about you?"

"Comfortable?"

DeNafria squeezed her hand.

Belzinger winked and said, "Why don't we make this dinner to go?"

•◆•

BOBBY DIALED THE apartment number while Father Scavo listened to an Average White Band CD through his headphones.

"I have something for you," Bobby told Lin Yao when she answered the call.

"Nice of you to call," she said. Her voice was cold.

"I'm hiding," he said.

"From what?"

Bobby didn't want to get into more than he had to. "I have your ring," he said.

Lin Yao didn't respond.

"Hello?"

"I heard you."

"I'd like to put it back on your finger."

Another pause.

"Honey?"

"You left me here yesterday and didn't call until just now. Except for what Father told me, I don't know what's going on. You tell me you're hiding. You haven't told me from whom or why. And then you say you have my ring, which means you had to get it from that animal. Is that what you're hiding from? Did you just kill him? I know my cousin had him."

"No, I didn't kill anybody. I busted him up a little, that's all."

Bobby saw Father Scavo had removed his headphones.

"Then why are you hiding?" Lin Yao asked.

"Because of your cousin, what he did."

"What did Ricky do?"

"It's not important now."

"What did he do? I went to him earlier. He said he's going to let the guy you beat up go."

"When did you see him?"

"Earlier. Two o'clock, two thirty. I don't remember."

Bobby realized it was before he had met with Zhu in the church. Whatever Zhu had told Lin Yao, it was probably to get rid of her.

"Bobby?"

"Just let it go," he told her.

"Is it my fault, because I told him about that animal?"

Bobby remained silent. The priest was watching him. Bobby shrugged.

"Now you won't even answer me," Lin Yao said. "How long will you be hiding?"

"Just until this is settled."

"Why can't you go to the police?"

"Just another day or two," Bobby said. "I promise."

The line went dead.

He called her right back. This time she didn't answer.

Father Scavo said, "You want me to talk to her?"

"No," Bobby said. "There's no talking to her now. I thought maybe if she knew I got the ring back it might soften her up."

"You keep making promises you can't keep. Even I can hear that in your voice. She's scared. She's afraid for you. She doesn't understand why you won't go to the law. Neither do I for that matter."

"Thanks for the insight."

Scavo ignored the comment. "What are you going to do about the money, Bobby? If you need some, I can get it."

"I have more than enough."

"It isn't worth the risk anymore. Pay them or go the police."

"I'm not paying Agro's bill for Mickey Nolan."

"Then pay that punk in Chinatown."

"Him I'd like to slap."

"Then give it to me and I'll bring it to him. This thing has changed now. Whatever you were hoping to accomplish, it isn't going to happen. Not after what they did to Lin Yao and what you did to that other guy."

Bobby shook his head no.

"You should've heard yourselves in church with those idiots," Scavo said. "It was like listening to a bunch of kids on a playground. Mine is bigger than yours. It was almost funny until that big ape showed the gun he was carrying. Then it became real again. You should go to the police and protect yourself. Protect Lin Yao, too."

"You don't know how much it galls me to pay them a dime now," Bobby said. "That idiot, Agro. And Lin Yao's cousin. I owe him a beating like the one I gave Nolan."

"Yeah, maybe, except it'll only keep this war going you do that. Think, man. How much you still owe, five grand?"

"Fifty-five hundred. It's what I'm willing to pay. They want more."

"So? You pay and it keeps Lin Yao out of it, right?"

"They won't go near her again."

"You don't know that. And even if you think you do, the money you owe isn't worth the risk you're wrong. Pay the fuckin' money or I will."

Bobby's head snapped. "Nice way to talk, Father."

"Don't be a jerk-off," Scavo said. "Come on, we'll go see this punk in Chinatown and pay him off."

Bobby held up both hands. "You've done enough. I'll bring it."

"You think that's smart? There might be people looking for you."

"There will be, probably, yeah."

"Then at least let me walk you. They won't do anything if a priest is walking with you."

Bobby was thinking of a way to get Lin Yao to hear him out.

"Hello?" Scavo said.

"I'll have to stop for the money," Bobby said.

"The apartment?"

"Yeah."

"Isn't that dangerous? In case they're watching, I mean."

Bobby was thinking about how he would get in and out of the apartment without a scene.

"Hey, genius," Scavo said. "Won't it be dangerous going anywhere near the apartment?"

Bobby said, "I'll have a priest with me."

CHAPTER 28

BOBBY AND FATHER Scavo took the short walk together from the church to Baxter Street. The air was thick with humidity. Both men were sweating profusely when they reached the apartment building. They were instantly relieved in the air-conditioned lobby.

Bobby and Lin Yao ignored each other in the apartment until he pulled the stereo receiver out and bagged some of the cash he had stored behind it. Lin Yao set her hands on her hips and asked him what he was doing.

"Paying them off," he told her.

"Since when is that there, the money?"

"A few weeks," he told her.

"Is there anything I do know about you anymore?"

"That I love you," he said. Then he fished the ring out of his pocket and set it on the dining room table on his way out.

Lin Yao said, "I won't put it back on until this is over."

Bobby stopped at the door. "Fair enough," he told her.

"Wait!" she yelled.

Waiting for more, Bobby stood in the doorway.

Lin Yao said, "Be careful."

Bobby smiled.

Out on the street again, Bobby and the priest quickly walked south toward Canal Street. He needed to pay Ricky Zhu to try and save Mickey Nolan. It hadn't been an easy decision to make, but it was the only way to clear his name with Nolan's gang. He would deal with Tommy Agro and the mob afterward. If they still insisted on shakedown money, Bobby would finally go to the law. He would still have close to half a million dollars to start a new life, even if it meant living in the mountains someplace.

He turned east on Hester Street and walked one block to Mulberry before turning south again. He was thinking that the people traffic on Mulberry was thick enough to protect them. Father Scavo, walking along the curb, was trying to provide extra cover. As they passed Luna restaurant, Bobby noticed a man standing on the curb switch his baseball hat from a red to a white one. Bobby instinctively sidestepped the priest and pushed him to the inside. He took a quick glance over his shoulder and saw a car pulling up fast. He heard the first pop before he could react. It felt as if he'd been punched in the left shoulder a moment before he heard the other shots.

Bobby spun counterclockwise before he lost his balance and fell to the ground. He noticed people diving to the sidewalk when he felt a second kick, this one just above his left hip. His head hit the sidewalk hard. He'd turned on his side to try and locate the priest when everything went dark.

•◆•

MICHAEL WARD HAD spent the early afternoon violently screwing Margaret O'Donnell. He had been angry she had fallen for Kenneth Ryan's trick in getting him to the apartment the day before. He took it out on her with raw anal sex.

He fell asleep sometime before two o'clock and woke up again at four. When he saw she was drunk, Ward went to the cabinet where she usually stashed money, removed what was there, then left without saying good-bye.

He thought he'd surprise his family by stopping at a local pizza parlor on his way home. It was grocery day. His wife would appreciate not having to cook after shopping. He ordered one pizza with anchovies, the way he and his wife liked it, and a regular pie for the boys. The counterman was boxing his order when Ward received an emergency call from Jerry Collins.

The detective turned away from the counter before answering his cell phone. "What is it?" he asked with clear disdain.

"Mickey Nolan," Collins said.

"What about him?"

"You said you wanted word when I knew something."

"Yeah, so?"

"He's being delivered in parts back to the neighborhood."

Ward told him to hold on. He paid for the pizza, then carried it out to the car before he spoke again. "What the hell are you talking about?"

"Somebody dropped off a carton of Chinese food at one of the bars with two of Nolan's fingers in the lo mein," Collins said. "This isn't good."

"I thought it was," Ward said. "You lose Nolan, that's half Ryan's strength. Should make your takeover easier."

"If the man was lost, yeah, but he's not. It looks like a kidnapping."

Ward said, "Yeah, so? What's the matter, Ryan still alive?"

"Don't bait me, okay, Michael?" Collins said. "I'll handle Ryan first chance I get. In the meantime, if Nolan was kidnapped and we don't pay to get him back, it makes us look bad."

"Who's behind it?"

"The Chinks took him, for sure, but maybe the other guy, the one beat him in the bar, set him up."

"Which you never bothered to learn about, why the guy beat him, did you? It might answer a lot of your questions if you found that out."

"Might be a robbery," Collins said. "The way it went down in the bar, the bartender said the guy beat on Nolan had a scar on his face. He said the guy made Nolan take a ring out of his pocket. He must've glommed it."

"Yeah, and what's that got to do with Chinks?" Ward asked.

"They knew each other, the Chinks and the guy beat Nolan. That's all I know about that."

"And you're calling me about this, why again?"

"There's no ransom demand," Collins said. "Nothing but the finger."

"Maybe they don't want the money," Ward said. "That should solve your problem."

"Who's gonna believe it? Ryan won't. Even if he does, he'll say he doesn't. It'll look like I didn't give a fuck, let the man get chopped up. Ryan can point fingers if that happens."

Ward added some sarcasm. "This the same Ryan is always dying, huh?"

"Give me a break with Ryan," Collins said. "The man's overseas I can't do anything till he's back."

Ward couldn't suppress a chuckle. "The fuck you want from me?" he said.

"Anything you can do will be much appreciated," Collins said. "Anything you can find out."

"It'll cost."

"Why it'll be much appreciated."

"I'll call you when I know something," Ward said, and then he killed the connection.

He looked at the clock in the dashboard and saw he was already late with dinner. He wondered if his partner knew anything about what was going on. Mickey Nolan had worked for Tommy Agro in the past. DeNafria had been watching the crew Joe Quack took over the past two years. He should know about Mickey Nolan. If he did, he was purposely keeping it to himself.

Then Ward thought about brokering a new deal with Kenneth Ryan.

Ward called his wife and told her something had come up and he couldn't make it for dinner. When she asked about the pizza, he told her to cook macaroni instead.

•◆•

DENAFRIA HADN'T MADE love to another woman since the last time he and Arlene Belzinger had been together. After he apologized profusely for not lasting long enough for her to reach climax, she brought him back to life. Then he surprised himself with two much longer encore performances. At least that's what Belzinger had called them.

When he left her apartment, DeNafria was feeling weak from his efforts. Then he received a follow-up phone call from Deputy Inspector Kaprowski about Tommy Agro's girlfriend with the broken nose. She had agreed to wire her apartment and the feds were asking the police to handle it.

DeNafria called his partner and gave him the good news. Ward yawned through the phone.

"Sorry to bore you," DeNafria told him.

"And the feds gave it to us?" Ward asked.

"Task force is handling it. Feds are still involved, but it's our wire, yeah."

"Anybody know why he broke her nose? Maybe she deserved it."

"He's slapped her around in the past. This time he was too drunk to use an open hand. Who knows?"

"Nice people, you Eye-talians."

"His girlfriend is Jewish."

"My apologies to the Jews."

"They're wiring the house as we speak. They're keeping her in the hospital overnight for appearances. Not that Agro'll stop by with flowers, but I guess to make it look good."

"Phone lines?"

"Soup to nuts," DeNafria said. "She wants him for this one. She's a brave lady."

"Or a stupid one. We really think he talks to her about what he does?"

"My guess is he makes calls from her place. Maybe he shoots off his mouth when he's drunk. It has good potential."

"Assuming he goes back there. Maybe he doesn't."

"He's been with her on and off more than five years. She's still a looker. She must be doing something right."

"Except for getting her nose broken."

DeNafria didn't get why his partner was being so cynical. He asked him. "What's with the negativity? Worst that can happen, the wire doesn't work."

"I guess," Ward said. "Tell you the truth, I was just on my way home with a pizza. Then I intend to get some sleep."

DeNafria remembered his partner's lie from the night before. "Right," he said.

"There a problem with that?" Ward asked with a measure of attitude.

"Only if you don't sleep."

"The fuck is that supposed to mean?"

"Nothing," DeNafria said. "Have a good night."

As soon as the connection was dead, he added, "And then go fuck yourself."

CHAPTER 29

MICHAEL WARD HAD been waiting more than two hours for Tommy Agro before the wiseguy was dropped off in front of his house. He was drenched in sweat as he stood watch from behind an oak tree until the car pulled away. When Agro spotted movement near the end of his driveway, he immediately reached for the stiletto he carried in his pocket.

Ward saw the blade and identified himself. "Easy does it," he said. "I'm a cop."

Agro took slow steps until he recognized Ward. He didn't put the knife away.

"I come bearing a gift," Ward said. "You can put the knife away now."

Agro did so slowly. "You can get yourself killed sneaking up on people."

"I apologize."

"Come to think of it, you're on my property. I'll assume you got a warrant."

Ward smiled and said, "I'm without papers. A WOP, just like you."

"You're a jerk-off is what you are."

Ward said, "Bad joke. Sorry."

"What do you want?" Agro said. "It's been a long day."

"What I said earlier. I come bearing a gift. There's a catch, though. I'll want a gift in return."

Agro gave a quick look around the area.

"I'm alone," Ward said. "This is definitely off the record."

Agro motioned at Ward to start down the driveway. He said, "You're gonna blow me, it shouldn't be out in the open like this."

When they were in the yard, Agro sat on one side of a picnic table. Ward sat across from him. Both men lit cigarettes.

"I'm listening," Agro said.

Ward said, "I need to know why some guy beat the piss out of Mickey Nolan and why some Chinks grabbed him off the street afterward."

Agro said, "Yeah, and?"

"I'm telling you what I need to know," Ward said. "I already know what you need to know."

Agro took a long drag on his cigarette. "We can go inside the house make sure you're not wearing a wire," he said. "Or you can tell me what you think I need to know and I'll decide whether it's something I need to know or not. Problem is the way you acted the other day, shooting your mouth off every chance you got, insulting people because you're wearing a badge, you can get away with it."

"Or insulting them so my partner thinks I'm gung ho."

Agro said, "It's still your move."

"You got a little overexcited the other night, or maybe she bit down on your cock with her teeth, but the woman lives over the old Fort Hamilton House went to the law."

Agro's face tightened. "She did, huh?"

"You broke her nose, Tommy."

"That what she's saying, the lying bitch. Actually, she hit her face on a kitchen cabinet."

"Whatever. Point is, she was upset and flipped."

"So how come I'm not arrested on this alleged charge?"

"Think about it," Ward said. "She didn't because they scared her into doing something worse. Something better for their cause."

"I'm not good at this game," Agro said. "You'll have to be more specific."

"First you tell me what I need to know, at least some of it."

Agro took another long drag on his cigarette. "Mickey Nolan? I heard, it's the same guy, I don't know it is, was picked up by some Chinks. Something to do with a broad, what he did to her. I don't know the guy beat Nolan, although I did hear about it."

"Guy had a scar, right?" Ward asked.

Agro shook his head. "That I didn't hear. Just some guy beat Nolan up and then the Chinks took him."

"How come there's no ransom?"

Agro shrugged. "Maybe they don't want one."

"You don't seem too upset. The guy used to do work for you."

"I'm not sure we're talking about the same guy," Agro said. "But that was business anyway, his relationship with me. Nothing dirty about it."

Ward smirked. "There a way Nolan will be released?"

"How would I know that? You're the one said there's no ransom."

Ward said, "There's an interested party wants to know."

Agro smiled. "Wants or needs?"

"There a difference?"

"What else was it you wanted to tell me?" Agro said. "What you were saying earlier, before you got sidetracked with what you need to know."

Ward nodded. "The woman with the broken nose, she—"

"Alleged broken nose," Agro said.

"No, it was broken all right. It's alleged how it got broken."

"Whatever," Agro said.

"She's letting us wire her apartment. You can find that easy enough, although my best advice with something like this is to send her some flowers and never see her again. It'll be twice as frustrating. The thing not to do is go off half-baked and whack her."

"I wouldn't think of it," Agro said. "What for, I've nothing to hide. And I can't imagine why anyone would want to hear tapes of her blowing me. All I do, I can remember right, is grunt a lot."

"There you go," Ward said. "Now, about Nolan, he going to disappear a piece at a time or all at once?"

Agro smirked. Ward knew the wiseguy was aware of the missing fingers.

Agro said, "We talking a long-term arrangement, me and you? Aside from your rudeness the other day, you might not be so bad."

"I don't know how long it'll be, I hope to go out on disability sooner or later, I've a bad back, but there's no reason it can't work both ways."

Agro nodded. "You need him released? Just curious?"

"I can see an upside to it, yeah," Ward said.

"Even if it does cost?"

"Within reason."

"Then I'll do my best."

Both men stood up. Neither offered the other a hand.

Ward said, "It's all a man can do, his best."

•◆•

WHEN FATHER JOHN Scavo saw the blood stains, he had thought Bobby was dying. He had just begun to issue last rites when his friend spoke.

"The hell are you doing?" Bobby had said.

"I, uh . . ."

"I'm not dead."

The priest was instantly relieved. "Where are you hit?"

"Left shoulder and hip, I think."

Scavo had leaned over and tried to examine the wounds without touching them.

"You're bleeding pretty bad."

"Because I was shot."

"Still a sarcastic bastard, though."

"My head hurts."

It was the last thing Bobby had said before he closed his eyes again. A few minutes later Scavo was riding alongside Bobby in the back of the ambulance to NYU Downtown Hospital. He had hung around the emergency room and made sure it wasn't serious before heading back to find Lin Yao.

Her first reaction had been shock followed by a bloodcurdling scream that shook the priest. Afterward she sobbed uncontrollably until she was exhausted.

When Scavo brought her to the hospital, she was assured by two different surgeons that Bobby would be okay. She asked to see him, but the doctors had insisted he would be unconscious for at least another few hours. Lin Yao was told that Bobby would be able to return home the next day.

Afterward Scavo explained what had happened and why they were headed over to see her cousin at the restaurant on Bayard Street. Lin Yao asked the priest if he still had the money.

Scavo had been carrying the small gym bag with him. He showed it to her. "I took it, yes. I have it here."

"I'll take it to my cousin."

The priest frowned.

"I'll take it," she repeated.

"Are you sure?"

"I'll take it."

"I'll go with you."

"No."

"Please, or I'll never hear the end of it."

"Please, no," Lin Yao said. "My cousin will think it's a trap if he sees you. I'll be okay. Ricky won't let anything happen to me."

Scavo said, "I really shouldn't let you go by yourself."

Lin Yao waited. The priest reluctantly handed her the bag.

CHAPTER 30

RICKY ZHU HAD become the leader of the Mott Street Shadows shortly after his thirtieth birthday. Two weeks ago he had turned thirty-two. He had served five years for a manslaughter charge when he was in his early twenties. He had committed another two murders he was never charged with in his rise to leader of the Shadows.

He had been embarrassed when his cousin started seeing the Italian a few years ago. When he heard Lin Yao had let Bobby Gennaro move in with her, it became a full-blown scandal.

Ricky was forced to confront his cousin about her living situation, but Lin Yao refused to listen to him. In the end, after a fifteen-minute yelling match and then staring each other down another few minutes, Ricky called Lin Yao crazy and walked out of the apartment. It had been one way to save face.

Today his gang had blown a chance to get rid of the Italian. Ricky was sure the Irish would be blamed for the ambush he'd arranged, but there could be no second attempt now that Bobby Gennaro had survived. Ricky would have to cover his tracks.

He did his best to act surprised when word came back about the shooting across Canal Street in Little Italy. He had hoped it would look as though the Irish had attacked Bobby Gennaro. As a staged response, he ordered the death of Mickey Nolan, then quickly rescinded the order when Tommy Agro called.

The wiseguy didn't know about the shooting in Little Italy but was suddenly anxious to vouch for the money to save the Irishman.

"Where the fuck is it?" Ricky said.

"It's coming," Agro told him. "If Gennaro doesn't bring it himself, I'll get it to you. Just don't do anything else to the Irishman or you'll have two wars on your hand."

Ricky said, "Don't threaten me."

It was then Agro lost it. "Hey, asshole, I've had about enough from you, okay?" he said. "The next Chink I talk to will be on the commission there where you roaches live. You don't want that, trust me. You're just another punk paying up, my friend. They'll squash you like a bug."

"Just get the money," Ricky said, and then he hung up.

Agro's threat to go to the Tong leadership unnerved Ricky, but he needed to hide his emotions from his gang. He ordered two shots of Du Kang for the sake of show. If Agro did go to the leaders of the Tong, it would be a problem. Killing the Irishman now didn't seem worth it.

When his cousin called and said she was bringing the money, Ricky was somewhat relieved. He called Tommy Agro and told him the Irishman would be released later tonight.

The wiseguy was insulting. "Figured out you're not king of the hill, huh?" he had said.

Ricky hung up on him. Then he drank another two shots of Du Kang before his cousin arrived.

•◆•

SHE'D BEEN ON the brink of happiness and tragedy so many times over the past few days, Lin Yao felt as if she were having a nervous breakdown.

By the time she found her cousin, she could tell he'd already heard what had happened. Five of his gang stood in front of the restaurant. A few more sat at a table inside.

Lin Yao had come with a game plan of her own. She talked with her cousin in private at his table. Ricky ordered a pot of fresh tea. The cousins spoke in their native Cantonese.

"I brought you the money for the Irishman," Lin Yao told him. "It's from Bobby."

"I shouldn't take it," Ricky said. "Not after what happened. Use it for his medical bills."

Lin Yao glared at her cousin. "What, you trying to make believe you're sorry now? Bobby was shot because of you, Ricky, and don't think the people who shot him won't know why if anything else happens to him. I'll be the one who tells them. Me."

Ricky looked away from her.

"Look at me!" she yelled.

He faced her again.

"You take the money and you give back the Irishman to his people and you let me come with you when you do it," Lin Yao said.

Ricky's face contorted. "What?"

"You give them the Irishman and I want to be there to make sure it happens. If anything else happens, I'll go to the police myself."

Ricky waved her off. "You're crazy."

"Or I'll go now," Lin Yao said. "I'll go to the police right now and tell them everything that happened. I have nothing to lose anymore, Ricky. Between the Italian Mafia, you and your gangsters, and now the Irish, what difference does it make? Bobby's already been shot. What else can happen?"

Ricky looked at the ceiling. "You're talking crazy," he said.

"They came after Bobby because of what you did to that animal. I could care less if you killed that piece of shit, but now they think it was Bobby that set it up."

"Yeah, and your white boy should've killed the Irishman when he had the chance."

"He might've, but then he'd be in jail, wouldn't he?"

"No disgrace if he saved your honor."

"I wasn't raped. I wasn't dishonored."

Ricky returned to speaking English. "Bullshit. Why you still with him anyway, fucking white boy?"

"Because I love him," said Lin Yao, also in English.

Ricky looked away again. This time she waited for his attention.

"Because I love him," she repeated.

She slid the money across the table.

"That's what you wanted," she said in Cantonese. "Now you have it."

"Whose money is it? I won't take yours."

"It's Bobby's money. He's in the hospital or he'd bring it himself."

Ricky smirked. "And what if the Irishman is already dead?"

Lin Yao didn't flinch. "Then you started a war," she said in English. "I hope you're prepared for it."

Ricky smirked again before taking the envelope. "I release him tonight," he said, also in English.

"Where?"

"Don't worry where. I release him."

"To who?"

"His people."

"I want to be there."

"What you talking about? You can't."

"I want proof the Irishman was released," she said. "I want to see it."

"I tell you I release him, I'll do it. That's your proof."

Lin Yao stared at her cousin.

"You're crazy," he told her. "I take care of it."

Lin Yao said, "I swear it, Ricky, if anything else happens, if you kill the Irishman, if you already killed him, I'll go to the police. You might as well kill me, too."

"I give back Irishman," Zhu said. "How many times you want me to say it?"

Lin Yao stared hard at her cousin. "I'm trusting you on this, Ricky. Don't lie to me."

"I tell you I do something, I do it."

Ricky downed another shot of Du Kang.

Lin Yao said, "I want this to end. I need this to end."

Ricky took a long drag on his cigarette. Lin Yao continued to stare at him through the smoke.

•◆•

"WAS SHE WEARING the ring?" Bobby wanted to know.

Scavo shrugged. "I didn't notice. She did bring the money to her cousin for you."

"I can't believe you let her do that."

"She said her cousin wouldn't take it if I went with her."

"Please."

"It's what she said."

He was waiting for the last set of X-rays. He'd been hit by two shots, one in the left shoulder and one in the hip. Neither had hit bone, but both were painful. They had hooked him up to a morphine drip to ease the pain.

"It made sense at the time," Scavo continued. "After hearing you and those gangster assholes in the church last night, almost anything makes sense."

"I didn't want her involved."

"Which is why it's time you talk to the police," Scavo said. "Before one or the two of you are dead from this bullshit."

"I'm not going to the law until I know what happened."

"What happened was you got shot, you dumb ass."

"I mean who did it."

"The Irish, obviously. Wasn't Agro's people, not in Little Italy. What's the difference anyway who's responsible? Jesus Christ, you're thick."

Bobby closed his eyes and tried to remember what had happened. He could see the guy switching hats, red to white, and then he remembered how the move had alerted him.

"They were waiting for me," he told Scavo. "The shooters were already in place."

"Obviously."

"They must've seen me going up to the apartment."

"And they waited until we came back down."

"Except I didn't notice anybody. You?"

"No, but I wouldn't know what to look for."

"And they could've shot you just as easy."

"I don't think they cared."

"It's a bold move," Bobby said, "and a stupid one."

"I didn't think we were dealing with a great deal of intelligence," Scavo said. "Present company included."

"The Irish wouldn't shoot a priest."

"Excuse me."

"It was Ricky," Bobby said, "her cousin. The punk hates me enough."

"You think it was Lin Yao's cousin?"

"Yeah, I do. It wasn't Agro. Like you said, not in Little Italy."

"What about Lin Yao? Is she in danger?"

"No, he's not that stupid, but I don't like the idea of paying the prick shot at me. Would you?"

"No, I don't think I would, which is all the more reason to go to the law and crawl out from this mess already."

"That'd be too easy," Bobby said.

"And smart. For you, I mean."

Bobby said, "It was the hats. They sell them all over the place. The white and the red."

"Excuse me?"

"Help me get out of here."

"Sorry, no, I won't."

Bobby strained to sit up, but the pain from the stitches around his hip stopped him.

The priest said, "You're not going anywhere."

Bobby said, "Wanna bet?"

CHAPTER 31

DETECTIVE MICHAEL WARD sat with Jerry Collins in a stolen Mercury parked one block off the West Side Highway. Collins was waiting for a call from the Mott Street Shadows. Ward was there as backup. His car was parked half a block away.

"You got a place to dump the car?" Ward asked.

"I'll leave it outside the bar on Eleventh Avenue until he's ripe enough somebody notices."

"You got a negotiator?"

"Once Ryan's gone I won't need one."

"And until Ryan's gone? You're gonna need one with the dagos after this stunt."

Collins shook his head. "We didn't shoot that guy today," he said. "That was the dagos or the Chinks."

Ward chuckled to himself. He had already assumed he'd have to kill Collins before he could retire free from loose ends. If the Italians or Chinese did the job, it was just as good. He was thinking he could expedite the matter with a simple phone call to Tommy Agro or maybe Kenneth Ryan once Nolan was dead.

He turned to Collins and said, "You better get this guy now. He shouldn't make it back to one of the West Side bars on his own. In the meantime"—he stopped to look at his watch—"I'm here in the city and I need to be home before sunrise."

"You a vampire, Mikey?"

"Fuck you, asshole."

"It's not like I don't appreciate it," Collins pleaded. "There's still ten grand in this."

"Should be twenty."

"I don't have twenty."

"Doesn't mean it shouldn't be. You got me another fifty-five minutes, boyo, and then I'm out of here and good luck. It isn't the worst thing in the world, Nolan makes it home. He'll be on a rampage soon enough anyway, they chopped his fingers off. He survives tonight, you can still get rid of him a few days from now and blame the Chinks."

"Except this way I don't have to worry he isn't pissed off we didn't come to his rescue fast enough," Collins said. "Which is exactly what Ryan'll say once he's back, and he'll have an audience, eh? Doesn't look good we let the man lose parts of a hand."

"Yeah, well, that isn't my problem right now," Ward said. "I got a regular job I gotta make believe I'm doing. This is all fun and games, but it's also on my sleep time and I'm losing a lot more than I'm getting. Enough so people're noticing. This don't go down in fifty minutes, I'm out of here. Like I said, good luck."

Collins lit up a fresh cigarette. Ward nudged him with an elbow for one. Collins passed him the pack.

Both men sat smoking in silence until Collins's phone rang. He answered it on the second ring.

"Yeah?"

Ward watched Collins talking on the phone. The conversation was brief. Collins turned to Ward when he was finished.

"Well?" Ward asked.

"Goes down at two fifteen."

"Where?"

"South of the Chelsea Piers."

Ward glanced at his watch. "Cuts it kind of close, no?"

"What do you want from me, Michael?"

"Fifteen," Ward said. "You can owe me the five."

Collins let out a lungful of smoke. "All right, man, okay," he said. "Fifteen. Done and done."

"Pleasure doing business with you," said Ward. "You can drop me at my car when you're ready to go."

"Anything else?" asked Collins, full of sarcasm.

Ward had already rested his head against the window and closed his eyes for a quick nap.

•◆•

"YOU'RE TAKING ME to a Howard Johnson's?" Lin Yao had asked the first time they spent a night together.

"I figure you have just enough booze in you so you won't have time to change your mind," Bobby had told her.

They had met at a deposition Lin Yao had shot for an insurance company lawyer a few weeks earlier. Bobby's best friend and roommate had been hit by a corporate limousine and had sued for damages. Bobby was there pushing his friend's wheelchair. The chemistry between them had been immediate. Bobby asked Lin Yao to have dinner with him later the same day. They hit it off and began dating the next week.

Two months later Bobby's friend was diagnosed with cancer. He died within six months. It was after the funeral when Bobby moved in with her.

Now she tried her best not to think about what a mess their life had become the last few days. She had decided to protect Bobby the only way she knew how. She would film the exchange between her cousin's gang and the Irish. Whatever happened, she would have it on film.

She had brought a bare minimum of equipment. Zooming in from three hundred yards would be good enough, she thought, although it was best if she could get closer. She had rented a black Ford Taurus and had followed her cousin's van when it left the garage on Broome Street.

Once they were on the move, Lin Yao smoked her first cigarette in five years.

She was trailing the van by a good distance. She followed it west on Canal and slowed down when it pulled to the curb after it passed the Holland Tunnel entrance.

Lin Yao saw her cousin was wearing a red baseball cap when he stepped out of the van with two others from his gang to urinate alongside a construction site. She pulled to the curb and turned off her lights until the van was on the move again. She sped up to make a light just before she turned north onto the West Side Highway.

She followed the van onto Tenth Avenue at the Chelsea Piers and then panicked when she saw her cousin get out of one van and into another. The first van turned back toward the West Side Highway. Lin Yao decided to follow it instead of waiting to see where her cousin went. She was hoping that Mickey Nolan was in the first van.

A few minutes later she watched through the lens of her video camera from a Chelsea Piers parking lot as a body fell out of the van she had followed. The body was tied at the wrists and ankles. It rolled onto the sidewalk along the West Side Highway as the van picked up speed and took off. Lin Yao kept her focus on the body and was relieved when she saw it was alive as it struggled to stand.

When she zoomed in on the face, she noticed the head was covered with a hood. Suddenly, a car made a screeching U-turn from the other side of the highway. It pulled up alongside the body standing near the curb. Lin Yao swung the camera just enough to get both the car and the man with the hood in the frame.

As she filmed, the hooded body jolted back a few steps before it fell to the ground. Lin Yao's heart was racing as she tried to steady the camera. The rear trunk hood had opened. The driver was out and heading around the front end of the car. He stood over the body and pointed a gun with an extension Lin Yao recognized as a silencer. He leaned down a few inches and his hand appeared to recoil two times. She was focused on the shooter now and could see him stashing his weapon a moment before he began dragging the body to the rear of the car.

Lin Yao filmed the driver as he struggled to get the body inside the trunk. She was shaking when he finally managed the task and slammed the trunk closed. She tried to focus on the license plate as the car took off and headed south. She wondered if her cousin had seen what had happened or if he had set it up himself.

Then she wondered if Ricky had lied to her about Mickey Nolan. If he had, she would take the film to the police in the morning herself. She had just set the camera on the floor in front of the passenger seat when a flashing light appeared in her rearview mirror.

•◆•

WHEN WARD SPOTTED movement inside the Ford Taurus in the outdoor lot, he thought it was a backup team of kidnappers.

When he realized it was a woman in the car, he waited until Collins had pulled away before cutting across the West Side Highway into the open parking lot. He slapped the portable light on the roof and turned it on.

Ward wiped sweat from his forehead before he pulled the Glock from his shoulder holster. He quickly surveyed the area from inside the car before getting out. He approached the driver with the gun pointed down.

"License and registration," he said when the driver's side window went down.

The woman leaned across the console. Ward quickly raised the Glock to cover her.

"Hands on the wheel," he yelled.

The woman turned to him. He immediately recognized her. He saw that she recognized him as well. He looked from her face to the floor on the passenger side and saw a camera.

"Get out," he told her. "Now!"

The woman was scared, but she didn't move. Ward pulled the door open. "Out," he said. "Let's go."

He was about to reach in and pull her out when he heard a shotgun being pumped. He turned toward the sound and saw two Chinese men holding shotguns on him. A bright light blinded him as a van pulled in behind the gunmen.

Ward couldn't see anything. Between the bright light and sweat, his eyes burned. He turned his face away from the light.

"Put gun on roof," somebody said.

"I'm a cop," Ward said.

"We blow your fuckin' head off," the voice said. "Put the gun on car."

Ward swallowed hard before setting the Glock down on the roof of the Taurus.

As his eyes adjusted to the light, Ward saw that a third Chinese man had appeared between the two holding the shotguns. He was a skinny man wearing a white baseball hat. He went to the Taurus and said something to the woman in Chinese. They argued in their native tongue a few seconds before the man waved at the woman and she climbed over the console into the passenger seat.

Then the man wearing the hat took the Glock from the roof of the car and sat behind the wheel. He said something to the men holding the shotguns before backing the Taurus out of the spot to make a U-turn out of the parking lot.

Ward stood watching as the Taurus headed south on the West Side Highway. Then one of the men with the shotguns went to Ward's car and pulled the keys out of the ignition. He tossed them into the darkness.

Ward was sure they wouldn't kill him now. He watched as one of the men held a shotgun on him while the other stepped inside the van. He was thinking he might be able to get to his own shotgun in the trunk of the car when he heard a blast. He hit the asphalt to cover up.

When he looked up again, the van was racing out of the parking lot. Ward crawled to his knees as the van turned south. He glanced at his watch, wiped more sweat from his face, and began the search for his keys.

CHAPTER 32

DeNafria had left for work early again, but today it was on purpose. He had decided to watch his partner again this morning. It was during the ride to his partner's house that he learned about the shooting in Little Italy the night before.

He turned down the radio and called in to check with someone from the organized crime unit. Five minutes later, he had learned little more than what the radio had told him.

Bobby Gennaro, a resident of Little Italy with a police record and alleged ties to the Vignieri crime family, was wounded in a drive-by shooting as he walked along Mulberry Street, just one day before the start of the San Gennaro festival. He is said to have been with a priest at the time.

When DeNafria arrived on the corner of his partner's block and saw that one of Ward's cars was missing, he noted the time on a piece of newspaper. Fifteen minutes later he saw Ward pull into his driveway from the opposite end of the street. DeNafria could tell his partner was agitated as he slammed a car door before grabbing something from the backseat. It appeared to be a bag.

Ward went inside the house but was out again a few minutes later and heading straight for his garage.

DeNafria sat and waited. He was determined to learn what the hell Michael Ward was doing in the middle of the night instead of sleeping. After ten more minutes with no sign of his partner DeNafria called Ward's cell phone number and learned his partner was taking another day off.

"What do you mean you're not coming in?" he asked. "Bobby Gennaro was shot last night. And Joe Quack is MIA."

"I'm not coming in," Ward repeated. "What's the big deal? Gennaro was shot, he's not going anywhere. I'm sick. I'm exhausted is what I am. I haven't slept right in months now and today I collapsed when I tried to get out of bed. You said so yourself, I look tired all the time. Well, today it caught up to me. I'm not coming in."

DeNafria was so frustrated he couldn't speak. He was tempted to ask Ward when he had collapsed getting out of bed, before he was out for the night or after he had come back home for a few minutes?

Or was it just now, inside the garage, when he collapsed?

"Right," DeNafria said instead. "Feel better."

It was then he called the deputy inspector and requested an emergency meeting.

Twenty minutes later he watched Michael Ward leave the house in what appeared to be a big rush. DeNafria would have followed his partner if he hadn't already requested a meeting with Kaprowski.

Instead, he drove back to Queens to a diner on Cross Bay Boulevard.

Kaprowski was waiting for him in a booth near the kitchen. The deputy inspector made DeNafria wait until he finished eating the top half of his purposely burned corn muffin. After he wiped his mouth, Kaprowski pointed to his wristwatch.

"Okay, John, now we're on the clock. The fuck is so important it couldn't wait?"

DeNafria explained the situation. Kaprowski frowned the entire time.

"And he took off, you're saying?"

"Like a bat out of hell," DeNafria said.

"And you didn't follow him because?"

"I already called you. Think about it."

Kaprowski made a face.

"Something isn't right," DeNafria said. "And this is already more than I'm comfortable doing."

Kaprowski pushed his empty cup of coffee toward the edge of the table for the waitress to notice.

"You know he had problems in the past, right?"

"We discussed it. I had similar issues. I understood how it can happen to a good cop. I didn't hold it against him."

"This makes my new day more fucked than my last one if he turns out to be dirty."

The waitress stopped by to refill both coffee cups.

Kaprowski said, "Any idea who he might be working with, he is dirty?"

DeNafria sipped his coffee. "I don't even wanna think about it, except he doesn't seem to have any love for wiseguys, he gets into it pretty quick with them."

"What about Joe Quack? Any word on where's he gone yet?"

DeNafria shook his head. "Either he had a deal with the feds and they scooped him up or somebody thought he did and made him disappear. We don't know, but Tommy Agro was getting a lot of attention about the same time Quack disappeared."

"There a chance Ward knows something?"

"I don't see how," DeNafria said. "I mean, I don't think so. Like I said, he doesn't seem to get along with wiseguys."

"Quack's nephew's fiancée is missing, too," Kaprowski said. "The kid called it in himself. Forzino his name is."

"The big kid. We already met."

"There weren't a couple detectives nailed for servicing the mob last year, all the help they provided over their illustrious careers, one of them went and wrote a book about it, I'd think it's a fantasy that Ward is involved. But there they were, living large out west."

"That goes back to the mob's fat days," DeNafria said. "They don't have that kind of juice anymore."

Kaprowski chuckled. "They don't, huh?"

"We have the time it'll take to get Internal Affairs involved?" DeNafria asked.

"No. Not without raising a bigger mess than we already have. And I don't know the special agent in charge has put somebody on Ward or not yet. He didn't tell me and I don't expect he will. About the only thing going for Ward right now is a shortage of manpower. Between terrorists and the Russian mob, there's a good chance Ward won't be watched anytime soon."

DeNafria said, "Well, technically, all we know is that he's out moonlighting or something."

Kaprowski said, "And that he lies to his partner about it."

"Maybe he's got a girlfriend."

"Then he'd be bragging."

"I'm just saying."

"Yeah, I know. And I'm the one's gotta deal with it."

Kaprowski finished off the rest of his muffin and wiped his hands with the napkin.

"I suppose I should bring it to Internal Affairs for now," he said, "but then I'll have to let the SAC know as well. Or I could just let him decide what to do next."

"The feds don't have their own IA?"

"Yeah, I suppose, but it's his task force, too, so why should I burden myself with this shit so early in my day?"

"Okay. And I do what in the meantime?"

"Watch your back," Kaprowski said. "Definitely watch your back."

•◆•

MICHAEL WARD HAD gone straight home from the city after the Chinese gangbangers took his gun away and left him standing in a Chelsea Piers parking lot. It had taken Ward more than twenty minutes to find his car keys.

He had hid the ten grand Collins paid him for the night's work in a fireproof strong box he kept behind a workbench in his garage. There was more cash in a few safe-deposit boxes spread around the city, but tonight's score was to be his last before he faked a back injury and tried to collect permanent disability.

It had been a good plan until Bobby Gennaro's Chink girlfriend had showed up and ruined everything. Knowing she had a camera and had probably filmed what had happened to Mickey Nolan, Ward didn't have many options about what to do next.

When he remembered what Collins had told him about the guy who had beaten Nolan the day the Chinks kidnapped him, he realized there was even more work to do.

"The guy beat on Nolan had a scar on his face," Collins had said.

Bobby Gennaro was the guy with the scar. The woman in the car at the Chelsea Piers was the retired bookmaker's girlfriend.

Ward knew he would have to kill Jerry Collins, and Bobby Gennaro and his girlfriend, as soon as possible. He might have natural cover whacking Gennaro and his girlfriend because of all that had gone down the night before. Nobody would think much of a former bookmaker with ties to a wiseguy who had turned rat getting whacked along with his girlfriend, especially after a first attempt to kill him in Little Italy had failed.

The key would be catching the couple together, preferably alone.

First, though, he needed to get rid of Jerry Collins. With Kenneth Ryan back from Ireland, it would seem like business as usual on the West Side. A guy looking to take over had miscalculated and got himself killed. There would be little tying him to Collins afterward. He could make sure by calling Tommy Agro and filling him in on what had gone down, minus a few details.

Ward was thinking he might even be able to play both sides of the coin and seek a bonus from Ryan for getting rid of his rival.

An anonymous call to his former precinct on the West Side would create a convenient diversion as well. Between the police having to deal with the bodies in Hell's Kitchen and the start of the San Gennaro feast downtown, it would be much easier to get to Gennaro and his girlfriend.

Ward drove over the Throgs Neck Bridge into the Bronx, then took the Bruckner Expressway to backtrack into Manhattan over the Third Avenue Bridge. He drove cross-town on 110th Street and parked on Fifty-fifth Street off Tenth Avenue.

He walked south to where Jerry Collins lived on Ninth Avenue off Forty-seventh Street. It was early enough in the morning for him to gain entrance to the building by waiting for someone to come out. He did so when an elderly woman struggled with the door.

Collins lived on the third floor of the walkup. Ward pulled down the baseball cap he was wearing and took the stairs two at a time. At the third-floor landing, he turned right and walked the short hallway to apartment 3B. He glanced once over his left shoulder before using a pick to unlock the apartment door.

As soon as he was inside, Ward could hear Collins snoring in the bedroom. Ward had already racked the slide on his throwaway piece, a Walther PPK. Now he attached the silencer and carefully sidestepped his way across the kitchen into the living room.

When he peeked around the corner, he frowned at the sight of a young blonde woman sleeping alongside Jerry Collins.

"Shit," he mouthed.

He decided to take out the woman first. He fired one shot into the middle of her chest. Collins woke when her body jerked from the impact. Ward leaned over and shot Collins in the head two times. When the woman started choking on her blood, Ward shot her in the forehead.

Then he went through her purse and Collins's wallet for whatever cash the dead couple had.

CHAPTER 33

"WHAT'S GRANDPA?" THE little boy asked.

"The one standing near the fireplace," Bobby said. "Anthony his name is. His friends call him Tony."

"What do I call him?"

"Grandpa Gennaro."

Bobby watched his father embrace the little boy in his dream. He saw his dad pointing to the picture of Tallulah Bankhead and then telling the boy about the Algonquin Hotel and all the celebrities that used to congregate there.

The dream moved outside the hotel to the street where Bobby could see Lin Yao leaning over to talk to the boy. Bobby tried to get close, but the San Gennaro feast crowd blocked his way. He felt anxious when he couldn't see the boy's face and pushed through the crowd, but the boy was gone.

He saw Lin Yao in the back of a taxi that had just pulled away.

Then he was upstairs in the apartment, he was looking down at the street. Ricky Zhu was smoking a cigarette on the stoop. Bobby's father stood behind him holding a strap as if he were riding the subway.

Anthony Gennaro was reading a newspaper. He stopped to point to his son's cheek and said, "How'd you get that?"

Bobby touched his scar. It was bleeding. "Prison," he said.

"What you do to wind up there?"

"I beat up a pimp."

Bobby turned away from his father and continued watching the street below.

"Tell the boy to be careful who his friends are," Anthony Gennaro said. "Those guys aren't as cool as he thinks."

Bobby could see the boy again. He was sitting on the stoop next to Ricky Zhu. He was playing with a plastic pail and shovel, the kind Bobby had used on the beach when he was a kid.

"There's nothing special about that life," Anthony Gennaro added. "Whatever they touch turns to shit."

Ricky Zhu handed the boy a cigarette. Bobby yelled down through the window. The music from the feast was too loud. The boy didn't hear him.

"All that money you stole," Anthony Gennaro asked his son, "what good is it now?"

"I don't care about the money," Bobby yelled.

He was frantically trying to get the boy's attention. The kid couldn't hear him.

"Watch your son," his father said. "You can lose him to those morons before you know it."

Bobby turned to his father, but Anthony Gennaro was looking down at his newspaper.

Bobby saw himself running down the stairs out into the lobby and then down the stoop to the street. When he finally saw the boy again, Ricky Zhu was walking him across Canal Street into Chinatown.

Bobby couldn't take the discomfort. He woke up. He wiped his forehead with the back of his wrist a few times before looking at his watch. He couldn't see at first. He realized he was squinting from the sunlight reflecting off the television screen. He had managed to sleep through the night. It was after eight o'clock in the morning.

He realized he was alone and began to panic. He called out for Lin Yao, but she wasn't there.

•◆•

FORZINO'S FIRST NIGHT at home alone had involved calling Sally's parents and telling them about her disappearance. He had purposely called late, in the hope that the answering machine would pick up, but it was Sally's mother who answered. They spoke for five minutes before he told her he had another call and lied about it maybe being the police. Mrs. Loomis didn't seem too concerned that Sally was missing, although she did ask Forzino to call them as soon as he heard anything.

Twenty minutes later the father had called back and wanted the details. Forzino hadn't given it much thought. He told Sally's father that he was going back and forth with the police, and then realized the guy might be taping him. Forzino told Mr. Loomis he would call back in the morning.

He could tell that the old man wouldn't let it go. He would have to ask Tommy Agro how to handle him. He called the police to report his fiancée missing and told them she'd been missing since this morning instead of telling the truth. He was told she had to be missing twenty-four hours before they would look into it. He told them he'd come down the next day if he didn't hear anything.

As soon as he had hung up, Forzino thought of a way to stall both the family and the police. He would claim Sally had called him in the morning and was having second thoughts about their relationship. He would say she was in Florida.

Forzino had poured himself a scotch before he finally fell asleep. The long day had ended on a good note. It would get better come the morning.

He woke up to 1010 WINS when his alarm clock went off at seven forty-five in the morning. The first news story he heard had something to do with Little Italy. Forzino used the remote to turn on the television before he turned the radio off.

ABC news was describing the shooting as "the Little Italy drive-by." When Forzino heard it was Bobby Gennaro that had been shot, he wondered who had ordered it.

Then, cursing under his breath as he flipped through channels, he searched for more information. Gennaro had been an irritation in the back of Forzino's mind since the day they had first met. For one thing, he couldn't forget how the retired bookmaker had caught him off guard and then cut off his breathing in the tiny elevator. It had become an embarrassment frozen in time.

The other issue concerned comments Gennaro had made about his bench-pressing. It had been an obvious insult when Gennaro asked whether or not he lifted with a pause. It had been a question asked for the sake of making him look stupid in front of Tommy Agro. Luckily, the wiseguy didn't understand what Gennaro was talking about and had defended his protégé.

The problem was Forzino did understand, and the remark continued to annoy him.

Today he was supposed to pick up Agro at eleven. He glanced at the clock and saw he still had a few hours to work out and vent some frustration.

He ate a quick protein breakfast shake before heading to the gym. When he was ready to test himself, Forzino had one of the personal trainers there spot him on the bench. He did a few sets of warmups, jumping from 225 to 275 to 350 to 400 before he felt ready to try for a maximum lift. He had purposely avoided doing repetitions to conserve his strength for an attempt at the 500-pound bench press, this time with a pause.

He focused on the bar as he lay underneath it. He remembered what the bookmaker had said and felt his adrenaline start to surge.

"He bounced it, it's more like four-fifty, maybe less," Gennaro had said.

Forzino blocked the thought out of his mind as he blasted 500 pounds up off the rack without the help of his spotter. He brought it down to his chest and held it there a split second before exerting all his strength through a guttural growl that hurt his throat.

The bar didn't move.

He tried to push again, but this time he felt dizzy from the effort. The trainer used both hands to help rerack the bar. A few minutes later Forzino removed fifty pounds.

The trainer said, "Maybe you want to skip that pause this time."

"Fuck that," Forzino said. "I'll get it."

He tried with a pause again and failed again, this time at 450.

He was embarrassed and angry. He left the gym determined to train his bench press with a pause from then on. First, though, he wanted to settle another issue between him and Bobby fucking G, and this time he had no intention of getting caught off guard.

•◆•

TOMMY AGRO COULDN'T sleep after the phone call from his new friend the undercover cop. Mickey Nolan was dead. Bobby Gennaro had been shot in a drive-by on Mulberry Street, of all fucking places. Another couple of bodies had been found by the police in Hell's Kitchen.

The cardinal rules about violence in Little Italy had been broken. Agro wasn't sure who had pulled the stunt there, but he knew it would come back to him.

A few minutes after his third cup of coffee an emergency page on his cell phone confirmed his suspicions. Agro recognized the number and cursed under his breath. He would have to answer the call from an outside line.

He quickly dressed and grabbed his car keys. He drove two blocks to where he knew there was a pay phone that worked. He used a phony phone card and punched in a number. Six rings later, "Fat Tony" Gangi, the underboss of the family, wanted to know what the fuck was going on in Little Italy.

It was a tough one-way conversation during which Gangi claimed the acting bosses of three of the four families in New York were breaking his balls about the shooting and that the heir apparent of the Irish mob on the West Side was demanding a sit-down, something about the bodies found in Hell's Kitchen, including some bigshot's daughter, somebody with something to do with the IRA.

Then Gangi went off about the San Gennaro feast and how much money they would lose if people didn't go because they were afraid of getting shot.

When the underboss of the family finally finished his monologue, Agro promised he'd take care of everything and swore on his mother that it wouldn't require violence.

"Good," Tony Gangi had told him, "because some guys are meant to be leaders and others are nothing more than muscle. How you handle this situation will determine whether we have the right guy in the right job."

Agro slammed the receiver down after Gangi had hung up. If he couldn't control the situation, his reign as captain of a crew might be the shortest one in mob history. He didn't know who he'd have to meet later from the West Side, but Gangi had made it clear the guy had clout and was to be respected.

Agro dialed John Forzino and was cranky with his protégé when he learned the big dope had spent the morning lifting weights. At least he would have the kid to dump on, he was thinking. Sometimes the best a skipper could do was push the shit downhill.

CHAPTER 34

IT HAD BEEN a long, uncomfortable night. The heat wave was in its sixth day. The putrid smell of rancid restaurant garbage filled the streets of Little Italy. The stagnant air and humidity retained the stench.

Bobby remembered how vendors for the feast of San Gennaro were still setting up their booths when the taxi had dropped them off in front of the apartment the night before. Father Scavo had helped Bobby get settled upstairs before returning to the church. The priest was upset with his friend for leaving the hospital.

Bobby had expected to see Lin Yao when he returned to the apartment. He was nervous when he didn't find her. He had called her cell phone several times, but Lin Yao didn't pick up. He left several messages. None were answered.

The painkillers helped him sleep again after his dream. He had forgotten to turn up the air conditioning and woke in a pool of sweat on the couch. His wounds gave him pain, but he was afraid the medication would keep him from leaving the apartment. He was making coffee when he heard the apartment door open. He stepped out of the kitchen and saw Lin Yao.

"Hey," he said. "Thank God you're all right."

Lin Yao remained silent.

Bobby said, "Father John told me you gave your cousin the money, but that was last night, right? The medication knocked me out once I got home. I woke up earlier and fell out again. I just woke a little while ago. I thought you were gone. I thought you had left me."

Lin Yao walked through the apartment to the living room. She sat on the couch. Bobby followed her. He sat in the recliner facing her.

"I followed my cousin and filmed the exchange," she said.

Bobby wasn't sure he had heard her. "What?"

"I followed Ricky to where they were dropping off Nolan," Lin Yao said. "They let Nolan go and then somebody killed him. Ricky has the tape."

Now he was squinting at her. "Why? Why would you do that? How does Ricky have the tape?"

She explained what had happened, including almost being pulled from the car by one of the cops that had talked to him on the street.

Bobby was furious. "Your cousin's guys kill Nolan?"

"No, someone else," Lin Yao said. "And then the cop recognized me. He wanted me to get out of the car. Ricky and his guys pulled up behind him. They had shotguns."

Bobby pushed himself forward on the chair. He could feel the stitches stretch around his hip wound. He winced from the pain and told her to start over, slowly, from the beginning.

Lin Yao told him what had happened since she'd brought the balance of Nolan's ransom money to her cousin. When she was finished, she said, "Ricky has the proof that you paid to get Nolan released. I'll go to the police if I have to."

"And you were with him since this fiasco last night, in Chinatown?"

"At the restaurant, yes. He wanted me to help him make copies of the tape. He wouldn't let me leave."

"Copies?" Bobby said. "We have to get you out of town."

"I'm not going anywhere," Lin Yao said.

"I'm serious," Bobby said. "You don't understand. You can't go around filming murders. Christ almighty, what the hell were you thinking? What the hell is that asshole cousin of yours thinking?"

"I'm not going anyplace, except to the police, and I'll tell them everything. If that's what it takes to end this bullshit, then I'll go there myself. I already told Ricky that. And he didn't ask me to film anything. He didn't want me there. I asked him first, when I dropped the money off, and he told me no way."

"Yeah, and then you went anyway and now he's got the tape."

"I told him if anything happened to you, I'd go to the police. He knows I mean it. He said to talk to you first. I am, but I'm not letting you talk me out of it."

Bobby was shaking his head. "What about the cop? What they do to him?"

"I don't know. We left and they were still back there, Tommy's guys. They had shotguns."

"Jesus Christ."

"But somebody killed Nolan and then put him in the trunk of a car. They were waiting for him."

"I don't know what that's about," Bobby said.

"The tape will clear that up," Lin Yao said. "I couldn't trust anybody anymore. I did what I had to do."

Bobby's mind was racing. He was sure it was Ricky Zhu who had tried to kill him. He couldn't tell her. "What was the cop doing there?" he asked.

"I don't know. Ricky said he was probably with the guy who killed Nolan, that he's a dirty cop. That's when Ricky saw my camera. He made me show him how to make the copies."

"Which cop was it? The tall one or the shorter guy?"

"The taller one, I think. The one with blonde hair."

"What he say, the cop? Anything?"

"He just wanted me to get out of the car."

"He see the camera, too?"

"I don't know. Maybe."

Bobby felt his teeth grind.

"We have the proof now. Ricky has it," Lin Yao said.

"Ricky is an idiot," Bobby said. "He'll probably try and shake down the cop too, he didn't already kill him. You can't admit to filming that anyway. You need to go away someplace, at least until this is settled."

Lin Yao shook her head. "I'm not going anywhere."

Bobby said, "Then help me get dressed."

•◆•

WHEN HE RECEIVED the heads-up call from his new friend the cop, Tommy Agro kicked at the bed and nearly broke a few toes. He limped around the room a full five minutes before he even tried to put pressure on his right foot again. Agro had plenty to yell about when Forzino picked him up and asked what was wrong.

"Nolan's dead, for one thing," Agro said. "A couple other micks, too. I don't know it was the Chinks or Gennaro or who the fuck else is involved. And then I almost broke my fuckin' foot. Couple little toes are all fucked up now. The nails already turning black. They fuckin' killed Nolan."

Agro realized he couldn't mention his cop friend in front of Forzino.

"I thought Gennaro got shot yesterday?" Forzino made the mistake of asking.

"You're a regular fuckin' student of the news, aren't you?" Agro said. "Yeah, he got shot. So, what the fuck does that mean? All I know is we gotta talk to the head mick today about all this and I don't know what the hell happened. Which is why we're going to Chinatown right now and find the fuck out. That little prick runs that half-assed street gang better have an answer to this, I can tell you that much. I got the underboss of the family up my ass and that's the last thing I need right now, less than two days I'm a skipper and that fat fuck is already breaking my balls."

It went on like that the next half hour until they parked in a lot on Mulberry Street and crossed Canal. They met with Ricky Zhu in front of the restaurant on Bayard Street and were brought down to an office in the basement. Zhu had a television and VCR set up on empty vegetable crate. Agro was about to explode when Zhu used a remote to turn the television on. He pointed to the screen and said, "Watch this before you make accusation."

He played the tape from start to finish. When the screen turned blue, Agro said, "Yeah, so? What the fuck is this, a Chinese fire drill?"

Zhu made faces. "What the fuck you talking about?"

Agro pointed at the television. "This fuckin' movie you made here," he said. "This made for TV Bad Boys shit. You're showing me this why? You think it's worth something to me?"

"You see Nolan is released?" Zhu said. "Or you fucking blind? Somebody else kill him."

"Really?" Agro said. "Like I can tell that wasn't one of your guys whacked him there. Like I know this isn't staged like some fuckin' home movie. This is nothing to me."

Zhu said something in Cantonese to one of his men.

Agro said, "And lay off the Chink rap now. You have something to say, say it to my face and in American."

"I said you full of shit."

"You think so, huh?"

Zhu smirked.

Agro thought about shooting the little prick where he sat with that arrogant smirk on his face, then remembered Tony Gangi had specifically said to resolve the problem without violence. He forced himself to smile.

"We didn't kill him," Zhu said. "Or you need to see it again. We get close up, you want it. That was a white boy shot Nolan, put him in trunk. Not Chinese."

Agro said, "Yeah, so what? Now you got a tape, you showed it to me, what do you think happens next?"

"We finished with business," Zhu said. "We get paid, we release Nolan. Somebody else kill him. We have proof."

Agro chuckled. "You obviously watched one too many kung fu movies, my friend. I'd like to see you use that tape outside this office? Where you gonna take it, the DA?"

Zhu popped the tape from the VCR. He extended it to Agro. "You want copy? No charge."

Agro stood up. "I thought there was a chance I could make sense with you," he said. "You're too fuckin' stupid."

Zhu flipped Agro the bird.

Agro forced another smile and then tapped Forzino on the arm. The two of them left Ricky Zhu smirking in his office.

•◆•

THEY ARGUED BACK and forth until Bobby gave up and called Father Scavo to ask him to stay with Lin Yao again. The priest, though still upset that Bobby had left the hospital, said he'd come to the apartment after a morning meeting.

Bobby had wanted Lin Yao to go to the rectory and wait for him there, but she was adamant about going to the police instead. She followed him into the bathroom and continued the argument while he dressed.

"I don't care if I get in trouble for filming a murder!" she insisted. "I didn't kill anyone. I did that for you, to prove you didn't do anything wrong."

"And what about your cousin? How do you explain to the cops about the kidnapping?"

"Then I won't mention the tape," she said. "But we can tell them what's going on without it. You were shot, Bobby, and it's not over yet. Now there's a dirty cop involved."

"Yeah, so you wanna go to them, the cops. That makes sense."

"Don't be sarcastic. You know what I mean."

"Yeah," he said, "I do know." He pointed to the scar on his face. "Remember where I got this?"

Lin Yao remained silent.

Bobby said, "We already know one of them is dirty, right? I'm not going to the law, Lin Yao. Not so long as your cousin has a tape of a murder you filmed."

"Ricky will never say it was me who filmed that," she said.

Bobby wheeled on her. "He wouldn't, huh?"

"No, he wouldn't."

"You're sure of that?"

She stood her ground. "Yes, I am."

Bobby was close to telling her it was Ricky who had tried to kill him the day before, but he asked for the detective's card she had grabbed the other day instead.

Lin Yao seemed hopeful. She retrieved the card from her purse and handed it to him when he stepped out of the bathroom.

"Maybe you should call the FBI in case that cop is dirty, too," she said.

"I'm not calling the cops or the FBI, Lin Yao. Not yet."

"I don't care if we have to move," she told him. "If we have to go into the witness protection program, we can do that. We can live somewhere else. At least we'll be safe."

Bobby went upstairs. She waited for him in the living room.

"What are you doing?" she asked.

Bobby came down the stairs holding a shotgun. He set it against the wall and then pulled one of his guns out of a cabinet and jammed it inside his pants.

"I'm going to look for Tommy Agro," he said. "Then I'll go the law myself."

Lin Yao blocked his path. "No."

"I have to find out what's going on."

"We already know what's going on. You need to call the police. Right now, or I will."

He stopped at the closet and opened it. He winced in pain as he reached up over the top shelf. He pulled out a box of shotgun shells for the Mossberg. Several shoe boxes spilled off the top shelf onto the floor.

"What the hell are those?"

"Shells," he said as he loaded the shotgun. "If you're not gonna let me take you to the church, you can sit on the couch there until Father John gets here. All you need to do is aim for the middle of something and pull the trigger. It'll take down anything in front of you."

"Are you crazy?"

"Not yet, no. When Scavo gets here, let him handle this."

"And you're going where with a handgun? They can put you away just for having that."

"It's registered. It's the only one that is. I'm not going unarmed."

She stood her ground. "No," she said.

"Father John will be here in a few minutes," he said. "Don't do anything until you hear from me again."

"Please, Bobby. Don't do this."

"I promise, I swear on my father, if I can't settle this today, I'll go to the law myself."

Lin Yao wasn't hearing him. "Don't leave," she said. "Stay here with me. We'll wait for the police here. Please."

"I have to find out about that cop and something else."

"What else is there to find out now?"

He tried to step around her and cringed from the pain. "Damn," he said. "Look, I need to go now. I promise it'll be okay."

Lin Yao continued to block his path. "I can't go through this again," she said. "Please don't do this."

He put a hand on her right arm to guide her out of the way. At first she resisted.

"Please," he said without looking at her.

Lin Yao stepped aside.

"It'll be okay," he said over his shoulder.

CHAPTER 35

Michael Ward had put on a wig and fake mustache before taking a room in a cheap Lexington Avenue hotel in Murray Hill. He watched the news on television and could tell the police were holding back information he had provided with his anonymous call.

Ward used a pay phone in the lobby of the dump and learned that Bobby Gennaro had already left the NYU Downtown Hospital during the night. He would have to try for Gennaro and his girlfriend at their apartment.

A few minutes after noon, Ward collected his things, wiped down the hotel room as best he could, and hustled out to the parking lot where he'd left his car. He was downtown in less than twenty minutes, but it took another half hour to fight through the feast traffic surrounding Little Italy. He parked in a lot off Broome and handed the attendant a twenty-dollar bill.

"Don't bury it," he told the Hispanic man. "Leave it out so I can get out of here fast."

The parking attendant pocketed the twenty and nodded.

Ward took his time walking south on Baxter Street. He was careful to keep his head down as he crossed Grand to the block where Bobby Gennaro and his girlfriend lived. He knew there was no turning back. The only chance he had of covering his tracks was to get rid of the bookmaker and his girlfriend and to make it look like retaliation for what had happened to Mickey Nolan and Jerry Collins. He could always plant the gun somewhere on the West Side after the fact and maybe tip off one of his former undercover colleagues as to where to find it.

Ward tugged down on the hat he was wearing as he approached the building where Gennaro lived. He showed his badge to an elderly Asian woman leaving the lobby before she let the door close. Ward thanked the woman for holding the door and then proceeded to the elevator. As he waited for the doors to open, he thought about his wife and two sons and how close he was to retirement.

Or losing everything.

When he was alone in the elevator, Ward glanced at his watch and took a deep breath. Just two more murders and he could be home in time for dinner.

•◆•

KENNETH RYAN LIED to Tommy Agro about where he'd been the night before.

"I'm not off the plane five hours and I'm told some of my people were massacred during the night," he said.

Ryan picked at the provolone cheese on a plate of cold antipasto. Tommy Agro was seated directly across the table. They were having an outdoor lunch at Christina's restaurant. Ryan preferred eating outdoors, even with the heat, because of surveillance bugs he'd been bitten by in the past. Agro wasn't crazy about sitting in the humidity, but it had been Ryan's request. He had the waiters arrange a pair of umbrellas to shade them from the bright sun.

Two of Ryan's men shared a cigarette with Forzino on the steps closer to the Second Avenue sidewalk. They each held handkerchiefs to wipe sweat from their faces.

"Now, truth be told," Ryan continued, "I can live without Jerry Collins. He's been a thorn in my side since the cops busted us up more than a year ago. He's made it hard to assemble a loyal crew. Always back-biting is his thing, if you know what I mean. Never a good thing to say about anybody."

Agro knew the type. "We deal with the same shit," he said. "Subversives are a fact of life."

"But the girl, Jesus, that was ugly," Ryan said. "She's family. The daughter of a man directly connected to boyos on the other side."

Agro didn't understand.

"IRA," Ryan said. "Those fuckers feel slighted, Tommy, we've got a problem neither of us can handle."

"You mean the army there?" Agro asked.

"Irish Republican Army," Ryan said. "Surprised you're not more familiar with them."

"You say it like that, I am. I understand. So, what, the kid was killed, the girl, her father is somebody with them?"

"Fuckin' A-right he is. He hears about this, he'll want answers. He'll want some heads, too."

"Yeah, well, let's not get crazy here," Agro said. "This ain't over there, okay. It's not the Wild West, contrary to recent newspaper headlines."

Ryan smiled. "Tommy, no disrespect intended, and I mean that in the most sincere way, but the boyos on the other side don't need to dick around like the Arabs to get a foothold here in New York. This girl was killed, Shannon Reilly, her old man wants to, he'll light up downtown like the Fourth of July, and he won't be sweating out the New York mob over it. Everybody has motives in what they do. Those people aren't about greed the way most of us over here are. To them it's the real thing, a war. You don't want to piss in Shaun Reilly's glass."

Agro was suddenly uncomfortable. He wiped the sweat rolling down his sideburns with a table napkin. He was thinking of what Tony Gangi had told him. He wouldn't be a skipper very long if the Irish started a war downtown. He wouldn't be alive very long, either.

"And what if it was one of your own killed Nolan?" Agro offered. "What if it was somebody looking to undercut you?"

"Like Jerry Collins?"

"If he was a subversive, if he was looking to cut you out, yeah."

Ryan smiled again. "Then who killed him?"

"I don't know. And I don't know who killed Nolan. I'm just saying."

"And I hear you," Ryan said, "but I'm going to have to have something and somebody to answer for what happened last night. Nolan was loyal to the people close to me. We let him work freelance for you and your people because it was his nature to stay busy. The other one, Collins, as I said, nobody will miss him. But the girl, I can't emphasize it enough, will require a marker. By now her family already heard, if the police notified them. I'll have to talk with her father soon as I leave here. He won't be happy she was hanging around the likes of Jerry Collins, which might mitigate the circumstances a cunt hair or two, but he'll still want the details of what happened and why. He'll also want news that we're on the animal killed her and that he'll be reading about it soon enough."

Agro gave it some thought. He could mention the tape or not mention it. If he did, there was a good chance he'd be drawn into sit-downs and compromises he'd have to answer for the next ten years. If he didn't mention the tape and the Chinese punk downtown used it to back off the Irish, it would be yet another strike against him for letting things get out of control.

A once win-win situation had suddenly turned into a no-win cluster fuck.

Agro rubbed his face a few times before he did a double take at the sight of Bobby Gennaro limping across Second Avenue.

•◆•

MOST WISEGUYS WERE creatures of habit. The organized crime task forces depended on it. Christina's was Agro's favorite place to have lunch, but he usually ate inside. Today the cops were lucky. Agro's party was sitting at an outdoor table recently wired by surveillance.

Agro had the waiters move the table an extra few feet away from the other tables for privacy. It was another move the surveillance team had counted on. The bad thing was the afternoon traffic on Second Avenue. Between the car horns and truck engines, it was sometimes difficult to hear.

DeNafria didn't know who the guy sitting with Agro was, except he looked Irish. So did two of the men standing with the big guy, John Forzino. DeNafria wished his partner was around to help with the names of the Irish players.

After a few minutes he noticed Agro doing a lot more listening than talking. He also noticed Agro wasn't as cocky as he usually appeared. Whoever the guy was sitting with Agro, he had said something to keep the wiseguy in check.

The one-way conversation at the table suddenly stopped when all heads turned toward Second Avenue. DeNafria looked in the same direction and saw that Bobby Gennaro had just stepped out of a yellow taxi. The retired bookmaker had been shot the day before. He limped to the sidewalk and appeared to struggle when he reached the stairs leading to the restaurant tables.

When he reached the bottom step, Agro's new playmate, John Forzino, reached an arm out to block his path. Gennaro twisted Forzino's arm into a half nelson and brought the big man to his knees. He leaned over and said something to the big man before he released the hold and had to steady himself again.

A moment later, up out of his chair, Tommy Agro was clapping.

DeNafria sat in his car parked on the corner of Thirty-fourth Street. He had been using a cell phone to maintain contact with the surveillance van parked across Second Avenue. After the action he had just witnessed, he decided it was time to sit in the van and listen to whatever he might pick up firsthand.

CHAPTER 36

I GUESS IT isn't safe for a girl to take out the garbage anymore," Lin Yao told the cop when she recognized him in the hallway.

He was holding a gun in one hand and his shield in another. He motioned for her to step back toward the apartment.

"How do you know I live in that one?"

"Because I read it on the directory downstairs," he said. "Let's go."

Lin Yao opened the door and then quickly tried to slam it shut behind her. The cop blocked it with his foot before slapping her across the face with the butt of his gun. Lin Yao fell hard onto the dining room floor. She sat there stunned a moment before she touched her cheek and felt blood.

"You prick," she said.

"Yeah, I know," he said. "I can get that way sometimes."

He locked the dead bolt and then motioned at her to move back on the floor. She did so slowly, sliding through the dining room into the living room. When she was alongside the television, he pulled a chair from the dining table and sat.

"What were you doing last night?" he asked.

"Doing where?"

"On the West Side Highway with that camera."

Lin Yao shook her head. "I wasn't anywhere near the West Side Highway last night."

"You don't want me asking the same question too many times," he said.

"I'm sorry, but I don't know what you're talking about."

"Where's your boyfriend?"

"Who?"

"Bobby G. Don't fuck with me, woman."

"He's out."

"Where to and for how long?"

"I don't know. He didn't say, but he is bringing someone back."

"The marines?"

"A priest."

"That's a new one."

"What do you want?"

"You really want to know?"

Lin Yao touched her cheek again. Her fingertips showed blood. The cop tossed her a dish towel from the back of a chair.

"I need to know what you were doing there last night," he said. "You and your camera."

"I think you have me mixed up with somebody."

"No, I don't. It was you."

"We all look alike."

"Yeah, you do, but it was you."

Lin Yao glanced at the clock in the kitchen.

"He coming home soon?" the cop asked.

"I don't know."

"What if I shot you in the knee, you think you might know something then?"

This time she was scared. "I don't know when he's coming back."

"Okay, but I won't play this game much longer," he said. "Now, what the fuck were you doing last night?"

•◆•

BOBBY WAS POSITIVE it had been Ricky Zhu's gang who had tried to kill him the day before. Now he needed to know if Tommy Agro had ordered the hit.

He could tell the wiseguy had spotted him when he got out of the cab on Second Avenue. There was someone else seated at the table Bobby didn't recognize. Another couple of goons he didn't recognize had been standing with Agro's muscle off to the side. When he saw Forzino staring him down, Bobby did his best to ignore the challenge. Then the big man stepped in his path and held up a hand. Bobby reacted from instinct. He grabbed Forzino's wrist and turned it upside down. He quickly twisted the arm into a half nelson and forced Forzino to his knees. Bobby could feel his stitches stretching around the bullet wounds. The pains from his hip and shoulder wounds were searing.

"I told you before to respect the experience," he whispered through clenched teeth into Forzino's ear. Then he let go.

When he turned around, Tommy Agro was standing up at the table giving him mock applause.

"Can we talk?" Bobby asked the wiseguy.

Agro motioned to the man at the table. "Kenneth Ryan. Kenneth, Bobby Gennaro."

The two men nodded at each other.

"Sit," Agro said.

Bobby glanced back over his shoulder. Forzino was rubbing his wrist. Bobby winced from the pain in his hip as he sat at the table.

"You okay?" Agro asked. "I heard about your accident yesterday. I'm surprised to see you out so soon, tell you the truth."

Bobby ignored the phony sympathy. "I was hoping we could talk in private," he said.

"There are no secrets here," Agro said. "Kenneth is from the West Side. Mickey Nolan was a good friend to him."

Bobby looked from Agro to Ryan and back to Agro again.

"Mickey was found in the trunk of a car today," Ryan said.

Bobby remained silent.

"There was another guy and a girl killed," Agro added. "Not too far from where they found Nolan. Kenneth here is asking about it. The girl was someone very close to him."

Bobby waited for more. It didn't come.

"What happened to you?" Ryan asked him.

"Like the news said, a drive-by," Bobby said. "Although some of your people think I had something to do with Nolan being kidnapped, which I didn't. All I did was bust him up some for assaulting my girlfriend."

Ryan smiled. "You're the wanker walked into the bar before the Chinks, are you?"

"I'm the one."

"Jesus, you've got balls, man. Do you know about the fingers? They cut off three of his fingers."

"I heard."

"And then they killed him anyway. I mean, what was the point of all that?"

Bobby turned to Agro. "I don't know about him being killed," he said, "except it wasn't the Chinese did that. I am wondering who took the shot at me, though, who ordered it."

"It was me you wouldn't be here," Agro said.

Bobby locked eyes with the wiseguy. "Yeah, well, it's somebody working with a cop," Bobby said.

Agro swallowed hard. He panicked and said, "This about that tape?"

"I don't know anything about a tape," Bobby said. "It's what I heard, though. Somebody killed Nolan when he was released and then a cop got involved. If there's a tape to verify it, maybe it's for real."

"Yeah, right," said Agro, pushing himself away from the table. "Well, I'm not about to watch another home video of what was supposed to be a fuckin' hit. And just for your information, my friend the retired bookmaker, I didn't see no cop on that tape."

Bobby smiled before shrugging. "I wouldn't know," he said. "I never saw it myself."

Ryan turned to Agro. "Well, I'd like to see it," he said. "I'd like to see it now, either of you don't mind."

•◆•

"HERE WE GO," Ward had said when the key turned the dead bolt lock.

He quickly stood up and moved inside the kitchen out of sight from the apartment door. He held the Glock up high when the door opened. He was surprised when he saw the man wearing a collar.

"What the hell happened to you?" the man asked the woman.

Lin Yao used her head to motion toward the kitchen. The guy turned and Ward saw he was in fact a priest.

"Jesus fuck," Ward said.

"Who are you?" the priest asked.

"He's a cop," the woman said.

"I am indeed," Ward said. "Move over that way. You can sit on the floor beside her."

"You going to kill a priest, too?" the woman asked.

"I'm not going to kill anybody," Ward told her. "I'm not," he reassured the priest. "Not unless I have to."

"What's it about?" the priest asked. His eyes shifted to the dining room table where Ward had set the Mossberg after he found it standing alongside the couch earlier.

"Ignore that, Father," Ward told him. "Just go take a seat on the floor."

The priest sat on the floor alongside the woman.

"He is going to kill us," she told him. "He has to."

Ward said, "Maybe I should, you're so fucking anxious to announce it every two seconds. I could wait for your boyfriend in peace I do that, couldn't I?"

"What is this?" the priest asked. "What's it about?"

"He's dirty," the woman said.

Ward glared at her. She was about to say something else and stopped herself. He had her attention. He could see she was scared. He shot her in the leg anyway.

CHAPTER 37

DeNafria bolted from the surveillance van as soon as he heard Bobby Genraro mention a cop. Every bad feeling he'd ever had about his new partner had magnified tenfold in the pit of his stomach. The first thing he did was flash his badge and grab Gennaro from the group.

"The fuck is this?" Agro wanted to know. "You pulling him off the street, the rat cocksucker?"

"What is this?" Gennaro also asked.

DeNafria walked Gennaro to his car, helped him get in the back, and then cuffed his right wrist to the bolts holding the front seat in place.

"I guess you made your deal, Gennaro!" Agro yelled. "You rat fuck."

"I don't know what's going on!" Gennaro yelled back at Agro.

"Yeah, right," Agro said.

DeNafria turned toward Agro and the other man he was with. Both of them had moved up the stairs to the sidewalk.

Agro said, "You better look after him better than you did the poor bastard got killed with his sister."

DeNafria said, "I'll be seeing you later, Tommy. Don't get lost."

Agro whispered something into the other man's ear. They split up and walked in separate directions.

DeNafria got in the car and immediately started the engine.

"The cop you mentioned at that table my partner?" he asked before pulling away from the curb.

"Yeah," Bobby said, "and the scumbag is working with whoever killed Nolan. What, you had the table wired?"

DeNafria ignored Bobby's question and headed south on Second Avenue. "You think or you know it was my partner?"

"It was him."

"He with Agro, too?"

"I don't know."

"When'd you see him?"

"I didn't."

"Who did?"

"My girlfriend."

DeNafria ran a red light on Thirty-first Street. He raced through the traffic heading downtown.

"She home now?"

"Yeah."

"She alone?"

"No, there's a priest with her."

"A priest?"

"From the parish there, Our Lord's Holy Cross. He's a friend."

Bobby thought about telling the cop about the shotgun, but decided against it. He couldn't be sure DeNafria wasn't dirty, too.

DeNafria caught a stretch of green lights and an open left lane. He raced four blocks before he had to slow down and weave through traffic again.

"My partner kill Mickey Nolan?" he asked.

"No," Bobby said. "But he was probably in on it."

"What do you mean?"

Bobby hesitated.

DeNafria lost his patience. "Hey, asshole, she might be in danger right now, your girlfriend," he said. "My partner called in sick to work today, only he didn't stay home, okay?"

"Jesus fuck."

"Yeah, Jesus fuck. What happened last night?"

Bobby told him about Lin Yao filming Mickey Nolan's release.

"And somebody clipped him right after?" DeNafria asked.

"Soon as the van dropped him off, yeah."

"Then the cop showed?"

"He stopped Lin Yao and must have recognized her. He told her to get out of the car. Her cousin's gang backed him down."

"So, he wasn't on the tape, my partner?"

"No."

"But she said it was him?"

"Yes."

"Would she know the car again if she saw it, the one the guy who killed Nolan was driving?"

"She had it on the tape."

DeNafria found another patch of clear space and floored the gas pedal until he was close to Houston Street. He avoided the cars waiting in the right-turn lane and made an illegal right onto Houston heading west. Then he saw the people traffic off Mulberry Street and remembered the feast.

•◆•

FATHER JOHN SCAVO used his belt as a tourniquet on Lin Yao's left leg. The bullet had missed arteries and bone and exited through the back of her thigh into the wood floor she was sitting on. There had been a lot of blood from the two wounds until Scavo cut the flow with his belt.

He had her lie on her back with her head on a couch pillow. Then the gunman had him tie and gag her. Now the dirty cop was standing at the living room windows and looking down into the street. Scavo knew they were all dead as soon as Bobby came home. He thought about rushing the cop, but the distance between them was too great.

He positioned himself on his knees in front of Lin Yao.

"You can take me as a hostage if you want," he said.

The cop barely glanced his way. "Thanks, but no thanks. I just want Gennaro and then I'm gone."

"Bullshit," Scavo said.

Now the gunman turned to him. "That any way for a priest to talk?"

"You can't think you'll get away with it. Not if you're a cop."

The gunman smirked. "You'd be amazed, Father."

Scavo didn't think he could talk the cop out of killing them, but he was hoping to distract him, maybe provoke him into taking a swing instead of using the gun. If he could get close enough, he would take his chances.

"So, what, you're going to kill three people? For what? You'll be able to walk away from this and nobody will figure it out? You really think this will solve whatever problems you have?"

The cop put a finger to his lips. "Shhh," he said.

"I'm trying to reason with you. This is crazy."

"I'll tell you what's crazy, Father. Going a lifetime without getting laid, unless you're the type likes little boys."

"I'd love to hear you say that without that gun," Scavo said.

"Would you?"

Scavo stood up. "Yeah, I would."

The cop turned and pointed the gun at Scavo's chest.

•◆•

THE FEAST OF San Gennaro runs along Mulberry Street, between Canal and Houston streets. It takes place east to west on Grand Street, between Mott and saxter Streets, and east to west on Hester Street, between Mott and Baxter streets. The pastor of Our Lord's Holy Cross Church had already walked through the streets of the feast and blessed more than three hundred vendors and merchants.

A Jay and the Americans tribute band performed on the Grand Street stand off the corner of Baxter Street. The crowd in front of the stand had spilled out into the intersection where revelers danced to the music.

The detective had driven up Lafayette Street the wrong way in order to save time. He had called for backup on the way. He left the car parked alongside a fire hydrant, then unlocked Bobby's handcuffs, and the two men headed east on Broome Street before turning up Baxter Street across from the old police headquarters building.

The detective hadn't noticed the Walther Bobby had jammed into the back of his pants. Bobby was careful to walk at an angle once they were out of the car so the gun remained concealed.

"There another way up to the apartment besides the front door?" DeNafria asked.

"You can get on the roof from the adjoining buildings," Bobby said. "You'll have to hug the sidewalk until you're close, though."

They reached the intersection of Grand and Baxter. The music from the bandstand was loud. Bobby could make out a Jay and the Americans tune, "Cara Mia," as he fought his way through the crowd. His wounds stung each time someone bumped into him. DeNafria tried to clear a path, but the people were in a frenzy partying.

When they reached the southwest corner of the intersection, DeNafria called his backup to try and pinpoint their location. He had specifically instructed them to stay off Baxter Street and to await his signal. Now it looked as though he was searching for them.

"You told them to stay off this street," Bobby said. "What are you looking for?"

"A guy wearing a white vest," DeNafria said. "It's a code. It means they're here."

Bobby knew the clothing code all too well. He said, "I didn't hear you tell them it was a cop they're looking for. That a code, too?"

"You didn't listen very good," DeNafria said. "I gave his name, but that isn't as important right now as getting upstairs, is it?"

Bobby's teeth were clenched. "Let's go."

They had discussed the game plan on the way over. Bobby would call and announce he was coming home if the answering machine picked up. He would say he had picked up a container of milk. DeNafria would climb across the adjoining roofs until he was above Bobby's apartment. Bobby would walk up the street in plain sight. If Ward was up there, he would move away from the window once Bobby was inside the building. DeNafria would take the stairwell down to the hallway and meet Bobby there. Backup would be waiting on his signal. When he heard the apartment door open, he would set the backup team into action before following Bobby inside the apartment.

Now it seemed impossible to pull off. The streets were jammed with spillover from the feast. DeNafria couldn't afford to wait out the backup.

They had argued about the Kevlar vest, but when DeNafria saw how the gauze covering the stitches was stained with blood, he let Bobby have his way.

Bobby said, "I need to get that milk."

DeNafria was still searching the opposite end of the street for the white vest. "I'll feel better when we have people in position," he said. "This isn't smart if I'm your only backup."

"You're the one told me that scumbag might be upstairs. I'm going for the milk and then I'm calling."

DeNafria gave in. "Go 'head," he said.

Bobby headed into a store on the corner. He was back after a minute carrying an orange plastic bag with a quart container of milk inside. He dialed his apartment while DeNafria ran up a stoop ten addresses from Bobby's building. Bobby waved when he heard the answering machine pick up.

He waited for the beep and said, "It's me. I'm on my way. I picked up milk for your cake. Love you."

He killed the connection and slipped the phone back inside his front pants pocket. Then Bobby pulled the Walther from his pants, slipped it inside the bag with the milk, and started for home.

CHAPTER 38

WARD HAD MOVED away from the window as soon as Bobby was inside the building. He had almost kneecapped the priest, but thought better of it and put a warning shot into the recliner instead. There was always a chance the wounded man would scream or cause enough of a racket to alert neighbors. As it turned out, the warning shot worked fine. The priest had stopped in his tracks.

Now he supervised as the priest helped the woman up onto the stairs leading to the second floor. He had them stop at the first landing where the second set of stairs turned up. He would aim at the woman but shoot the priest as soon as Bobby was inside the apartment.

He waited off to the left of the door again, parallel to where someone would be standing once inside. He still had a clear shot at the woman and the priest.

A few minutes passed before Ward heard the elevator door out in the hallway. He wiped sweat from his forehead and put a finger to his lips for the priest again.

A minute later he heard the door lock turn. It opened and Gennaro, holding a plastic bag, stepped inside. When the retired bookmaker looked up, he was staring at the barrel of the Glock.

Ward motioned him inside. "Let's go," he said.

Gennaro hesitated and then Ward shot at the priest.

•◆•

DENAFRIA FOUND THE door to the roof locked and had to use the fire escape to gain access to an adjoining apartment. He tapped on the glass once before pulling the window up and entering the bedroom. He called out without yelling, but no one responded. He quickly found his way to the apartment door and glanced through the peephole. He was staring at the stairwell doorway.

DeNafria carefully opened the door. He saw that Gennaro had already reached his apartment door and was about to go inside. DeNafria spoke into his cell phone to give the verbal signal to the backup team. Then he slipped the phone into its holder and stepped out into the hallway with his Glock leveled at Gennaro's back.

He heard the doorknob turn up ahead and saw Gennaro step inside the apartment. He followed in a shooter's crouch. He could feel his heart racing as he approached the open doorway. Then he heard Michael Ward's voice and his adrenaline kicked in.

"Let's go," Ward had said.

Gennaro wasn't moving. There was a phht-like sound and Gennaro dropped to the floor. Swinging his weapon to the left, DeNafria charged inside. He leaned against the closet doors and leveled the Glock just as Ward shot him in the chest.

•◆•

AS SOON AS he saw the gun with the silencer, Bobby froze. The Walther was inside the plastic bag, which he'd left open by carrying just one of the handles. He could reach in and get it, but not before Ward reacted. He would have to wait for a better opportunity.

Then Ward fired toward the stairs and Bobby dropped to the floor. He reached for the Walther when DeNafria stepped between him and Ward. Bobby could hear the phhht-like sounds over and over and then DeNafria landed in his lap. Bobby couldn't tell if the detective was dead. He looked up and saw Ward trying to angle the gun for a better shot. Bobby pulled the Walther out with his right hand. He poked it between DeNafria's right arm and ribs and fired two quick shots.

The return fire came a moment later. At least one of the bullets hit DeNafria again. The other had just missed Bobby's left ear.

He pushed DeNafria to the left to free his right hand for a better shot and noticed that Ward had taken a bullet in his right leg. The dirty cop was changing an ammo clip when a chair crashed against his head. Ward slammed into the kitchen counter before losing his balance and falling to the floor. Bobby was about to shoot again when he felt pressure on his hand pushing the gun down. Then he heard the shots and could feel the recoil.

It was DeNafria. He had fired two shots. Both had struck dead center in Ward's chest as the dirty cop tried to sit up. Now he lay dead still.

Bobby waited a second before yelling Lin Yao's name. He panicked when he didn't hear her answer.

•◆•

THE PRIEST HAD seen the gun move to his left when he heard the apartment door open. He was assuming the dirty cop was anxious to kill Bobby first. Then the banister to his right splintered.

Scavo froze when several shots were fired where Bobby would've been standing. Then he heard two more shots and saw the dirty cop buckle where he stood.

It was then that Scavo jumped off the landing and grabbed the closest thing, a dining room chair, and flung it as hard as he could. The chair struck the dirty cop across the left side of his head and he crashed into the kitchen counter. Scavo was reaching for a second chair when he heard another couple of shots. When he looked at the dirty cop this time, he was already dead.

Scavo turned the corner and saw Bobby and another man struggling to stand.

"You okay?" Bobby asked the man.

"Just sore," the man answered.

Scavo saw the holes in the man's shirt and realized he was wearing a Kevlar vest underneath. He made the sign of the cross.

"You're not kidding," the man said.

•◆•

SHE HAD THOUGHT she was dead when he shot her in the leg. She was surprised when the cop let Father Scavo tend to her wounds. Then she was gagged and tied again.

She fought to stay conscious and alert.

When she heard Bobby's voice on the answering machine, she felt nauseous but couldn't vomit from fear of choking. She looked up at Father Scavo and could tell he was scared, too.

Then the cop stepped away from the window and made them move to the first landing on the stairway. She saw the cop was pointing the gun at her and felt defiant again.

She heard the door open. Her anger had turned to rage. The cop fired a shot and the banister splintered to her right. She was clenching her teeth when more shots were fired. She tried to sit up and see when Father Scavo jumped from the landing. She saw him grab the chair.

There was a final series of shots she heard before she saw the dirty cop lying on his back. Then she could see the blood spots on his chest.

She heard Bobby's voice and knew he was alive.

It would take hours before she could stop shaking.

EPILOGUE

IT WAS FIVE DAYS after John Forzino had made a second call to his fiancée's parents informing them about Sally's change of heart and apparent abandonment when he had her possessions shipped to Michigan. Two days later he was confronted by Mr. Loomis in a strip club formerly owned by Joe Quastifare. Forzino did his best to explain to the distraught father that he had no idea where Sally had gone or why she had left, but Mr. Loomis became surly. Two bouncers forcibly removed him from the club.

•◆•

TWO DAYS AFTER the body of Shannon Reilly was interred in a Belfast cemetery in Ireland, Ricky Zhu's head was found in a plastic garbage bag in front of his hangout restaurant on Bayard Street. The offering was believed to be the Tong leadership sending a message to its member gangs operating in Chinatown.

•◆•

THE SAME DAY Ricky Zhu's head was found, Tommy Agro was stripped of his rank and demoted to acting captain of a small crew operating out of Maspeth, Queens.

•◆•

THE NEXT AFTERNOON Detective John DeNafria was presented with a departmental citation and was given a Gold Shield. His relationship with Detective Arlene Belzinger was successfully rekindled when she gave up her plans to move to the Southwest.

•◆•

ONE WEEK TO the day Tommy Agro was demoted, John Forzino was inducted into the Vignieri crime family along with two other associates. The ceremony took place on a private yacht that had been chartered for the occasion. After becoming a made man, Forzino spent most of the night with a sixteen-year-old blonde-haired Russian girl. The next morning when the yacht docked at a West Side pier, Forzino brought the girl home with him to Brooklyn. He threw her out in the middle of the night after catching her going through the change on his night table.

•◆•

ONE MONTH TO the day when Bobby Gennaro and Lin Yao Ji made love without protection, she learned she was pregnant. Later the same day Father John Scavo married them in a private ceremony at Our Lord's Holy Cross Church. The newlyweds spent their honeymoon night in a suite at the Algonquin Hotel. The next day they listed the Little Italy condo for sale and began a search for a small house somewhere in upstate New York.

ACKNOWLEDGMENTS

I'LL START WITH Peter Skutches and Ann Marie, because the truth of the matter is nothing would ever get beyond the messes I make without them. I owe Peter for editing five books now and I don't know how you start repaying his expert guidance. Ann Marie has made all the difference in my life and that's the truth of it.

I dedicated this book to Craig McDonald for the reasons already stated. I treasure our friendship with all my heart.

Others I need to thank include: Jim "Doc" Nyland, once again for his help with the guns; the Average White Band—the coolest funk band in the land; and, as always, the guy who got me started with this writing stuff (and who also advised me to "show rather than tell" some of this novel), Dave Gresham.